VANILLA BEACH

Peter J. Venison

Clink
Street

Published by Clink Street Publishing 2023

Copyright © 2023

First edition.

ISBN: 978-1-915785-33-6 paperback
978-1-915785-34-3 ebook

To Diana, loved by everyone, but mostly by me

Preface

The events that take place in this book are based, in the main, on actual occurences on the islands of the Comores and Mauritius in the Indian Ocean.

The characters in the story are entirely ficticious.

Chapter One
"Sloane Towers"

Roger Brown was a harmless sort of bloke, not someone who went looking for trouble, but sensible and well organised. He was the junior assistant manager of the Sloane Towers, a luxury hotel in Kensington, London, with three hundred guest rooms and two fine restaurants. He had been doing the job for just under two years, since he had been promoted from an analyst in the back office. He was popular and easy going, although well trained and efficient. The guests of the hotel liked his quiet but purposeful manner and the staff recognised him as someone on whom they could rely, provided they carried out their duties satisfactorily. Roger was married to Constance, a South African girl whom he had met on a number nineteen bus. They had been married for four years and, as yet, had no offspring. Roger was a good-looking young man but he considered himself fortunate to have landed Constance, because in his eyes, and many others, she was a very beautiful young woman. Their friends were surprised that they had not made babies.

Roger had been born and brought up in suburban London. He was the product of a stable marriage, commuter-belt living, local school and high school, rugby, tennis, sailing and, latterly, a course in hotel and catering management. The family had lived in a semi-detached house with small gardens, front and back, in a tree-lined street. His mother had been the dominant adult in the partnership. His overseas adventures, as a child and young man, had been confined to camping trips in France, early on with his parents, and then later with his male chums.

Roger's upbringing had allowed him opportunities that many young men of his age had not experienced, but his roots were decidedly suburban. His parents, who had certainly "bettered" themselves beyond their own expectations, were, nevertheless, relatively uncultured people. Although they possessed a gramophone, they did not own one classical music record and the home was almost devoid of books. In all their years of marriage they had never set foot inside a hotel and rarely attended the theatre, save for Christmas outings to the pantomime. To the best of Roger's knowledge, his parents had never been to an opera, ballet or classical music concert. Rarely was there an intellectual discussion in the home and, although Roger's mum and dad enjoyed a healthy sex life, they would never dream of discussing anything of this nature with their son, and certainly neither one of them was brave enough to explain the birds and the bees. Luckily, Roger was a quick learner and his physical attractiveness to the fairer sex had been helpful. His lack of exposure to the more cultured things of life, however, troubled him and he learned how to bluff in covering up his lack of knowledge about the finer things of life. As Roger's career had developed, and as his journey exposed him to men and women, often from a higher social rank than himself, he began to realise what he was missing in terms of education and exposure to the arts. The more he realised he did not know, the more he bluffed. He had become an expert bluffer. Roger did not like to look foolish, so he made sure he rarely did. This shortfall in experience was, in Roger's eyes, a severe disability for him in his chosen career, or so he thought in his early days of hotel management. Most of his hotel guests were more worldly people than himself. Luckily, Roger was a fast learner.

There were a few things, however, that Roger was very good at, not least listening to and understanding other people. People, whether they be hotel staff or guests, felt that Roger was listening to them – and hearing them; they felt that he understood what they had to say or what they needed. Coupled with his ability to be practical and logical, he was able to come up with plans and solutions that everyone could agree to. Roger could size up situations and sort them out, when they needed sorting. Somehow or other Roger seemed to have an ability to get things done. He was a good manager and a good organiser. As a result, he had made rapid progress in his early career.

Constance was a true product of the sunshine of South Africa. Born in the days of Apartheid on the Highveld, she was, firstly, privileged to be white and, secondly, to be the daughter of a wealthy industrialist and a stay-at-home mum. She had attended university in Cape Town with no particular distinction and then hot-footed it to England for the "experience", where she joined forces with many expatriates like herself at the Overseas Visitors Club in Earls Court and eventually secured the job as a secretary to an executive in a leading advertising agency in Duke Street. Her appointment had more to do with her good looks than her experience. She was an extremely attractive young lady who quickly gathered a wide circle of friends in her new environment.

Despite her upbringing in the "colonies", Constance's education, both at school and from her parents, was far broader and more rounded than her new husband's. The standard and scope of her whites-only school in Johannesburg and subsequent university in Cape Town was much higher and all-encompassing than Roger's suburban grammar school and technical college. She was familiar with, and fond of, most of the higher forms of art and music, but that is not to say she was a snob. Constance could have as much fun in a disco or night club, as any other young lady. In fact, some, that knew her well, would say more. Her mother had, at an early age, explained the basic facts about sex, but, until she reached university, Constance had not been sexually active. By the time she had landed at the Overseas Visitors Club in London, however, Constance had gained considerable experience and this was the ideal place and time to have some fun. At first glance, it looked as if Roger could provide some of that fun. Although the pair came from such different backgrounds and had developed, as a result, very different interests, one thing bound them strongly together. Physically, they were extremely attracted to each other. They became constant companions whenever their careers allowed and, very quickly, they considered themselves, not only to be lovers, but also "in love".

Their chance meeting led to a short courtship and then marriage, much against the wishes of Constance's parents in distant South Africa. Constance had fallen for Roger's good looks, his charming smile, his wavy blonde hair, and tan, acquired from his frequent sailing activity. Roger thought that Constance was the most beautiful girl he had ever met and was proud to have captured her attention. At five feet seven inches tall, with flowing blond hair, sparkling blue eyes, and a well-toned shapely sun-tanned body, Constance was a fantastic catch for any young man and Roger was astonished that he had been the lucky one. Since their relationship was heavily weighted to their mutual physical attraction, it would remain to be seen whether this would be enough to sustain a long-term partnership, but in the first few years of marriage life could not be rosier. They made love at every opportunity. At the same time, they took precautions. At this stage of their lives, they did not want the encumbrance of a child. On that they were in complete agreement.

At work Roger reported to Antoine Mersky, the general manager of the Sloane Towers. Antoine was a large loud man, who claimed to have come from a titled European aristocratic family. Roger wondered if that was true. If so, why would he be working as an hotel manager? Roger also wondered what Mersky had been doing during the war. Mersky spoke several languages but his mother tongue was German. When he spoke English, it still sounded German and his lips twisted into a snarl. When he smiled, which was rare, it was more of a sneer. When he walked, he did so with a very slight limp. Roger always wondered why.

Mersky was a bully and a tyrant, the product of a bullying Austrian father and a once-pretty, but now meek, German mother, whose family had actually been the ones with the money. Mersky was not really fat, but heavy and solid. He had a jowly sort of face with almost no neck and very large feet, highlighted by the fact that his black hard-leather shoes were always shone so impeccably that they stood out like two large rocks on a beach. One leg was slightly longer than the other; his tailor never seemed to get this just right, so he was always tugging at one leg or the other in an attempt to even up the hems. At the hotel he wore a formal morning suit with grey and black striped trousers and a black jacket. He was extremely experienced in his trade but this was the first time in his career that he had been in charge of such a large hotel, and certainly the first time he had worked for American owners. This was difficult for him because he had a low opinion of Americans. He was appalled when an executive from the company in America showed up off the night flight from Boston wearing sneakers and a sweat shirt. In Mersky's world such attire had no place in the first-class cabin of an aeroplane and certainly not at the Sloane Towers, other than in the gym.

As assertive and aggressive as he was to his staff, he was, of course, the complete opposite when dealing with the actual

American owners of the hotel, to whom he almost bowed and scraped, as if they were from a superior rank in the army. This need to kow-tow only caused him to bottle up his resentment, which, when the bosses had left, spilled over into wrath in the direction of the nearest unfortunate employee. His poor secretary, Marianne Treadwell, was the most likely recipient of his pent-up wrath. "Vat the fuck are you smirking about?" he would yell at her no sooner had the Americans left. Marianne, by dint of her position in the hotel, would have to bear more than her fair share of Mersky's bad temper, but she had never completely acclimatised to it. Most of the staff of the hotel were frightened by Herr Mersky and, those that could, did their utmost to keep out of his way. There was no hiding place for Marianne, who not only had to bear the brunt of her boss's wrath but also his sexist comments about her backside or breasts when he was in his "playful" mood.

There were two other assistant managers. One, Hans Ofal, was also German, although from Berlin rather than Bavaria, from whence he believed Mersky hailed. Ofal was exceptionally correct: shiny black lace-up shoes that matched his jet black greased-down hair and immaculately pressed pin-striped suit that matched his pin-striped face. He spoke with a clipped German accent, each sentence being concluded with a "Ja?" as if trying to force everyone into agreement. He was a few years older than Roger and considered himself to be infinitely superior. "Vat do the English know about hotel-keeping?" he would frequently mutter to himself. Roger secretly thought that Ofal must have been trained in the Nazi Youth. But Hans was completely intimidated by Mersky, who frequently swore at him in German. Although Roger could not understand the exact meaning of all the words, he knew they were bad because Hans literally shook in his black shoes whenever Mersky approached. Unfortunately for Hans, his rigidity was also a handicap in his dealings with hotel guests.

When a guest would approach him with a minor complaint or even request, his stiffness came across as aloofness, even rudeness. He was completely lacking in warmth. The only time that he laughed was at his own jokes which, infrequent as they were, always concluded with a double "Ja?"

The other assistant manager, Louis Voullemin, was considerably older than either Roger or Hans and, therefore, much more experienced. His specific responsibility was food and drink, or "food and beverage" as the American owners insisted on calling it. Whereas both Roger and Hans were always immaculately dressed, particularly Hans, Voullemin always seemed a bit sloppy. His trousers were often crumpled, his shoes scruffy and his lank hair falling over his forehead. Louis never walked; he shuffled. Mersky, naturally, was extremely frustrated by Voullemin's unkempt appearance, but no matter how much he ordered the man to smarten himself up, it never happened. When Mersky shouted at Louis, however, it just seemed to roll off him with no affect at all, normally accompanied by a shrug, which further infuriated his boss. A strange half smile would come over Louis' face as Mersky admonished him. The louder Mersky screeched, the more Louis' half smirk extended across his face, further infuriating his boss, who eventually would turn away, swearing under his breath with exasperation.

Nobody on the hotel staff of almost five hundred employees liked Mersky. Not one. Some, such as Andre Flamant, the ultra-smooth chief concierge, knew how to charm him and, probably more importantly, cater to his needs. Flamant was the perfect London hotel concierge, oozing in obsequious charm. He wore his black hall porter's uniform with pride, always immaculately pressed and sporting a shiny crossed-key badge in the lapel. Mersky was partial to visiting various dubious clubs in London when it was quiet at the hotel in the afternoons. Flamant, through his contacts, always knew where Mersky had been and Mersky soon realised this. He was not keen that "Baroness" Mersky should find out, so the silence of the concierge was much appreciated. To his face, Mersky would treat his concierge like a best friend. He would lean over the concierge's high desk with his elbow nonchalantly resting on the top as if he were talking to his friendly neighbour over the garden wall. Flamant would produce his phoney smile and occasionally let forth an appreciative little forced laugh. It was as if they were swapping dirty jokes. But although Andre hated Mersky as much as anyone else in the building, he knew how to play him, just as he knew how to play the myriad of super wealthy guests for whom he produced daily miracles.

The three assistant managers took it in turns to be "duty manager", working specific shifts during which they had to deal with whatever operational or guest-related problems came up on their watch. Outside of these hours they each had definitive and distinctive operational responsibilities. Louis, as previously mentioned, was in charge of food and beverage. Hans was in charge of the rooms side of the business, and Roger looked after the personnel function as well as "maintenance". Mersky handled Sales and Marketing although this was clearly not his forte.

Roger did not get shouted at by Mersky. A possible reason was that he had been recommended for his job by the human resources director of the American company, who was well respected by the head office in Boston, USA, and who, therefore, had a certain influence on Antoine's remuneration package. To upset Roger might mean upsetting the man in Boston, which was not a risk worth taking for the cash strapped "Baron".

Andre Flamant and Roger, therefore, seemed exempt from Mersky's wrath, as was the pretty assistant housekeeper, whom Antoine fancied, and the ultra-smooth linkman who "guarded" the front entrance of the hotel. This man, George, was Antoine's eyes and ears. He knew everyone that entered and left the hotel and persons of interest were noted for onward transmission to the boss. George, known around town as Gorgeous George because he was exceptionally handsome, had a charming word for everybody who stepped through the portals of the place, many of whom he was able to address by their name. He had special pockets in the tails of his uniform jacket to store the tips. George was certainly richer than his boss, Antoine. The Linkmens, as they were called, were jobs highly sought after by hotel employees. The level of their compensation was impossible to ascertain by the Inland Revenue Service.

Within the hotel, another of Antoine's informers was Daniel, the subservient elevator operator. From his privileged position this shrivelled-up little man, with a slight hump on his back, could monitor the movements of almost all guests and, indeed, some of the management. Antoine Mersky was quick to prise information from sneaky Daniel.

Other than this small cadre of employees, Mersky was universally feared and detested by everyone else who worked in the place, since, almost everyone, from the lowest of the low to the first tier of management, had, at some time or other, been on the receiving end of his temper and foul mouth. The smallest incident would set him off, and, although he was right to be pointing out shortcomings in performance, he failed to realise that most of these failings had occurred as a result of his unlistening style of management. Instructions issued one day would be changed the next; policies agreed upon at a weekly meeting would be altered without notice. The lack of consistency in every respect caused chaos. The only thing that was consistent was Antoine Mersky's bad temper and that, of course, made it hard for Roger, the personnel manager, who had to cope with multiple instances of distraught supervisors and employees as well as a very high staff turnover. This, in turn, led to more inefficiency, which, of course, led to more shouting and admonishment by the man in charge. It was a vicious and unpleasant atmosphere in which to work, and one which placed a severe strain on middle management and supervisory staff, including, of course, Roger.

The trait that angered Roger most about his boss, however, was the way he treated the female staff, continuously plying them with barely hidden suggestive and sexually oriented comments. He would slide up to the front office cashier's desk and, almost under his breath, make sexually suggestive comments to the girls that worked there. Or he would prowl the hallways of the hotel looking for the prettiest room maids to pester them. And yet, he was so overbearing that none of these victims could face up to bringing any action against him. Often, they would just leave the job. Sometimes they would register a complaint with Roger in his personnel office but never did they have the guts to take him on in law. When Roger had tentatively and somewhat nervously raised these complaints with Mersky, he had merely laughed them off, saying that women get a kick out of such things. When Roger told Constance about this, she was livid. "What that man needs is an encounter with a baseball bat," she would exclaim. "One day I will do it myself!"

Yet, despite this, the hotel was a success. Not because of the way it was operated but because of a shortage of first-class rooms in the city, which was emerging buoyantly from the dark days of the war. The Sloane Towers was the first new luxury hotel to be opened after the carnage of the Blitz. As far as the American market was concerned, there were no other hotels. The traditional, established, English hotels had been severely run down when they had been used as barracks or makeshift hospitals during the war. Some had been severely damaged in the Blitz. Their financial health was shaky. There simply had not been the money available to refurbish them, so the spanking new Sloane Towers was in a class of its own. Even its browbeaten staff could not endanger its success, which, of course, resulted in better wages and better tips for its employees. It was worth taking a beating from the lunatic in charge because there was nowhere else in town where one could earn so well.

From his role in "personnel", Roger could see that the hotel could be even more successful with a better organised and less destructive manager, and he did his best to pass this message on to his "bosses" in America, but, from their perspective, even with this autocratic manager, the "numbers", as the Americans called them, were staggeringly good, so why risk a change? Not only that: on the owners' fleeting visits to London, Mersky was charm itself, particularly, they observed, with important hotel guests, whom he addressed in a blisteringly subservient manner. It would seem that there was nothing Roger, nor anyone else on the staff, could do about Antoine Mersky's unpleasant and damaging management style. They would just have to make the best of it or leave for pastures greener.

At the weekends the three assistant managers took it in turns to be in charge of the hotel for twenty-four-hour shifts, which meant, of course, that they needed, on their shift of duty, to sleep over in the hotel, albeit "on call". It was during these long shifts that Roger developed good relationships with the other weekend supervisors, which included the two restaurant managers, Bruno and Christian, as well as the banqueting manager, Monty. As their names implied, Bruno was Italian, Christian French and Monty hailed from the east end of London. All three knew how to kow-tow to Mersky when required, but all three hated and despised him.

Bruno looked and spoke like a character from the Chicago Mafia, yet he had been born in Soho, London, to Italian immigrant parents who owned a café in Greek Street. He resembled a mobster: thick set, swarthy, with a crumpled face and a drawl. The tuxedo he wore as head waiter never quite fitted, the black trousers always slightly too long, causing a little pile of black cloth on the upper part of his shoes. Nevertheless, despite this somewhat scruffy appearance, he was well known in the trade and he certainly knew how to look after his regular customers, who included a fair sprinkling from the world of entertainment. Bruno's genuinely warm welcome and his clever mixture of friendly chat, whilst knowing his place, had won him many loyal customers. His big smile of greeting was an indelible feature of the room.

Christian, who ran the fine-dining restaurant, one floor above Bruno's steakhouse, was the exact opposite of his Anglo/Italian colleague. Younger, by a decade, he was smooth and suave, deferent and charming. The "society" ladies of Knightsbridge and Chelsea adored him. He fitted their image of the perfect French maître d, always polite, always charming, and as smooth as polished glass.

There was nothing smooth, however, about the third member of the "club" – Monty, the banquet manager. Somewhere, deep in history, Monty's family had also hailed from Italy, but any trace of an Italian accent had long gone, replaced by the distinct strains of a Londoner. Indeed, Monty was a Londoner through and through: a big confident handsome man, oozing self-assuredness, but with a charm that could upsell his product with importunity. Monty could be all business when it came to the complicated matter of organising major functions but his sense of humour and charm were never buried beneath his businesslike approach. Although Monty was at least ten years older than Roger, the pair quickly developed a strong bond.

At the weekends Mersky would retire to his country house in the Cotswolds, so his presence in the hotel was negligible.

That did not prevent him, however, from making surprise visits to the property. Since he never signalled his intention to do so to the duty manager, the supervisory staff had devised a "look out" system to give early warning of a Mersky visit. Within minutes of him being spotted getting out of his car or even walking in the direction of the hotel, the warning signs would flash around the place and everybody would be on high alert. Even so, Mersky always found something wrong, something to cause the closest member of staff to him at the time to be at the receiving end of vitriolic abuse. The effect that this had on the supervisory staff was interesting. In a strange way the common enemy of Mersky moulded together those that worked for him into a team: a team that was united in one thing – hatred of the boss.

When Roger was on weekend duty, it became his practice to have a late-night beverage with the two restaurant managers and Monty. Long after the last diners had departed and the last table cleared, they would chew the fat, sitting around a restaurant table with clear views in several directions in case Mersky were to pay a surprise visit. It became a game, and the frequent topic of conversation, for them to dream up ways to eliminate the boss. Suggestions varied from taking a pot shot at him from the roof or the fire escape, to poisoning his morning coffee. These murderous ideas were, of course, fanciful, but not without a large slice of wishful thinking. The "murder club" would meet for an hour or so every Saturday evening at around midnight each time Roger was on that shift. It became a game to dream up the most gruesome way to remove the tyrant from their lives. The laughter at each outrageous plan was just the tonic they all needed.

One evening, the little group's discussions took a distinctive turn towards reality. Monty's first assistant, an attractive tall brunette, had reported to her boss that she was being sexually harassed by Mersky. These "approaches" always took place when Janet, the assistant, was in charge of functions in the absence of Monty. They generally took the form of sexually suggestive comments about Janet's figure, but were now heading in a more active direction. Mersky had been trying to get Janet to accompany him to a suite. When Janet had refused, Mersky had later reported to Monty that she had been mismanaging the function in Monty's absence. Monty was now faced with a tricky situation. He had taken Roger, as the personnel manager, into his confidence. Janet was an efficient deputy to Monty; he did not want to lose her and he certainly did not relish the thought of firing her just because she would not succumb to Mersky's advances.

Roger, as head of the personnel function, knew that he had to act. He decided to confront Mersky. For a fellow who did not look for trouble, he knew that this would be trouble with a capital "T".

The following Monday, after Mersky's customary morning meeting with his department heads and assistant managers, Roger asked if he could stay on as the other participants were leaving. Mersky rarely closed his office door, so, as his department heads sidled out, he was somewhat surprised that Roger shut the door behind them and stayed in the room.

"Mein God," exclaimed Antoine, "it must be something serious. Has there been a rape?"

"Not quite," said Roger, still standing, but thankful for the opening, "but something along those lines."

Mersky was instantly interested. His eyes gleamed with anticipation. "Sit down, young man. Tell me about it."

Roger did his best to delicately describe the girl's allegation that she had been inappropriately approached. He was nervous, but he gritted his teeth and attempted to describe the young lady's accusation. Mersky immediately cut him short. His eyes now flashed with anger. As he spoke, he banged his fist on his desk. His coffee cup rattled on the silver tray. "The young lady is lying. The truth is that I had to reprimand her for sloppy work in managing the function. I have told Monty that she must go."

Roger bravely stuck to his guns. "But, sir, if you persist you run the danger of her pursuing these allegations. Of course, I accept your word," he lied, "but if you fire her, we could find ourselves facing public scrutiny. And, in her defence, we have previously only had good reports about her management of functions. Maybe we should give her a second chance?"

"No second chances," Mersky almost shouted at Roger. "I don't give second chances. The girl must go. Do you understand? The girl must go!"

By now, the man was in a rage. His famous temper had kicked in and Roger knew, that, whatever he said, it would be useless. He would just have to see to it that Janet received the most generous of severance packages and set about finding a replacement. He hated himself for being so weak. When he later told Constance about his conversation with his boss she was not impressed.

A few weeks later a similar problem found its way to Roger's personnel office in the form of Mrs Perkins, the head housekeeper. Molly Perkins was a perfect fit for her job. Her experience was unsurpassed. Her last manager called her "Perfect Perkins". She had been head housekeeper at both Claridge's and the Savoy before being lured by Antoine to the Sloane Towers with a hefty salary increase. She was an organised and efficient manager, respected and loved by her employees and well received by the hotel guests. She ran a tight ship and when, on occasions, any of her staff had been directly reprimanded by Mersky, she had had the courage to take the matter up with him.

"If you have something to say to members of my staff, then you must say it to me and I will deal with it," she had, on more than one occasion, had cause to tell her boss. By and large, this had worked and Antoine had not over-meddled in her affairs. But, unfortunately for Molly, Antoine had taken a shine to one of her assistants, Marylyn, who, sensing an opportunity, had, unlike the hapless Janet, encouraged him. Housekeepers are in the perfect position to carry on a dalliance with the boss; in this case she had the keys to three hundred bedrooms.

Marylyn, knowing that she currently held some sway over Mersky, had decided that his desires would be better catered for if she were to be promoted to head housekeeper. This would mean, of course, that Molly Perkins, had to go. Molly was too long in the tooth to not notice what was going on. Mersky was becoming more and more critical of her performance and increasingly unpleasant and curt in his dealings with her. He knew that it might be difficult and unpopular to fire her, which is what Marylyn was encouraging him to do, so he had resorted to one of his fall-back techniques, which was to make things so unpleasant for an employee that they decided to leave. Molly was not having any of this. She decided to enlist the help of Roger.

The late-night chat at the weekend meeting of the murder club turned serious. Although it was a breach of confidence, Roger shared with his colleagues the latest predicament regarding the head housekeeper. Monty, who had already lost his best assistant, Janet, as a result of Mersky's sexual appetite, was incensed. "We have to stop this bastard," he exclaimed. "If you can't get any help from the Americans, then we will have to do it ourselves!"

"Do what?" asked the others, almost at once.

"Remove him. Fucking kill him. That's what I mean!"

"Are you serious?" chimed Roger and Christian, again almost in unison.

"You bet I am. What say you, Bruno?"

Bruno thought about it for a moment, then, in a slow and serious tone, replied, "I think the man deserves it."

"He might well deserve it," said Roger, "but the usual penalty for mistreating employees is decided by the courts, though there aren't too many employees who have the means or the will to take this route."

However, there was no doubt in the minds of the four late-night plotters that Antoine Mersky's abuse of his position and his ongoing intimidation of people, who were in no position to defend themselves, needed to be brought to an end. But killing him, in Roger's eyes, seemed over the top. Not only that, but it was, of course, illegal, in the eyes of the law but also by the word of God. Nevertheless, at this moment, Roger did not intervene. In fact, worse than that, he even contributed to the plot.

When the discussion continued, now fuelled by a few more brandies than normal for this late-night gathering, the subject of "method" came up. Mersky's murder had to be accomplished in an untraceable manner. Shooting him was one possibility, but the risks involved seemed precarious and, anyway, none of the "club" owned a firearm. They could, of course, hire an assassin, but this posed the obvious threats of later blackmail and other, as yet unforeseen, problems. After twenty minutes or so of discussion the group settled on poison and here Roger was helpful. He had recently read a novel where the villain had been poisoned by a substance, which apparently left no traces. The little group signalled their approval of Roger's suggestion. Then came the inevitable discussion about which of the four should be the assassin. Nobody volunteered. It was Bruno who broke the silence.

"I 'ave the method," he suddenly exclaimed. "One of us will do this thing, but the rest of us must not know which it was."

The other three were puzzled.

"This is what we do," continued Bruno. "We take four playing cards – the Jack, the Queen, the King and the Ace. We shuffle them around and put them on the table, face down.

We decide before that the persons who draw the King and the Ace, will be the – 'ow you say? – the designated killers. Nobody will tell anyone else in the group which card they drew. Two of us will know that we are not selected to kill and two of us will know that they have been chosen. Each of the chosen will not know who is the other chosen. Both of those chosen will set about poisoning, or otherwise despatching, the evil man. Whoever succeeds will never be known to the other three. Comprendi? This is old Italian recipe."

Roger and the others thought about it for a moment. Then Christian, the restaurant manager, piped up, "If I am the one with the King, why wouldn't I wait for the one with the Ace to go ahead and do the poisoning, or why wouldn't he wait for me?"

"Good question, Christian. I suppose it will come down to which of the chosen has got the balls to do it – but two chances are better than one."

A silence fell. Their minds, previously dulled by the brandy, were now churning. This was a wonderful method of committing the murder, yet staying anonymous. But would any of them, in the cold daylight, have the guts to go ahead? Roger thought about what he would do if he drew the Ace or King. He would probably hang back and hope that the other lethal card holder was braver than him and the probability was that the other "cardholder" would do the same. "What a fascinating scenario," he thought, not quite sure of what would happen next, but rather certain that nothing would.

"Okay," said Monti suddenly. "Let's do it, before we change our minds. Get the cards, Bruno. I know you have some in your locker."

The brandy glasses were refilled. Minutes later, Bruno returned with a pack of well-worn playing cards.

"Which suit?" he asked.

"Who gives a fuck?" said Monty

"Well, clubs it is," said Bruno, as he placed the Jack, Queen,

King and Ace of clubs on the table. Now he turned them over and shuffled them around until only a wizard could have known which one was which.

"Now, just to be clear. We will each pick a card. We will not show our card to anyone here, but will slide it back into the pack. If you pick an Ace or a King you are one of the designated killers. No one must ever know which card you picked. You will not know who the other designated killer is. You must act independently. Whichever of you murders Antoine Mersky must take that knowledge to their grave. You swear that you will never discuss this pact with anyone, including the persons sitting round this table. Is that understood and agreed by all here?"

Suddenly, the mood of the four men grew sombre. The earlier jocularity had evaporated. What had commenced as a crazy idea was quickly becoming a reality. They were about to be complicit in a murder; they might even be required to carry it out. Roger silently prayed that he would not draw the murderer's card.

"Agreed," said Monty with some enthusiasm.

"Agreed," mumbled the other three, almost in unison.

With that Bruno reached forward and took a card. He glanced at it and pressed it to his chest. Not a flicker of emotion crossed his face. The others reached in and retrieved a card. Nobody uttered a word. The cards were one by one slid back into the pack, face down. The gaiety of an hour ago had gone, replaced with a deep sense of trepidation. An eerie silence followed. It seemed to last forever. The silence was broken by Roger. "Well, fellas," he started, "I'm pretty tired. I'm off to my bed. Who knows when I will get disturbed." With that he headed for the elevator. He wanted to call Constance to tell her what had just transpired but that would break his promise. After ablutions, he climbed into the fine sheets of the Sloane Towers. Sleep eluded him.

Three weeks later Antoine Mersky dropped dead on the tennis court in the manicured gardens overlooked by the hotel. An ambulance was called by his opponent, but by the time the paramedics arrived he was well and truly gone. His death certificate indicated that he had suffered a heart attack. There was a collective feeling of relief at the Sloane Towers, for all except four men. They too were happy that this awful man was no longer in charge, but their collective guilt hung over them like a heavy cloud. Had he, they wondered, died of a heart attack, or had one of them actually honoured the pact? They would never know, but that collective guilt would never disappear. For one of the quartet it could be that the guilt had been earned.

It did not take long for the American owners to react. The junior management of the hotel and the staff assumed that a new experienced general manager would be recruited or drafted from a sister hotel in the States. They were quite surprised, therefore, when it was announced that Roger would be appointed general manager, jumping over the older, scruffy, Monsieur Voullemin and the more experienced but sterile Hans Ofal, neither of whom were impressed with the decision. Roger was stunned. The rest of the supervisors and staff were pleased. Roger was a popular choice, albeit that he was younger than most of those that would be called to work for him.

Although surprised by his sudden promotion, Roger took it in his stride. Constance was extremely proud of her young handsome husband, now the youngest general manager of a large London hotel. In the stuffy and hierarchical world of European hotels, Roger would have had to wait many years for his turn to be in charge, but, thanks to the Americans, he had now been given his chance at a very early age and was determined to make the most of it. For her young husband to be the general manager of one of London's fanciest establishments was socially very uplifting for Constance and she planned to take full advantage. Where better to entertain her friends than the Sloane? As the manager's wife of one of the city's most prestigious establishments, her standing in the world of advertising agency executives had been greatly enhanced, even if she was only a secretary.

One year after Roger's elevation to management, with the hotel going from strength to strength as the improved environment translated into better service and standards, Roger's feeling of pride and satisfaction received a sudden jolt. A policeman visited him in his office.

"We are wondering if we could question some of your employees about the death of your predecessor. There appear to be some unanswered questions that need to be cleared up."

Roger froze. One of the four must have spoken.

Chapter Two
"Vanilla Beach"

As police enquiries intensified over the next couple of months, Roger became increasingly concerned. Although he had not drawn one of the killer cards, he feared that, should one of the four members of the murder club be talking to the cops about their arrangement, he might be seen as some sort of accomplice. Up until this point the death of Antoine Mersky was still officially due to a heart attack, so why, Roger wondered, were the police so interested? Presumably they had also interviewed Monty, Christian and Bruno but none of them had mentioned it to Roger. This seemed really strange and, in some way, ominous. Roger had never spoken of the murder club to Constance, but she now sensed his tenseness. At first, she put it down to the pressures of the job of general manager. After all, Roger was very young and inexperienced to be managing a luxury hotel in London. The pressure of being in charge of over five hundred staff, she thought, must be very high. It was strange, because when he first took the job, he had seemed amazingly relaxed; latterly he had become tense and often distracted.

Fate, however, now intervened. The American owners of the Sloane Towers had hit some financial difficulties in Europe. In order to finance further properties in Germany and France they had borrowed heavily in D-Marks and Francs. The international exchange rate had swung vehemently against them and they were having difficulties in servicing the debt. To ease the pressure, they decided to sell their jewel in the crown, the Sloane Towers. The new buyers had not previously been in the hotel or tourism business, so they were keen for Roger to stay on. Roger was not sure he could see a future with them, since this could be their only hotel, but, more to the point, the sale gave him an opportunity to collect a sizeable redundancy payment and leave. In his mind, not only could he leave the Sloane Towers, but also England, thereby escaping, he hoped, the unwanted attention of the police.

Constance could not have been happier. The chance to go home with her handsome husband, to be close to her family and childhood friends seemed wonderful. She could not wait to swap the relentless greyness of London for the sunshine of South Africa. She worried that Roger might struggle to secure a job as good as the one he had in London, but his confidence that things would work out and his outstanding track record persuaded her otherwise. The time had come, she thought, to start a family of their own. What better place to do so than in South Africa with the support of her family and plenty of cheap labour to help?

But fate had a different plan for the Browns. When Dusty Evans, one of Constance's uncles, who held some mysterious position in the South African foreign ministry, heard that Roger and Constance were coming home, he was delighted. Roger could be just the man he needed.

During the 1960s and '70s, the South African government's policy of Apartheid was fully entrenched, as was opposition to it from every other country in Africa. As a result, the air space above all African countries north of South Africa was closed to South African aircraft, be they commercial or military. This made it very difficult for South African Airways to operate long haul commercial flights to Europe or Asia, since, in those days, the range of aircraft meant that planes, even military ones, had to land somewhere in Africa to refuel.

One of Dusty's tasks in the Foreign Office had been to identify island nations, off the coast of Africa, where South African planes could land and refuel. Large sums of money and other benefits were offered to Cape Verde off the West Coast of Africa and the Comoran Islands, off the East Coast, to let South African planes land. In both cases Dusty had been the man who had negotiated the deals, which entailed South Africa building and financing airstrips and airport buildings. Dusty was the right man for the job. Unlike almost all of his colleagues in the Foreign Office, Dusty was one of the few English descendants in government amongst a raft of Afrikaans-speaking colleagues. As such, he had been far more acceptable to the respective governments in the islands off Africa.

In the case of the Comores, part of the deal also involved the financing and building of a tourist hotel, the one and only resort in the country. This had happened, but what Dusty and his colleagues now realised was that building a hotel is one thing, but operating it is another, especially in such an economically backward country as Comoros and on a remote island, to boot. The hotel, the Vanilla Beach had, in two instances, been leased to operators, both of whom had failed and eventually walked away. Attempting to run a hotel in a location with extremely limited airlift and a tortuous supply chain had just proved impossible and the hotel had been closed down and "mothballed". Dusty had helplessly witnessed his government's investment deteriorating. He desperately needed someone who knew what he was doing to salvage the situation. When he heard that his nephew-in-law was coming to Africa, his interest was piqued. This young man had done so well in the hotel business in London at such a tender age. What was to say he couldn't be just the man his country needed?

Constance and Roger had imagined settling down in the leafy suburbs of Johannesburg or the beautiful countryside of the Cape, where Roger would in some way enter the tourism business and the pair of them would raise a lovely family. Dusty had other ideas. And so it was that Roger and Constance decided to take a look at the challenge of the Vanilla Beach, persuaded by the offer of twenty percent ownership of the hotel on the basis that they would put in a five-year stint, and a management contract which, if things went well, could be three times the salary Roger had been earning in England. This was Roger's chance to earn some real money and, although he and Constance realised that this would not be what she had had in mind for their new life in South Africa, Constance was comfortable with the decision. "What have we really got to lose?" She convinced herself. "If it doesn't work out, we can always come home. Let's at least go and take a look – and we can make babies anywhere!"

Less than three weeks after the couple had left London, they were setting foot on Ngazidja, more easily known as Grande Comore, one of the three major islands in the independent nation of the volcanic Comoros Islands. Very few scheduled airline flights landed in the Comores. In fact, the only two remaining international flights were a weekly flight from Paris on a cattle truck of a 747 which had five hundred seats crammed together and stopped en route at six other African countries, where most of the passengers disembarked, and a weekly small passenger jet from Johannesburg operated by South African Airways and subsidised by the South African government as part of the "landing rights" deal. Both planes frequently arrived in Moroni, the capital, with less than ten passengers on board.

Roger's first impression was encouraging. The runway seemed to be in a good state of repair and the airport buildings, although modest, were relatively new and in reasonable condition. Dusty had accompanied Roger and Constance on this first trip in order to show them the hotel and introduce them to the island authorities. Before proceeding to the Vanilla Beach, Dusty decided to take them to the little town of Moroni and the port, which was the lifeline of all the imported products that the hotel would need to operate. The town itself was, in fact, a development that had sprung from the harbour. It consisted of one once-grand street, lined on both sides with handsome royal palms, leading from the port to the now dilapidated Palace. The palms, once magnificent, were now unkempt and untidy and their roots had curled across the sidewalk like Quatermass, lifting the blocks here and there enough to make walking precarious. The formerly imposing avenue was edged by crumbling buildings in the style of the famous boulevards of Paris, but they were now peeling and dirty, giving the overall impression of grandeur long gone. Other than that, the rest of the town was a muddle of little row houses and grubby untidy and ill-stocked shops, apart from a square, which showed signs of its old landscaping and was still the site of a weekly market. The architecture was distinctly French colonial, but here and there were signs of Arabic infiltration; the main feature being a mosque with a prayer tower. The once-white walls of the mosque and the surrounding houses were now stained and filthy. The water that lapped at the rocks on which the mosque was built was full of discarded household and ship's waste. Rusty tin cans clanked against the harbour pier in a constant smooch with plastic waste, and the water's edge smelled bad. The actual harbour wall had almost disintegrated and a newer wooden pier had been constructed which extended several hundred yards into the ocean. Perched on the end of the pier was a small rusty steel crane and Roger noticed it was emptying goods from a container ship into tiny wooden craft. He later discovered that these boats were known as pirogues; they were little more than wooden canoes with a stabilising outrigger on one side. It all looked romantic, but very inefficient.

"As you can see," said Dusty, when he saw Roger staring at the unloading process, "there is no deep-water harbour here. Everything has to be unloaded from ships into these little wooden boats to be brought to the shore. It is a slow process. Shit, man, you cannot imagine what it was like when building the hotel."

From the rather dismal water's edge they made their way up the palm-lined main street to a colonial-looking building at the end. This, they were informed, was the Presidential Palace and House of Parliament. The grubby white building was surrounded by a rusty ironwork fence. The grand plastered pillars defining the building were scarred and flaking. Outside, in a sentry box, slouched a solitary uniformed guard, clutching an AK47 and sweating in the morning heat.

"We'll come back here tomorrow," announced Dusty. "I've arranged for you to meet the President and a couple of his cabinet. Now, let's go to the hotel." With that, he instructed their driver to proceed to Vanilla Beach. Roger was impressed with his wife's uncle; his swashbuckling approach was as far away from Roger's image of a civil servant as one could get. With his sporty casual clothes and his flamboyant moustache, Constance's uncle was like a character from a Rudyard Kipling book. Roger liked him a lot.

The potholed road took them through the shacks that made up the suburbs of the little town and into the countryside beyond. The road roughly followed the rugged coastline to their left. To their right towered a huge dark mountain, or, to be more precise, volcano. The remains of an eruption were evident everywhere. Roger wondered how long it had been since the mountain had been active. "Not in our lifetime," he was informed by Dusty. However, the soil was black and rock-hard lava trails still fanned out on both sides of the road, punctuated here and there with vanilla trees and a few wooden shacks. After twenty minutes of driving, on a barely tarred road, mostly in contemplative silence, through this rather bleak landscape, the countryside suddenly became green and the sea, to the left, glistened blue. They were now several hundred feet above sea level and ahead, bathed in sunshine, they could see in the distance what appeared to be a long white sandy beach, stretched between two land promontories and edged by brilliant blue water. The black mountain had given way to rolling green hills on one side and the sparkling blue ocean on the other.

"There she is," exclaimed Dusty, almost with pride. "There's Vanilla Beach." For a few moments, in the distance, a long off-white building could be seen, as the bright sun shone on its walls. Then it disappeared as they began their descent. The road wound down through quite dense green jungle. Here and there were little patches of sugar planted in man-made clearings and dotted about were shacks for human inhabitants, although very few people actually appeared. When they did, Constance noticed how different they were from the blacks in South Africa, who, as they emerged from the bush would almost certainly be carrying something on their heads. Here, the few people that the popped out of the bush wore cloth on their heads in the Arab way. As they descended the air became noticeably more hot and humid but the sunshine was glorious after the greyness of London. To Roger this was all new and exciting. To Constance, it felt like Durban, South Africa's premier resort town on the Indian Ocean, renowned for its humidity.

The hotel, which had not been visible from the road at any point after their first brief sighting, suddenly appeared to their left. A three-storey building, of no particular architectural interest, stretched out along the length of the beach, or, to be more accurate, along the length of one of two beaches. On a small promontory between the two beaches stood what appeared to be the main facility block of the hotel. At least, thought Roger, this building had some appeal, with some interesting Arabic-looking towers and a tiled roof.

The real attraction of the place was, unquestionably, not the buildings but the beach. Although now strewn with seaweed and other miscellaneous flotsam, this was, without doubt, an impressive mile-long stretch of white sand, fringed with the bright blue water forming a natural swimming pool between the beach and a barely visible reef. This was the sort of beach that Europeans yearned for; the sort of beach that could make the headlines of the Sunday newspaper travel supplements; a beach that could not be found in the Mediterranean. The man-made hotel buildings could do with some work, thought Roger, as he took in the scene, but Mother Nature's side of the deal was spectacular.

Constance was impressed. "There are no beaches like this in South Africa," she offered.

"You're right there," said Dusty, with a tinge of pride, as if he had been the explorer who had discovered it.

As their battered little taxi pulled up into the potholed turning circle in front of the closed doors of the hotel entrance, a black man wearing a dirty brown jacket and shorts emerged from a side door. On the pocket of the jacket there appeared to be a Vanilla Beach logo, now almost faded beyond recognition. His smile of welcome was as big as a salad bowl. "Happy noon," he offered with an outstretched hand to Dusty. "Nice to see you again, Mr Dusty."

"Likewise," said Dusty as he took the outstretched hand, "I'm so glad you're still here."

"I go nowhere, Mr Dusty. It is my duty to be here. And I'm awaiting for my money!"

"Good," said Dusty with a broad smile and completely ignoring the reference to payment. "Let me introduce Mr and Mrs Brown. Mr Brown is to be the new manager of the hotel."

On hearing this, Ibrahim, the caretaker, executed a sweeping low bow in front of Roger and Constance.

"It will be my honour so serve you, Mr Brown – and also Lady Brown as well."

"Thank you," said Roger, when the bowing had finished. "I'm sure Mrs Brown and I will appreciate that."

Introductions over, Dusty suggested they start the tour of the hotel. For the next hour or so the little party trudged through the sad neglected-looking property, starting with the restaurant, bar, reception area and lounge. There were cobwebs, dust and miscellaneous debris in every nook and cranny. Everything smelt of the sea. "Christ!" thought Roger, "what a mess!" All of these public areas, in one way or another, were partially open to the elements. This open air feeling, designed to provide the guests with the kiss of the ocean breeze, a respite from the buzz of central air conditioning, and the view of the spectacular beach, had provided little protection for the furniture, which, piled untidily in various corners, was looking stained and severely weather beaten. The back-of-house areas had fared somewhat better, but several layers of grime had built up on most of the equipment. "Somewhere, beneath that dirt," Roger mused, "maybe lies some decent stainless steel." Despite the weather- beaten state of the spaces, Roger could see the validity of their design. He was certain it would have to be completely re-equipped, but the fundamentals of good planning were there. And, to be fair, the actual architecture of the main building, with its various roof lines and towers, was actually quite attractive.

Next, the little party trudged along the long beach, popping in to the ground-level guest rooms from time to time to sample their condition. The bedrooms were a good size, but much of the furniture was missing.

"Do you have a furniture store?" Roger asked Ibrahim, rather speculatively.

"No, Mr Roger. Most of the furniture has been stolen. If we go to the villages, we will find it."

At the far end of the beach sat a wooden building, which was the boathouse. There were no boats left, just signs that they had been there, but the building seemed adequate and was surprisingly intact. Two rusty outboard engines and various oars and paddles were strewn across the floor. All the boats had presumably been stolen. From this end of the site, one could get the feel of the whole place; a sweepingly long white sandy beach, flanked by brilliant blue water, trapped by a reef several hundred yards to sea, on the one side and striking volcanic mountains on the other. Nestled on a little promontory a mile away sat the restaurant, bar and reception buildings, with their slightly Arabic architecture. It seemed to fit.

On the return journey towards the hotel core, Roger suggested that the little group walk back along the two upper floors. All the hotel bedrooms on all three floors were sea facing, with a concrete walkway running along the rear. On the two upper floors the bedrooms had small balconies with wooden crisscross design railings, whilst on the ground floor, they had little patios covered with stone paving, now smothered in weeds. The paint was peeling badly from the bedroom doors which, strangely, opened outward towards the walkway. The walls between the bedrooms and the walkway were punctuated by little ugly frosted glass windows, designed to let light into the showers within, many of which were stained and cracked. The landscaping at the back, on the other side of the buildings from the sea, had once been neatly kept but it had now run wild, covering, in many places, the walkway. A major clean-up and replanting job would be necessary. The rooms on the first and second floors had more furniture in them than those below, presumably because the ground floor rooms had been easier to steal from.

When the little party finally arrived back at the lobby,

two hours after they had set off, Roger was having second thoughts. There was no question that the site was, or could be, terrific. But the condition of the infrastructure and equipment indicated a mountain of hard work for whoever took on the challenge. Furthermore, the remoteness of the place and the obvious lack of transportation links, both for customers and for goods was alarming. Two experienced hotel operators had tried and failed to make this work. "Why should I be any different?" thought Roger. "And, what would Constance do in a place like this? She would go mental." Strangely, Constance had said very little during the walkabout.

"Well," piped up Dusty, when Ibrahim had gone to seek some fresh water for the little touring party, "what do you think, Roger?"

For Roger, who had recently operated in the pristine world of a newly built luxury hotel in the heart of one of the greatest metropolises in the world, the shock of seeing the dilapidated state of this resort hotel was almost overwhelming and certainly depressing. You did not need to be an expert in hotel-keeping to see that this place needed a shitload of work. Was this the work that Roger really wanted to be involved in? Was this the sort of work that he could realistically be successful at? These were the questions that Roger was wrestling with. And yet, should he be successful, the possibility of actually owning a healthy slice of this real estate was something that he probably could not expect in the real world. Then there was Constance. Could a beautiful young woman like her really make a life in such a backward place? What on earth would she do with herself? She had never played a part in his professional life; would she want to do so now? He knew that she wanted to start a family, him too. How could one bring a child into such a remote place? What on earth would the medical facilities be like? This was not exactly Chelsea! And Constance was such a social creature. In London she had many friends and a very active social life. She knew how to amuse herself when Roger was working his long and unsociable hours as hotel manager. In South Africa, her homeland, she would have no difficulty in reconstituting her circle of friends, but here, on a beach in the Comores, her social life could be negligible, except for the hotel guests who would be like ships passing in the night. Roger needed more time to think. There were so many things to consider.

"Well, Dusty," he finally began. "The site is beautiful, but the place is a mess. If we are to have any hope of success, plenty of money will need to be spent. At this stage I can't even guess what that number is, but, if I am to take it on, that money must come out of the South African government's pocket, and none of it from mine. Before we proceed with any deal, I will need to work up some estimates of how much and how long it will take to ready this place for business. There's no way I can come up with a definite cost without some help from a quantity surveyor, but I can have a rough crack. And then, Constance and I will need to talk; she will need to be part of the decision."

At the back of the main hotel building was a small suite of offices. It was agreed that for the rest of the afternoon, Roger would utilise one to start figuring out a refurbishment plan and cost thereof, whilst Dusty occupied another to attend to other South African government business, before returning to Moroni where he had arranged for them to stay overnight in the local government's guest house adjacent to the Presidential Palace. Having blown the dust and dirt from a couple of desks, Ibrahim disappeared for a while to organise a lunch snack for the little group and Constance decided to take herself and her thoughts for a stroll along the beach and a little sunbathing.

Roger's outline budget for refurbishing and reopening the Vanilla Beach posed more questions than it produced hard and fast numbers, but he diligently worked his way, undisturbed, through the absorbing process, trying to ignore his dusty, dirty surroundings. Constance meanwhile trudged halfway down the beach in the hot midday sun. She cut a lonely, but strikingly beautiful figure. The brilliant shimmering water looked so inviting. For a while she sat on the beach, deep in thought.

"What a spectacular place," she mused to herself, "and what a fascinating island. It's a real time warp. There must be so much to explore and to learn here. This is a dream come true."

The hot sun beat on her back. There was no shade at all on the beach.

"Screw it," she suddenly said out loud, "I'm going for a fucking swim." Since being on the site with Dusty and Ibrahim she had not seen another living soul. She stood up and looked up and down the length of the beach and back towards the wall of empty hotel rooms. Nobody to be seen. So, without further hesitation, she stripped off her clothes, including her underwear, and placed them neatly in a pile on the sand. She had a magnificent body. She was proud of her figure and regularly worked at keeping it in good shape. She knew that Roger appreciated it. Slowly she eased her way into the water until the warm ripples covered her firm round breasts. The feeling was just delicious. The freedom of swimming naked on her own mile-long beach was something she had never experienced before. She wished that Roger was there to share the moment with her.

It did not take long for the Comoran bush "radio" to alert every male islander within a mile of the beach that a naked white lady was taking a dip. Access to the hotel rooms from the green jungle was not a problem, since most of the doors had been left unlocked. As Constance splashed around in the sea, the occupancy of the sea-facing guest rooms rapidly began to grow with islanders, all careful to stay hidden from her view. Their Arab religion did not allow women to show their faces, let alone their whole bodies, so here was a treat sent straight from heaven. Amongst their number was Ibrahim.

As Constance waded out of the water, heading for her little pile of clothes on the beach, the full glory of her magnificent body was on view to the men behind the dirty drapes. For a while she lay on the beach naked allowing the hot sun to dry her body and her wet blonde hair. As she slowly put her clothes back on, the gallery of men once again disappeared into the jungle. This had been a special gift – and one, God willing, that they might see again. Later, when the small group of Dusty, Roger and Constance bade farewell to Ibrahim before heading back to Moroni for the evening, there was a sparkle in Ibrahim's eyes which had not been there in the morning.

"I do hope your day has been as wonderful as mine," were Ibrahim's parting words as the little group climbed into the waiting rusty taxi.

The following morning, Dusty's little group proceeded on foot to the Palace to meet the President. Dusty had advised Constance that it would be polite for her to cover her head; she borrowed a napkin from the guest rooms for the purpose. The dishevelled sentry opened the rusty gate to let them in, from whence they were guided by another half-uniformed guard to the ruler's quarters.

President Saif bin Sultan was a stern-looking figure in white dish-dash. The shiny black shoes that peeked from beneath the robe seemed incongruous. It was well known that he was gay, a rumour that Dusty had shared with Roger and Constance the evening before. Constance did her utmost to be polite and deferent but all she could think of during the audience was Saif bin Sultan engaged in gay things. Roger hit it off well with the old man. It turned out that Saif bin Sultan had stayed recently at the Sloane Towers on a visit to London. Roger had not known about this at the time because apparently the President and his young companion had been incognito.

The interior of the Presidential Palace was a strange mixture of Asia and Africa with a few European (particularly French) touches. The antique European chairs in the hallway were covered in dust. Although the walls were thick the hot humid air had found its way inside and the high ceilings were dark and dotted with damp spots. By contrast, the room in which the President received his visitors was light and cool, enhanced by a through-the-wall air-conditioning unit, which continuously rattled. On the large wooden desk and on the walls were photographs: some of local ceremonial events but many of Saif and his friends on various jollies, including skiing and sailing. Both Roger and Constance each noticed that the photos featured only men.

The meeting itself was rather short; it did not include other ministers, as advertised. Dusty was obviously seen as a reliable friend and ally. The President did not seem too perturbed that the only hotel of international quality on the islands was currently inoperable but, nevertheless, offered his cooperation in regard to any efforts that might be made by Roger to reopen it. Obviously, the provision of more jobs and renewed foreign exchange could only be good for his nation, but, somehow, they had managed to jog along without the hotel for years before and would, apparently, do so again should needs be. Presumably, thought Roger, the French would be there with handouts, as usual in this part of the world. After twenty minutes or so of chat, Saif bin Sultan abruptly stood up, indicating that the meeting was over. He once again welcomed Roger and Constance to his island and promised his support, and then they were dismissed. Neither Roger nor Constance was terribly impressed but Dusty, now used to the ruler's seeming indifference, assured them that this had been a good, and necessary, meeting.

On the evening before, Roger and Dusty had agreed that Roger and Constance would stay on the island until the next weekly flight from South Africa appeared. Since the plane they had arrived on was due to depart back to Joburg at 1pm, Dusty took his leave. It had been agreed that Roger would use the rest of the week on the island in an attempt to assess the cost and timescale of getting the hotel open again and that they would meet again in South Africa in a week's time to map out the way forward, if any. Roger and Constance had debated whether Constance should return with Dusty, but she had opted to stay with her husband. A week on the island to explore should be enough for her to contribute to the decision that Roger and she would need to make and, besides that, she really loved having her husband in her bed each night under the African skies – so much more romantic than the inner suburbs of London.

In the days that followed, whilst Roger busied himself with assessing the costs and the logistics of reopening the hotel, Constance, in between carrying out errands for him, explored more of the island, each day gathering facts and information that were quite useful to her husband. In the afternoons she would swim. The occupancy of the beach-facing rooms grew exponentially as the week went by. Constance still did not have a bathing costume.

Chapter Three
"Murky Water"

Exactly one year after their first visit to the island, the revamped hotel would open to the public. Roger negotiated hard with the South African government to fund a new capital investment programme, a new pre-opening marketing programme, and a pretty useful salary for himself for the pre-opening year so that he could supervise the renovations and hire and train the operating personnel. At the same time, he had convinced the government that his eventual "free" shareholding should be raised from twenty-five percent to fifty-one percent once the government had received back its reopening investment. Dusty, on behalf of his government, had come to accept that without Roger's professional help they might have nothing. Better half of something than all of nothing. And, in any event, the main purpose of creating the hotel was to secure landing rights, not to make a profit from it.

For most of the year Constance worked as her husband's secretary and assistant. Her help was invaluable, particularly for the first part of the year when the couple had no expatriate staff at all. They lived in one of the few habitable suites in the hotel and hired a local villager to cook for them. They were overwhelmed with work but they were in it together. For months they were in each other's pockets, but at night, in the cosy quarters of their suite in the empty hotel, they enjoyed each other's company in bed. In the days they quickly learned that the locals, although generally amiable and willing, were, through no fault of their own, not used to the concept of work on an organised and routine basis. Furthermore, it soon became apparent that the islanders did not really care for the concept of service or giving service. When it came to recruitment, in almost all cases, local applicants were looking for jobs that they considered to be uplifting, such as accounts clerks or front desk personnel. Not too many wanted to be cooks or waiters or even housekeepers. Roger devised a quick sifting mechanism before he interviewed any local for a job. Each applicant was supplied with a form asking them to tick on a multiple list of jobs, not in the hotel, any occupation that appealed to them. Most ticked "policeman", "school teacher", or "hospital worker"; the first two because they were positions of power, and the last because the French government, short on health workers, was willing to pay fares to France for persons to work as hospital orderlies. Anyone who ticked these boxes on the form was not invited for an interview.

Roger's concern that island life, with no opportunity for spending time with her friends and family, might be too much for Constance to take, did not materialise. There was just so much to do in regard to re-establishing the resort and Constance proved to be such a useful resource that there was no time for her to think about her missing social life. There was also a goal to achieve and focus on: a goal that came nearer and nearer every day. Roger had set his mind on reopening the hotel within one year and he meant to achieve it. Nothing was going to derail him. By the time Roger and Constance climbed into their marital bed, exhaustion, both mental and physical, often overcame them. What had been at first a very active sex life began to tail off. Initially this was not a problem, but, as the year progressed, Constance, particularly, began to wonder why. "It's not just men who need sex," she often thought to herself, but she desisted from raising the subject with her busy husband. She could see that Roger had undertaken a monumental task in getting the abandoned hotel back into working order. He had been literally swamped with difficulties and logistical challenges, from dealing with construction crews to hiring around four hundred operating staff. Things were always going wrong. Roger needed to think on his feet almost every day. It was no wonder that he was too tired at night to have sex with his wife. On the other hand, it was also a little boring to hear of nothing else but the problems of the job. Their social life had disappeared completely. At least, if the hotel had been up and running, there would have been activity to talk about around the guests; there would have been life after dark. As it was, during the pre-opening period Roger just kept working away long after the sun had gone down. Although Constance could share in many of the challenges, Roger did not involve her with everything he was doing. If truth be told, Constance was, despite all that was going on in Roger's world, becoming a little bored; both of the island and even Roger himself. On the other hand, she kept reminding herself, she had willingly entered this challenge with her husband, so, to some extent, she only had herself to blame if she was unhappy. "Things will change once the hotel is open," she kept telling herself. Meantime, in terms of sex, she would just have to take matters into her own hands.

By and large, Roger, with a calmness that amazed and inspired those around him, tackled the various challenges that opening a hotel on an island threw at him. Early on he had decided that the rather boring architecture of the hotel's room blocks needed to be softened in appearance, and that the key to this would be in the landscaping. On the beach side of the property he could not improve on Mother Nature, but on the land-facing side, he believed there was a huge opportunity to create a wonderful tropical garden, which would be the first thing that arriving visitors would see, rather than rows of buildings punctuated by bedroom doors. To this end, Roger had hired a French landscape architect who had been recommended to him by a hotel manager in Paris. Patrice LeBlanc was a strange man, but truly a genius in regard to horticulture. Patrice had long lank brown hair which he never seemed to wash. He wore the same t shirt each day, which he rinsed out at night and hung on his balcony. He refused to present Roger with a plan of how the gardens would be laid out, stating that Roger would just have to trust him. He would disappear for days at a time, gathering plants in the jungle. When it came to the actual planting, he threw a sheaf of arrows over his head and plucked out the arrows one by one as he was followed round the site by his helpers. Where an arrow landed was where something had to be planted. When he was finally finished the garden looked spectacular, full of interesting indigenous and colourful plants. But, and as far as Roger was concerned, there was one big drawback; there were no palm trees. Roger was careful how he approached the matter with Patrice, whom he had learned did not like palm trees because they were not indigenous to this particular area of the Comores. "But the tourists like palm trees," explained Roger to Patrice, "they expect to see palm trees. Palm trees fit their image of a vacation paradise."

"Well, they're wrong," was all Patrice would say. "I am not planting palm trees, and that is that." The debate, or lack thereof, went on for several minutes.

Finally, Roger, completely out of character and probably as a result of many frustrations, suddenly lost his rag. "Listen, my French friend. My kitchen equipment is at the bottom of the ocean, the legs on my beds are falling off, the cutlery has been sent to Tokyo, my wife is hardly talking to me, and all I am asking for is some fucking palm trees. Please, Patrice, plant the fucking palm trees and then fuck off."

Patrice was shocked – but he planted the trees. This was the first time that any of the staff had seen Roger lose his temper; maybe the intense pressure was finally getting to him?

Roger quickly realised that the level of supervision required to run an efficient hotel would be extremely high and that a local supervisor would find it hard to discipline someone from the same village or even the same extended family as them. Gradually a few stars emerged: locals who were able to take responsibility, but even in these cases, they did not have the necessary experience to administer and provide standards of international service. Roger knew that he would need to inject some experience into his team if he were to operate a first-class resort, which he fully intended to do. He decided that, at minimum, he would need a European chef and sous chef, a restaurant and/or food and beverage manager, a housekeeper, a maintenance engineer, and at least one bookkeeper/accountant. Due to the ongoing refurbishment work and planning thereof, Roger did not feel that he had the time to go on extended recruitment trips to Europe, so, at first, he relied on agencies in London and Paris to find the right people. He soon discovered that nobody of any experience or quality wanted to come to an island with no track record of hospitality and only one resort hotel, especially one they had never heard of. He tried his hand in South Africa but people in the industry were wary due to the earlier failures of the property. Finally, he struck gold. Other Indian Ocean islands, he realised, had already developed a well-established tourism sector, and a cluster of resorts of international standard had been operating for several years. The islands of Mauritius and the Maldives were two cases in point. Surely those trained supervisors would have a closer understanding of island life and the opportunities it could support? Surely these islands could be a happy hunting ground for some experienced supervisory personnel who would be willing to swap one island for another as long as it advanced their careers and filled their pockets? It also cost much less time and money to pop over to Mauritius on the hunt than to search in Europe or the Far East.

This strategy seemed to work and a few months before the reopening, Roger had successfully filled his vacancies with a collection of individuals who were soon to become his Comoran family. He had discovered his new chef at the Club Med in Mauritius, which he and Constance had used as their base whilst scouring the island for likely candidates. They had been impressed by the variety and imagination that the chef put into his daily menus. The food was not only tasty and visually appealing but, somehow, fun. Chef Jimmy Sparrowhawk was the reason. This huge north-country Englishman sported an impressive handlebar moustache. His face was ruddy, presumably from the constant exposure to hot stoves and ovens. He stood over six feet five inches tall in his kitchen clogs. You could always identify the soup of the day by the colour of his moustache or, if that failed, the splashes on his white jacket. Jimmy, as Roger was soon to discover, had a sudden and violent temper, but he was a creative genius in the kitchen. His short temper had severely tested his relationship with the rather delicate French manager of the Club, and Roger, luckily, had made his approach just after there had been a huge and divisive eruption between the two. Jimmy had had enough of "this little French twerp" and agreed to join Roger on the spot. Jimmy appeared to have no family ties at all, which, maybe, was his problem. One thing he definitely did have, however, was immense skill and imagination in the kitchen. That was the most important factor in Roger's thinking. He was prepared to live with the crap. According to Chef Jimmy, he was free from baggage: no wife, no girlfriend, no boyfriend, and no kids, so, a transfer from one island to another would not be complicated. "Everyone has some baggage," thought Roger as he signed Chef Jimmy's new employment contract. "No doubt we'll soon learn the truth about Chef Jimmy."

Roger's selected food and beverage manager and maître d was not what he had set out to find. In fact, Dinesh Hare was a product of the island of Mauritius, a blend of imported Indian and local islander of French descent. Roger had observed him at work on a dinner trip to the Saint Georges Hotel and Casino on the other side of the island from the Club Med. Dinesh's way with the guests was exceptional and he had "film star" good looks. He was smooth. He seemed to know every diner's name and was greeted with genuine warmth by all who entered the restaurant or the attractive pool bar. It had been more difficult to interest Dinesh in leaving Mauritius, but Roger's offer to elevate him from restaurant manager to food and beverage manager was enough, it seemed, to secure him. What Roger did not know, at the time, was that Dinesh's charm had won him a place in the hearts, and some cases, beds, of some of the most beautiful guests of the hotel, including several celebrities. Dinesh's conquests included many married women; in fact, he derived particular pleasure from them. Roger's attractive wife, Constance, seemed a very plausible target and as good a reason as any to go to the Comores. Nothing was off limits to Dinesh. All Roger knew was that Dinesh was charming, experienced, well trained and single. He would make an ideal addition to his management team.

It was Dinesh who recommended Roger's final recruitment coup on the island. Brigitte was the young head housekeeper at the Belle Mare. Brigitte was French. She had been raised in an orphanage in the suburbs of Paris. She had followed a boyfriend from Paris to Mauritius but had since ditched him. At the age of twenty-five, she was quite young to hold the position of executive housekeeper at such a prestigious establishment, but, according to Dinesh, she was very well regarded.

She was also a very pretty blonde with a cheeky smile and a charming French accent when she spoke fluent English. Roger thought she was cute. Dinesh and Brigitte had dated a few times. She liked Dinesh but was well aware of his reputation as a ladies' man. Maybe, she thought, if she went to the Comores, as he was planning to do, she could get his exclusive attention. For Roger, the possibility of securing Brigitte as his housekeeper at the Vanilla Beach was extremely attractive. After a couple of meetings with her and the offer of a lucrative contract, Brigitte was persuaded to join the Comoran team. Constance, who only met her after she had signed, was not so sure that this particular appointment was a good idea.

But, at least, the trip to Mauritius had been a welcome break from the pre-opening travails back in the Comores. Constance had also been able to do some much-needed shopping. For several weeks she had been mulling over a trip to South Africa to do some personal shopping. She was concerned about the state of her wardrobe, particularly in regard to playing the role of the manager's wife once the Vanilla Beach was open. She had absolutely nothing to wear for the opening of the hotel or, for that matter, thereafter, and even her underwear was becoming tired. Mauritius, she found, catered for a luxury market and, although the prices were sky high, Constance found several boutiques offering designer summer clothes from Europe, at least as good as she would have found in Johannesburg or Cape Town. In the Comores there were no shops like this, so Constance, with Roger's encouragement, went on a spending spree, including a couple of nice little numbers that she hoped would appeal to him.

Roger and Constance did agree on one important recruitment decision. Constance absolutely loved the resident Mauritian band at the Club Med. They seemed to be able to capture the mood of the crowd; in fact, they created the mood. They were fun to listen to and fun to dance to. They were totally engaged in the action on the little dance floor in front of them and they cleverly adjusted their programme to the mood of the crowd. Constance thought they were just terrific – and very sexy. She implored Roger to hire them for the Vanilla Beach. Roger could see her point and set out to do so. He succeeded.

The trip to Mauritius had been fruitful but Roger was still short of an experienced maintenance engineer and an accountant, neither of which were available, it seemed, in Moroni or Mauritius. On a fleeting trip to South Africa to negotiate increasing airlift to the island, Roger had got lucky. Sitting next to him on a plane from Cape Town to Johannesburg was a middle-aged man with whom he fell into conversation. It turned out that the man's son was the maintenance engineer at the Admiral Crighton Hotel in Cape Town. One thing led to another and, a few weeks later, Colin Freeke had agreed to come to the Comores, with his young wife and baby daughter. That left the bookkeeping vacancy, which, through an agency in London, was duly filled in the form of Hector Watkins, a recently qualified accountant in search of adventure. Hector had come to the right place.

The reopened hotel had been completely refurbished and was now sparkling. This process had been very hard since the difficulties of unloading cargo at Moroni harbour had been immense. A container full of replacement kitchen equipment had been dropped to the bottom of the ocean and many other items needed to be airfreighted at huge cost in order to circumvent the harbour. Of the five hundred or so beds in the hotel, at least two hundred had been stolen. The original bedframes had been made locally on the island. They were quite crude; Roger preferred to call them "rustic". Despite this, Roger took the decision to have the replacements manufactured in the same workshop that had produced the original beds. This was a mistake because, one by one, as guests started to use them, the legs fell off, eventually prompting the need to replace them all with beds manufactured in South Africa.

But Roger's biggest problem had been airlift to the island. It was all very well having a beautiful resort, but how were the guests supposed to get there? South African Airways, despite the government's commitment to fly a weekly service from Johannesburg to Moroni, had tired of the low passenger count and decided unilaterally to discontinue the flight. Roger, of course, had been banking on this service to provide seats for the guests he had secured through his pre-opening marketing efforts in South Africa, his largest potential market. Now he was stuffed. With no planes to bring his customers his hopes for a successful relaunch would be ruined. There had been no other possibility left to Roger other than to charter a commercial plane, which he had done to replace the weekly SAA service. This arrangement, although expensive unless he could fill all the seats on a regular basis, only secured business in South Africa. What Roger really needed was air service from the lucrative European market as well.

It was Constance who came to the rescue. She, like many South Africans, had friends and relatives who were working in Dubai, the home of the ever- expanding Emirates Airlines. One close friend, it seemed, was working for Emirates and secured an introduction for Roger and Constance to meet with the airline's marketing director. At the time Emirates was not flying from Dubai to South Africa, having been unable to secure rights from the South African government who could not share in the route due to overflying bans on the African continent. Roger had, rightfully, surmised that if he could convince Emirates to fly to Johannesburg via Moroni, they could use the legitimate rights of the non-functioning (and non-existent) Comores Airways to land in South Africa. Operating this route could open up the Comores to traffic from all over Europe, via Dubai, as well as traffic for the Emirates from Dubai to South Africa. Roger believed he could fill a weekly flight to Moroni from Johannesburg with his South African guests and fill the same plane between Moroni and Dubai with Asian and European guests. All he needed to do was convince the Emirati owners of his plan. This suggestion had worked and, after a site inspection of the runway in Moroni, Emirates agreed to commence a weekly service from Dubai to South Africa via the Comores. All that Roger needed to do now was fill the seats.

As Roger's self-imposed deadline of opening one year after his renovation programme had commenced, the pace of activity quickened even further. Roger was convinced that by having a firm date for taking in paying customers the huge amount of work that needed to be done to be ready would crunch itself into the time allowed. Any sort of soft or floating opening date, in Roger's view, would have meant that the pre-opening preparations would spread out into the time available, at huge cost to the hotel and Roger personally. The hiring and training of the completely raw islanders gathered pace and the difficulties of teaching rural village-dwellers the skills and requirements for serving the needs of sophisticated Europeans on holiday became apparent. It was hard enough to achieve success in the pre-opening simulated exercises and practice. Roger was fearful about what it would actually be like with real guests. Most of his friends in the business back in the UK had suggested to Roger that he go for a "soft" opening; that is to start with a deliberately low room occupancy and build up slowly in numbers thereby giving the new staff a chance to learn and gain experience in a gradual curve. Roger did not agree. His strategy was to open, if possible, to a full house and hit the staff hard. In Roger's opinion, most guests experiencing low levels of service at the opening would be quite tolerant and, in recognition of this, Roger was prepared to offer a very low room rate for the first few weeks of operation: better to have the staff experience what the pressure would be like going forward than let them settle into an easier life. Constance argued with Roger about this approach, as did Dinesh, but Roger was unbending. "The quicker they see what the real pressure is like, the quicker they will learn to cope." This was Roger's mantra and everyone would just have to put up with it.

To achieve his goal of an instantly full resort, Roger had offered a ridiculously low room rate to the travel industry in France and South Africa. You could stay at the Vanilla Beach for five dollars per person sharing in a double room. The proper and published rate was closer to sixty. Within days of offering this introductory rate, the hotel had been sold out. Roger's theory of a hard opening was about to be tested.

As Roger and Constance welcomed their first guests, directly off the inaugural Emirates flight, in the lobby of the hotel, something strange and rather ominous occurred. A loud thud from somewhere in the distance resonated across the lobby, followed a few minutes later by another – louder and obviously nearer. The thuds got closer and louder and more frequent. Colin Freeke suddenly appeared in the lobby, just as all of the lights went out. "What the fuck is happening?" yelled Roger at Freeke.

"The underground power line is exploding. It's throwing great clouds of earth up into the entry road. With a bit of luck, it will stop at the transformer box near the entrance," replied Freeke with absolute coolness.

As they spoke, the emergency generator kicked in and the lights were restored, but the thudding noise continued to come closer and closer. As it reached the transformer the two men held their breath. There was a long pause. It seemed like a fortnight. Then, silence. The transformer had done its job. The progress of the exploding electrical cable had been halted. No damage had been done to the newly renovated hotel, only to the grass verge at the side of the entry road and to the cable itself, and that could easily be fixed.

It was not long, however, before the second potential disaster manifested itself. As the new arrivals scattered to their rooms, the sudden rush to use the bathrooms after a long flight emptied almost all the toilet cisterns in the guest rooms. Unfortunately, the cisterns did not refill. Somewhere, somehow, the water that had been run off in flushing was not replaced. Fresh water was not reaching the hotel rooms. It was not long before the front desk and the hotel switchboard were inundated with complaining guests. All eyes were again on poor Freeke. Most men in Roger's position would, by now, be yelling at their engineer, but Roger, sensibly, realised this would not help. What needed to be done was to solve the problem. Somewhere, between the loos in the rooms and the main supply pipe, water was being lost. They would just have to dig up the pipe until they found out where. Roger could have cried as men with spades set about digging across his newly landscaped gardens, tracing the line of the feeder pipe. For twelve hours none of the newly arrived guests could flush their toilets or take a shower or bath, and there were simply not enough buckets in stock to help everybody out. Roger toured the property continuously, talking to his irate guests but, after a while, the anger seemed to change to sympathy. Everyone knew that he and his staff were doing their best to solve the problem. Some guests even volunteered to help with the digging. At last, the offending leak was found and repairs carried out. Roger threw a freebie cocktail party in the lobby and everyone rejoiced. Roger and his staff had made friends with their first guests and the tolerance levels for the ongoing mistakes of his rookie staff were phenomenal. It seemed that Roger had got away with his opening tactics, and the second guessing from his management team was stopped in its tracks. Constance too had been invaluable. Her helpful involvement with the guests had been terrific. The introduction of fresh blood to the island by way of over two hundred guests had invigorated her. There was no time for boredom now.

Dinesh, however, really had his work cut out in the dining room and bars. Local young men whom he had been training as waiters were initially overwhelmed. Although all wait staff had been through Dinesh's course on wine recognition, with detailed instruction on the differences between the winelands of France and elsewhere, almost all of this had been forgotten in their initial panic to serve guests. What had been detailed and rehearsed descriptions of wines were now reduced to simply describing their colour. "White, pink or red?" Somehow, since their smiles were infectious, this actually added to their charm and, somehow, at five dollars per night, almost anything was forgivable.

To announce to the world that the Vanilla Beach was open and ready for business Roger decided to throw an "opening party". To this end he hired a public relations firm in London which had branches in both Paris and Johannesburg – all three were potentially lucrative markets for the resort. The agency asked that Roger negotiate with Emirates for ten free seats to Moroni from London, Paris and South Africa so that they could invite a handful of celebrities from each place, together with a clutch of photojournalists. The plan was to give the celebs a few wonderful days at the hotel whilst being photographed and interviewed by the press, particularly the glossy magazines. Getting real celebrities to take a week out to go to an island they had never heard of and which certainly was not in the class of Saint Barts or Monte Carlo had proven to be a difficult exercise. So it was not a surprise to Roger (although it was a disappointment) that the characters who stepped off the plane from both directions were definitely not class A celebs; class C would be a better description. Nevertheless, the glossy magazines were not too picky about whom they wrote, as long as they looked glamorous; so several good pictorial spreads soon appeared in magazine stands on the Champs Elysées, Sloane Square and the cafes of Cape Town.

Roger had arranged three days of activities, culminating in a grand opening dinner with sumptuous feast and fireworks, to which the President, Saif bin Sultan, and his friends and senior colleagues would be invited. Roger sat at the top table, hosting the President, whilst Constance sat at another with the dishy third-rate European actors. Jimmy the chef had planned to excel. However, this was the first banquet that he and his new crew of islanders had been asked to prepare and tensions were running high in the kitchen. Yet another water pipe burst, this time under the kitchen floor, adding to his difficulties. His cooks were having to dodge around great holes puncturing the kitchen floor.

Whilst Roger and Constance engaged in small talk at their respective tables, there seemed to be a very long wait for the main course to arrive. On a couple of occasions Roger managed to catch Dinesh's eye, but all he could see was panic. After a while Roger excused himself from the table and headed for the kitchen. On the menu was a vol-au-vent dish. As Roger passed through the second of the swing doors into the kitchen, he was hit by a barrage of little pastry vol-au-vent cases. He instantly realised what was happening. Jimmy, the tall chef, had lost it. Out of complete frustration with his newly trained local brigade and having to deal with the chaos in the kitchen due to yet another water leak , he had flown into a rage that was making matters infinitely worse by throwing little brown pastry bombs at anyone who came near him. "Stop," yelled Roger, as he deflected the flying pastries. "You can throw as many as you like, but please, please save enough for the President's table." For some reason, Jimmy thought this was funny. Whether it was the sight of his boss in the kitchen or the thought of only managing to serve one table at the banquet, Jimmy somehow pulled himself together and, although he continued to swear profusely, set about resuming the food delivery process. Luckily for Roger, the so-called celebrity crowd knew where their bread was buttered. They were on a freebie normally reserved for real celebrities; they were not going to rock the boat over a little slow service or some missing vol-au-vents, nor were the photojournalists. They had all grown to like Roger and, in some cases, particularly his lovely wife, so they were not going to do anything to spoil the party.

Notwithstanding the chaos in the kitchen, the opening party was actually a great success, mainly, as it turned out, due to the nonstop energy of the Mauritian band. Most of the guests had no idea the musicians were also imported. To them, the party was an all-Comoran affair, and one that they loved. As Constance had predicted, the band read the mood of the crowd perfectly. From quiet melodic numbers during the meal, allowing the guests to talk, eat and drink (especially drink), to fast and furious songs après dinner, to slow romantic melodies in the wee hours, they got it just right. The circular dance floor, sited as an island in the blue lit pool, was ablaze with the vibrant colours of the ladies' dresses and the men's carnival-coloured shirts, and the bright stars over the Indian Ocean illuminated the magical and romantic scene.

For one brief moment Roger felt the thrill of success. With the help and support of Constance, they had actually done it. They had taken the derelict dump that they had inherited and turned it into a living dream.

Constance had acted as the resident public relations manager for this gala opening week and played her role to perfection. One of the visiting actors, Alain Gabor, had really fallen for her and she was enjoying the attention, especially since her husband had recently been too busy to give her any. Gabor was only to be at the Vanilla Beach for seven days but this was long enough for him to know that he just had to get the hotel manager's wife into his bed. Gabor was a man used to getting his way, especially with young women. In her role as acting public relations manager for the hotel, Constance felt that it was her duty to spend time with Alain, or so she rationalised. She was actually flattered by his Gallic charm, but, despite being incredibly attracted to him, managed to resist his flagrant advances. She found herself fantasising about Alain Gabor. She knew it would be easy to succumb to his charms but her sensible self told her this would lead to disaster. On the night of the party, she wore a particularly provocative dress she had found in Mauritius, which hugged her body like a tight glove. It certainly appeared to her admirers that she was not wearing underwear. Gabor was particularly keen to find out, as was Jean Pierre, the band leader, but Constance kept them guessing. She would let Roger find out when the party finally fizzled out at 2am. Despite the shambles in the kitchen, the visiting "celebrities", the Presidential party and the other paying guests had the time of their lives, and Roger's route to putting the Vanilla Beach on the map had begun. Unfortunately for Constance, by the time Roger joined her in the marital bed, he was exhausted, and the body-hugging party dress was back in the closet – unnoticed.

Two days after the party the C-listers left on their freebie flights back to Europe and South Africa. Constance had managed to avoid the advances of Alain Gabor. That had not been easy. First, because he pursued her with some intensity, and second because she actually thought he was gorgeous. Roger was too busy to notice.

Although Gabor's amorous intentions had slipped from his grasp, he determined that he would one day return. To him this parting was not adieu, but simply au revoir.

And so it was that the Vanilla Beach reopened its doors.

Roger launched marketing initiatives in South Africa and Europe, with financial backing from the airline, and he was suddenly in business. The newly renovated hotel was an instant success in both markets. Due to the infrequency of the airlift, all guests had to stay for at least a week, which did not seem to be a problem, since the Vanilla Beach was a perfect holiday destination. Sunshine, sand, palm trees, and the waters of the warm Indian Ocean. What more could anyone want?

The hotel was providing employment for over four hundred local people, which meant it was probably directly supporting over three thousand Comorians. The room occupancy, within a few weeks of trading, had reached a staggering eighty-five percent, Saif bin Sultan was a happy man, the sun was shining – what could go wrong?

It did not take long for Roger to find out. They were in a part of the Indian Ocean subject to occasional cyclonic conditions. Full blown cyclones, though, are rare in the Comores; they occur more frequently in the islands further into the Indian Ocean where the wind picks up power over a broader stretch of water. In the Seychelles, Reunion and Mauritius, cyclones occur at least once or twice per year, causing much damage. Their frequency is such that it is almost impossible to get storm insurance on those islands. But in the Comores they were not regarded as a threat. However, not long after the launch party at the Vanilla Beach, the effects of an offshore cyclone gave Roger a very worrying time.

The normally calm waters inside the reef had been unusually stirred up by the effects of a building cyclone several miles off the coast. The crystal clear water within the reef had briefly turned murky as disturbed water flooded through the gaps in the barrier. According to the locals, this condition was not new. It happened from time to time when there was a particularly bad storm out in the ocean. The dirty-looking water normally cleared after a few hours, returning the bay to its normal crystal clear and brilliant blue form. Unperturbed by the cloudy water, a healthy young Belgian guest had gone for a dip. As he headed out towards the reef, he was suddenly attacked by something, unseen, in the water. Whatever it was, it had dug its teeth into his left arm; the pain was indescribably awful. The creature had bitten right through. He yelled in pain as he thrashed around trying to shake off his attacker. His screams knifed through the air but there were very few people on the beach to hear them. Luckily for him a solitary hotel guest heard the shouts and, looking up from his book, saw a figure splashing around about fifty yards into the water. The onlooker dropped his book and ran into the sea in the direction of the troubled swimmer. He was quickly joined by another guest who had heard the screaming from his room. Together they grabbed the stricken Belgian and dragged him to the shore. Even in the unusually murky water the trail of blood could easily be seen. By now a cluster of onlookers had gathered on the beach. As the unfortunate swimmer and his rescuers reached the shore it was clear to those watching that the man's left arm was hanging off his body, almost severed by a huge and ragged gash. Blood was pouring from the wound. Roger's boathouse staff, who had now arrived on the beach, had been trained in basic first aid, but they had never experienced anything like this before. They did understand, however, that they needed to stop the flow of blood, which they managed to do by applying a tourniquet of beach towels. The poor Belgian was rushed in Roger's car to the small hospital in Moroni, with Roger at the wheel, accompanied by Ibrahim who knew where to go. The blood was everywhere as the tourniquet began to fail. Roger just prayed that they would reach the hospital in time. The hospital was basic, to say the least, but the local doctor knew what to do. The blood flow was stopped and the arm was saved. Roger was terrified, looking at the state of the hospital, that his hotel guest would eventually emerge from the place with something far worse than what he had entered with. The ramshackle wooden building was seared from the sun; paint was flaking from most of the walls. A few old wheelchairs were littered in the tight corridors; the chrome had worn away from their frames. The whole place looked unloved, unkempt, and decrepit.

"Thank Christ," thought Roger, "that Constance is not pregnant. I would never want her in this dump."

Roger was, of course, extremely grateful to all who had helped, especially the two guests who had swum out to drag the poor Belgian to the shore. It appeared that a barracuda, somewhat disoriented by the storm at sea, had inadvertently, in the murky water, strayed through the gap in the reef to the shallow water. This, apparently, was most unusual, so Roger soon learned. According to Ibrahim, there had been no such attacks on this beach as far back as anyone could remember. "On the other hand," thought Roger, "nobody has been swimming there for many years."

Roger's next problem was that about two hundred extremely annoyed and unhappy guests who had paid for a beach resort holiday were now too frightened to venture into the water, even though it had quickly cleared to its normal pristine state. A quietness had fallen across the hotel like a blanket of fog. The piped music that normally wafted through the public areas at mid- morning was now playing to no one. The normal sounds of happy holidaymakers had disappeared. The place was like a morgue. Nobody had ventured into the sea. A delegation of discontented and morose guests demanded to see Roger, insisting they get a refund for a wasted holiday. Other guests had assembled in the restaurant, expressing their fears to an unnerved Dinesh, whose charm, for once, did not seem to placate them. Roger immediately offered some minor concessions but insisted that this was a once-in-a-century accident and that it was perfectly safe to swim again. To prove the point, Roger instructed his boat-house staff to immediately recommence the water sports with a demonstration of water skiing. Roger then donned a costume and took to the waters, although his skiing proved to be more amusing than proficient, and Constance changed into a little red bikini and joined the boathouse water skiers in solidarity with her husband. This was the first time she had needed to wear a costume.

For two days none of the guests would venture into the water. The atmosphere at the resort remained sombre – funereal. But gradually, one by one, their confidence returned. Luckily for Roger, the only new arrivals to the hotel would come on the once-per-week Emirates Air flight. That was also when the current crop of guests would be leaving. He would need to make sure that the "leavers" at the airport could not speak to or meet the "arrivers". If he could do that, he might be able to keep the whole incident quiet, at least for long enough for confidence to be restored. A few dollars into the hands of the airport manager seemed to do the trick. A temporary plywood wall suddenly appeared in the little airport building, screening off any view that had existed between arrivals and departures, and diminishing any chance of the two groups communicating. When the fresh group of vacationers walked into the hotel, they had no idea what had taken place a few days before and, much to Roger's relief, business resumed as normal.

Roger also visited the invalided Belgian every day in the grubby little hospital, taking him delicious treats prepared by Chef Jimmy. Naturally he offered the Belgian a total refund for his vacation as well as payment for all hospital treatment. The unlucky swimmer acknowledged that he had been a little silly to swim in such poor conditions and did not blame Roger nor his staff. Roger and the Belgian became quite friendly. Roger offered to extend his guest's free stay for as long as he wanted upon his release from the hospital. In recognition, the Belgian promised that if questioned by the new batch of tourists at the hotel, when he returned, he would say that he was recuperating from an accident elsewhere. Disaster had been averted, but lessons were learned. In future hotel guests would be warned not to swim in murky conditions, which, fortunately, were very rare. Despite this, Roger privately wondered if this had been an omen. He hoped not.

Chapter Four
"The Crash"

Jimmy Sparrowhawk's loss of control under pressure at the opening party banquet had troubled Roger. Since that day there had been no further outbreaks of Jimmy's violent temper nor lack of control, but he had not been under such huge pressure. Roger worried about the possibility of a reoccurrence, but he was also concerned for Jimmy on a personal level. Jimmy's cooking and his training of the local staff had been superb. The Vanilla Beach was gaining a reputation in the travel trade for culinary excellence, which was all down to Jimmy. Roger could not afford for Jimmy to go off the rails again. He needed to get to the bottom of Jimmy's demons, not only for Jimmy's sake but also for the health of the business.

However, there was a more urgent behavioural problem than Jimmy's mental salvation. Brigitte and Dinesh had seriously fallen out, posing the threat that one or both might leave. Brigitte's strategy of following Dinesh to the island to get his sole attention had seemed to work. During the pre-opening period there had been no distractions for either of them. They were both busy in organising their respective departments but did not have the added pressure of dealing with hotel guests. Although Roger had allocated them each a small staff bungalow in the grounds of the hotel, it was not long before they had moved into one. Roger was, of course, delighted because it freed up accommodation for other staff. But once the hotel had opened for business, cracks started to appear in this arrangement. Dinesh had plenty of opportunity to charm a continuous flow of young ladies on vacation, many of whom fell easily to his allure. There had obviously been occasions when Dinesh could not help himself from satisfying their needs, particularly in the afternoons when he had less to do and Brigitte was busy. Conveniently, all his conquests had available bedrooms; he did not need to sully his own quarters and, so far, Brigitte, although suspicious, had no actual proof of his infidelity.

Brigitte too had plenty of admirers amongst the hotel guests. There seemed to be an endless stream of young men, both from Europe and South Africa, who really took a shine to her in her cute little head-housekeeper uniform. She would have had no difficulty in conducting numerous liaisons with handsome young men, but she showed little inclination to respond to their flirting since nobody had the charm and panache of her Dinesh. However, one afternoon, as Brigitte was doing her rounds, checking up on the work of her room cleaners, she let herself into a guest bedroom with her master key only to find Dinesh and a pretty little South African blonde naked in the bed. Brigitte was beyond furious and, naturally, extremely upset. She managed to hold it together until she reached Roger's office, where, once inside, she burst into tears. Sobbing, almost hysterically, she demanded that Roger give her back the little bungalow she had vacated for the love nest with Dinesh. Roger was taken aback by the normally chirpy housekeeper sobbing uncontrollably in his office. He did the natural thing and wrapped his arms around her to give her comfort. As the sobbing subsided Roger did not immediately release her from his embrace. He could feel her shapely body pressed against him. Despite the drama and the weeping, the movement of her body against his was, to his embarrassment, hugely erotic. He held her a fraction too long. For two reasons. Firstly, she noticed the reaction of his body. Second, because, at that very moment, in walked Constance.

Whatever might have happened as Constance saw her husband in an embrace with the pretty housekeeper we shall never know, for just as Constance was taking in the scene an almighty screech and thunderous roar enveloped the whole building like an underground train approaching a platform. It was the unmistakeable sound of jet engines and it was as if they were in the very room itself.

"What the fuck is that?" yelled Roger. Both women screamed in terror. The sound subsided somewhat but was quickly followed by others: tearing metal, explosions and screams from people outside, who obviously could see what was happening. The booming explosions stopped, but not so the screaming of panicked humans.

The Ethiopian Airways jet liner that had narrowly missed the hotel buildings crashed into the sea just beyond the hotel beach. One wing had dipped into the clear blue water between the beach and the reef. The plane had then cartwheeled as that wing broke off and the fuselage crashed into the deep water, bouncing off the reef as it did so, throwing some of the unlucky passengers into the air, still, in some cases, strapped to their seats. The commercial airliner was carrying one hundred and sixty passengers plus crew.

Ethiopian Airways Flight 166 had left Addis Ababa on schedule and en route to Nairobi just ninety minutes earlier. Shortly after take-off, three armed terrorists had forced their way into the cockpit carrying guns and hand grenades. They told the captain that they wanted him to fly to Australia. The captain kept his nerve and entered into dialogue with them, as two remained in the cockpit whilst the third went aft to control the passenger cabin.

"We don't have enough fuel to reach Australia," said the

captain. "We'll need to refuel somewhere; which means we will have to land to do it. Do you understand?"

The hijackers' knowledge of English was not good, but they seemed to get this message. The captain then suggested that the Comores would be a good place to stop for fuel. He hoped of course that, somehow, he could get a message to someone on the ground to forewarn them. However, at the controls of a jet with an armed terrorist, fingers on the pin of a hand grenade, standing over him, the captain was far from sure things were going to work out well. He explained his plan re the Comores and showed his capturer where it was on the map. The man with the grenade seemed to be satisfied that it was on the way to Australia. The captain wanted to make some sort of announcement to his terrified passengers and crew to calm them, but the lead hijacker refused. The captain gritted his teeth and flew on. Outwardly he remained calm. Inside his stomach was churning with fear. He kept reminding himself that over a hundred and sixty people, and his crew, were now totally dependent upon how he handled himself. It was a massive responsibility and one that he had hoped he would never have to deal with. But this was for real. It was actually happening; not to someone he might read about in the paper, but to him. Meanwhile, the passengers remained glued to their seats as the terrorist in front of them waved a hand grenade and stared them down.

As the hijacked plane approached Moroni airport, the captain tried to explain that he needed to overfly the airport first to ascertain that the runway was clear. The hijackers jabbered away to each other in Arabic. They seemed to be nervous of the captain's intentions. As the plane circled above Moroni the lead hijacker seemed to change the plan. He had spotted the Vanilla Beach a few miles from the runway. From what he could see it was a resort. He could clearly make out white bodies sunbathing on the beach. It looked like a typical scene of Western-style hedonism: something that, if destroyed, would be worth dying for. He abandoned his plans to visit Australia and started barking instructions to his colleagues. The captain had no idea what was going on, but sensed a change of plan. His alertness, already high, was now off the charts; he had to find a way of preventing disaster.

As the plane circled again and the Vanilla Beach came into view, the chief hijacker started making all sorts of gestures to the captain and, in his broken English, made it clear that the captain should crash the plane into the hotel and hotel beach. It was crystal clear to the captain that, if he did not follow these new instructions, the pin would be removed from the grenade right in front of his and his engineer's face, blowing the whole plane into smithereens.

Once again, the captain circled the airliner and lined the flightpath towards the central building of the hotel. Lower and lower he flew. The eerie voice of the altimeter count sounded like a death knoll. "One hundred, ninety, seventy..." Lower and lower, straight towards the roof of the building in which Roger was holding Brigitte tight. Closer and closer came the jet, until the buildings filled the windows of the cockpit. Then, suddenly, at the very last minute the captain yanked on the stick and the jet's nose lifted. The undercarriage clipped the radio masts, but the main structure of the plane scraped above the roofs by inches.

Shocked at what had transpired, the hijacker pulled on the pin of the grenade. Nothing happened. The captain had to keep flying the plane, but the engineer, seizing his moment, leaped onto the hijacker and a struggle ensued which, if he had not been strapped in, would have knocked the captain out of his seat. What control he had was lost. The plane dipped. The right wingtip hit the beach in the shallow water. The plane did a slow cartwheel as the wing broke off. The main fuselage and remaining wing crashed onto the reef. The passenger cabin fractured into two pieces, one falling back into the shallow water and the other, together with the other wing, into the deep shark-infested water beyond. Unbuckled passengers fell headlong into the water screaming. Those strapped in went with their seats. The panicked cries of the passengers could be heard clearly on the beach. Some onlookers would never forget them. Some were cries of fear, some of gruesome pain.

Out of the one hundred and sixty passengers, eighty-five were saved, including the captain and most of the cabin crew. That was a miracle. As it happened the Vanilla Beach, at the time, was hosting a conference of French doctors, thirty in all. When it became apparent that there had been a crash, the staff from Roger's boathouse mobilised every piece of equipment that could float. Several brave hotel guests rushed to help them and soon a little flotilla of assorted rescue craft including windsurfers and boards was headed to the carnage of the crash, which quickly spread over several hundred yards.

On shore the doctors mobilised themselves with the help of Roger, who had rushed in horror from his office to the beach. Banquet tables were hurriedly set up on the sand, and as the boat house staff dragged more and more casualties from the water, they were instantly triaged and treated in the make-shift beach operating theatre. Blood was everywhere – on the tables and spattered all over the beach. Bodies were constantly being dragged out of the water by boathouse and security staff and several willing hotel guests. One by one they were lifted onto the tables for examination. Banquet tablecloths were spread on the beach into which the dead bodies were wrapped. Ghastly bloodstains soaked through the flimsy material as the bodies were piled up – no time to waste on the dead; the focus had to be on those that could be saved. The noise was ghastly. The doctors could hardly hear each other over the awful screams and wails of the injured passengers. The meagre first aid kits from the hotel were unable to cope with the need. Doctors appealed to the onlooking guests for anyone who had access to painkillers to donate them. Chef Sparrowhawk, seeing a doctor trying to amputate a limb with something akin to a Swiss army knife, rushed to the kitchen to produce some sharp butcher's blades.

Inside the hotel function room, with the help of some of the medics, Roger frantically organised another makeshift operating theatre. Constance and Brigitte, putting aside their mutual suspicion, suddenly found themselves acting as nurses, following the barked Anglo/French instructions of the doctors, which Brigitte was able to translate to Constance and others. Margaret Freeke, the engineer's wife, had quickly joined them, whilst her husband marshalled all the power and water supplies that the doctors called for. Bloodstains were everywhere. The scene was horrific and the cries from the injured and the dying were indescribable. The three volunteer nurses would never forget them.

The team of doctors performed miracles. Nobody really seemed to take charge; the combined effort was remarkable. As were the efforts of the waterborne lifesavers – not only the boat-house and security personnel but also many willing hotel guests. The shallow water within the reef had turned red; it was strewn with body parts. Nothing like this had ever happened before in a resort hotel. Roger's worst nightmare could not top this.

Not all guests, however, joined in the action. Many just gathered on the sandy beach to watch, as if the hotel had pre-pared some amazing afternoon entertainment. Videos taken at the time recorded several gin-swigging, wise-cracking, bikini-clad holidaymakers chatting to each other gaily as if they were at a cocktail party where the cabaret was a plane crash. However, they, and, unfortunately, many other hotel guests who had been heroic, got their comeuppance when they eventually returned to their rooms. Whilst the hotel staff, including all the security personnel, had been gallantly helping with the injured and dying passengers, robbers had visited. Hotel rooms, which had been quickly vacated in the excitement, had been ransacked. Anything of value had been taken and was now safely tucked away in the surrounding villages. As if Roger did not have enough to deal with, he was now accosted by angry hotel guests complaining about their losses, threatening to sue and cause all sorts of trouble.

This mini guest riot, however, was soon ended by another unwelcome visitor. Within a couple of hours of the disaster on the beach, a small swarm of official government vehicles and army equipment swept up the driveway to the hotel. They were led by the gay President in his old Austin Princess. With as much pomp as he could muster, he told the astonished Roger that he and his army general were taking over control of the entire site, at the request of the United Nations, the CIA, the FBI, and anyone else he could think of. The site would need to be sealed off for evidence. Hotel guests must, for the foreseeable future, stay in their rooms. They must not be allowed to walk on the beach or go into the sea for fear of tampering or spoiling evidence. This was now a crime scene and the world's detectives would need time to assess the situation and apportion guilt.

"Oh shit," thought Roger. "If my guests are unhappy about being robbed, what the hell are they going to say if they have to stay in their rooms for the rest of their holiday?" Throughout the emergency Roger had, miraculously, kept it together. He had not panicked. His natural organising ability had kicked in and his calmness in action certainly saved lives. Now, a gang of "experts" had arrived to help and, apart from looking after his guests, Roger was relieved of the responsibility of saving lives. He went into his office, shut the door and cried. Some of the things he had just seen were gruesome. This was all too much for one man to take. They did not teach this at hotel school.

It took over a month before the Vanilla Beach could open again for guests. For a few days the water inside the reef was red with blood. Several body parts kept drifting up onto the beach. Pieces of metal, plastic and the odd seat cushion from the disintegrated plane kept appearing, gruesome reminders of the crash. Basically, the place was a mess. But it was also crawling with army and intelligence personnel from the USA, Ethiopia, France, the UK and so on. The captain of the plane had survived, but the hijackers had not; they were now with their virgins. The captain had, of course, been able to explain exactly what had happened, so there was no mystery to uncover. But the beach did need clearing up. And the publicity that the hotel had experienced was not the sort it really needed. Roger, faced with the thought of feeding nearly four hundred guests in their rooms for several days, and soon to be overwhelmed by the clean-up exercise, decided that it would be cheaper and easier to charter a plane to send them all home. As usual, he received excellent cooperation from Emirates. However, he was forced to cancel other incoming reservations for weeks ahead and many other bookings going forward were cancelled by travel agents or the prospective guests themselves. In short, it was a financial disaster for Roger and no insurance company, government or international agency was willing to reimburse him.

On top of all of that, the woman in his life had not forgotten that, seconds before the plane crash, she had caught him in what appeared to be a deep embrace with the sexy little housekeeper. Whatever disasters may have overtaken them all since they had arrived in the Comores, in Constance's eyes, this was the worst. Two could play at that game.

Chapter Five
"Coup D'État"

A few months after the hijacking incident things at the hotel seemed to be getting back to normal, as was the marriage, at least on the surface, between Roger and Constance. To relieve them from the pressure-cooker atmosphere of running the resort they had agreed that Constance should take a trip every few weeks to South Africa to see her folks and friends and restock her wardrobe. Roger had also invited his ageing parents from the UK for a few weeks' visit and Constance was terrific with them. The disruption to business caused by the hijacking had put a major dent into the finances of the resort, but, reasoned Roger, the fundamental business, based upon his early success, was sound. Sooner or later any negativity in the market as a result of the bad publicity would dwindle and eventually disappear and the hotel would return to high occupancy and profitability. Roger had begun to have thoughts about adding rooms and facilities to the property. After all, the second beach, on the other side of the main buildings was entirely undeveloped. It would certainly be possible to add another hundred or so rooms. He also had thoughts about adding a small casino building. Whilst in Mauritius he had noticed that most of the hotels operated casinos, not for the use of the islanders, but exclusively for tourists and hotel guests. Roger knew very little about the casino business, but one thing seemed sure; it generated high revenues. There were, however, two problems facing Roger in this regard. First, the Comores was predominantly a Muslim country; its President was Muslim, as were all his ministers of state. The religion classified gambling as unholy and Muslims were not allowed to gamble under any circumstances. Or so they were told.

The second impediment was that neither Roger nor any of his staff, knew anything about the operation or management of a casino. This problem, of course, could be solved, but the first hurdle might prove too difficult to overcome.

Roger had made a habit of regularly meeting with President Saif bin Sultan in the interests of ensuring smooth passage for his business. He had also become familiar with most of the President's chosen advisers and ministers, partly through introduction by the President but also because, to a man, they seemed to think that the Vanilla Beach was their playground and one in which it was not necessary to pay their way. Roger had soon found out that he needed a licence for everything. First there was the musical entertainment licence, then there was the liquor licence (notwithstanding that alcohol was banned by Mohammed), then the tobacco licence, then the licence to operate a boat, and so on. Although the payments for these licences were often quite small, it quickly became apparent to Roger that the payment needed to be given to the individual minister in charge. These payments had, of course, to be made in cash and obviously not in front of any witnesses. Roger knew that none of these funds ever found their way into the public purse. He shuddered to think what the back-hander would be for a casino licence and to whom it would need to be paid.

Roger first broached the subject of opening a casino with the President when he was alone. Said bin Sultan was silent for a long while. The rattling of the air conditioning unit filled the silence. Finally, he replied that it was not possible, but that maybe Roger could sort out a route with his minister of finance, in complete secrecy, of course.

"There will be much opposition to this idea," the President explained, but his eyes said something different. "There must be no connection to me."

Roger left the meeting rather pleased. "Much opposition," he knew, meant a substantial backhander, but for a casino, it might be worth it. The meeting with the minister took place in the jungle, beyond prying eyes. A reasonable sum was agreed for a casino licence and an unreasonable payment was handed over to the minister in a brown envelope. The casino project had a green light.

And so, to the second problem; how to run a casino? Roger would need someone he could really trust. His first choice would be his wife. Lately, she had become a little pensive, even, he thought, distant. Maybe a spell off the island would do her good? Roger's plan was to send someone to London to attempt to enrol at one of the casinos as a croupier. He had assumed that new recruits were given a thorough training in how a casino works before being released on the gaming floor. If he could get someone he could trust to go on this mission, it would be extremely helpful. The problem was that this exercise would take a minimum of a few months and he did not like the idea of Constance being away for so long. Neither, he assumed, would she.

The other candidate would be Hector Watkins, his book-keeper. He was a single young man, so there would be no family complications. After all, Hector came from London; the costs of his residency there might be cheaper, especially since he offered to stay at his parents' home, and, in the end, he would be responsible for the control of the casino accounts at the Vanilla Beach. Although Hector had settled in well, his social life on the island was less than exciting. It had been difficult for him to make friends, since there were so few expatriates living in

Moroni. He did fancy Brigitte, but first, she was already taken by Dinesh and, second, he did not believe it would be wise for him to fraternise with other employees when he was, as the bookkeeper and controller, actually, in a sense, policing them. He had enjoyed a few dates with the daughter of a French sugar-broker in Moroni, who had been visiting for a month, and also with the expatriate teacher at the school in the town, but neither of these affairs had blossomed into anything other than friendship. Not that he was unhappy, far from it. He loved being on the island, and on his infrequent days off he would happily hike into the jungle to explore. However, the chance to return to the UK for a few months was an unexpected bonus, as well as the opportunity to expand his professional horizons. So, when Roger approached him, he jumped at the chance. But who would do the books whilst he was away? Roger had, whilst at hotel school, taken a course in basic accounting, so maybe between himself and Constance they could fill in the void for a few months, if Hector could give them a crash course of the necessities before leaving for London. This also, hoped Roger, would give Constance something to get her teeth into to take her mind off whatever was bothering her. Also, Roger did not want to spend several months apart from Constance. Now that the hotel was settling down, what he wanted was for Constance to produce a baby.

Hector was quick to agree with the plan and set about applying for a trainee slot in some London casinos using his mother's home address in Streatham. Given that he already had an accounting degree and could be considered to be quick at numbers, it was not long before several casino operators replied, offering him spots in their training programmes. An accountant who was willing to learn how to play the games could be huge asset. Hector, in discussion with Roger, opted to sign on at the Playboy Club. This, thought Hector, could be more fun than the stuffier Les "A", which was also keen to employ him. So, off went Hector to London where his new employers had no idea he was actually a spy.

Hector found himself in seventh heaven. For someone who was quick with arithmetic, the course, although interesting, was also a doddle. It was not long before he was dealing in the real casino, surrounded by the prettiest bevy of waitresses and croupiers he had ever set eyes on, in their bunny costumes.

"Stay for three months," instructed Roger. "Learn all you can and then come home. And, keep your hands off the girls!"

Hector took some of the advice.

Meanwhile, back at the Vanilla Beach, Roger concentrated on building an extension to the hotel to house a small casino, just big enough for half a dozen tables and fifty slot machines. Constance tackled the bookkeeping. This was exhausting work which, to Roger's disappointment, left no time for baby-making. Notwithstanding all Roger's efforts, a distance had opened up between the pair. Constance almost seemed bored in his presence. There was little time for lovemaking and when it did take place Constance appeared disinterested. Almost against his will, Roger found his thoughts frequently wandering to his pretty housekeeper.

Brigitte had moved back into her own bungalow. Her relationship with Dinesh had broken down completely. For a while Roger had been concerned that this would lead to Brigitte leaving the island. This would be a huge blow, since she was really good at the job and would be very hard to replace. As a result, Roger went out of his way to make sure Brigitte would carry on, despite her treatment from Dinesh. It seemed to Constance, and others on the staff, that Roger was spending an unusually large portion of his time with the pretty housekeeper. When a small number of expatriates are forced to live in proximity in a foreign place there are bound to be interpersonal relationships that form and reform continuously. Roger's little group was no exception.

Something else, however, was bothering Roger. In an attempt to keep abreast with island politics, Roger had kept Ibrahim on the payroll. He had appointed him as the hotel concierge, but his real job was to keep Roger informed about local affairs and assist him in relations with the President and the numerous other politicians and local chiefs. Roger had learned that Ibrahim came from a well-respected and important local family. He had his ears to the ground regarding the island's politics and was able to connect Roger to any local contact he might need. Ibrahim soon became the conduit through which Roger paid for licences and other favours he needed.

For several weeks, since the air-hijacking incident, Ibrahim had been warning Roger about the instability of the government. There was, it appeared, not a lot of love for the gay President and his cronies. Whilst many people on the island were suffering economically, Saif bin Sultan seemed to have a charmed life. Compared to the rest of his fellow countrymen he lived in luxury. He controlled the tiny army, the police and, of course, the telecommunication systems. The most important of these was the radio station, there being no local television service on the island. According to Ibrahim, a lot of people, including some of the wealthier families, were not thrilled about Saif's leadership, and there was a lot of talk about necessary change.

Roger had, of course, invested a lot of time and money in keeping close to the ruler. Any change might present some difficulty. On the other hand, the Vanilla Beach would be a source of revenue to any government and, regardless of who was in power, would, if left alone, continue to be one of the nation's largest employers and generators of foreign exchange. "Whoever is in power," Roger told himself, "will need the Vanilla Beach." Notwithstanding that, Roger also knew that political unrest could lead to bad publicity which, in turn, could lead to a drop in tourism. It was in his interests to make sure, where possible, that the island remained stable and peaceful. The fact it might not was troubling to Roger.

Not long after the hotel was again running at full capacity, an odd couple checked in, having arrived via the flight from Dubai. According to their passport details, as supplied to the front desk, they were French: Monsieur Claude Vatinelle and Madame Diane Largesse. Claude was a weaselly little man with thin tangled brown hair and round-lensed spectacles. Diana was squat and looked somewhat severe. She wore short hair and long khaki shorts. If they were not a couple, Roger would have sworn she was a lesbian. Although they did not claim to be married, they certainly behaved as a "couple" and shared the same double room. This room was cluttered with artist's equipment, such as oil paints and canvases but, strangely, these never seemed to be used. During the day they rarely took advantage of the beach or the ocean, preferring, instead, to hike off into the jungle. Each evening they would arrive at exactly the same time for dinner and, having made sure that Dinesh was well looked after, they sat at the same table. They rarely spoke to the other holidaymakers.

What also made them stand out from the other tourists was their length of stay. Initially they checked in for a week, like almost all the rest of the clientele. However, at the end of the week, they approached the front desk and asked if they could extend their stay for a further two weeks. The receptionist, Priti, was able to oblige, but thought it strange they had not asked for a better room rate, considering their length of stay would now be three weeks. In passing, the desk clerk mentioned this to Constance, who was now occupying Hector's office behind the front desk. That evening Constance advised her husband that Monsieur Vatinelle and Madame Largesse were staying on, thinking that he might wish to thank them at the dinner table that evening or even offer them a free beverage or whatever. Roger duly did his thing as hotel manager and greeted the couple at their table, thanking them for their extra business and enquiring if there was anything he could do for them.

"As a matter of fact, Monsieur Brown, there is something," Vatinelle offered. "A few of our friends from Paris have decided to join us here next week. I do hope you will be able to accommodate them."

"Of course," replied Roger, "how many rooms will they need?"

Roger was quite surprised when Monsieur Vatinelle told him there would be eight more people, requiring four more rooms.

"How long will they be staying?" asked Roger.

"At least two weeks, maybe three," came the reply.

This was even more surprising to Roger but he accepted the booking without raising an eyebrow, thanked Monsieur Vatinelle for the business and made his exit from the table, promising to put a note of confirmation under his guest's door.

"What on earth are these Frenchies going to do here for all those weeks?" he asked Constance, when he reported back to her. "There's something very strange going on."

Before even two of the three weeks were up, Roger found out. One morning, at the first hint of daylight, he was alerted by his front desk night staff, that a cargo ship had anchored in the deep water outside the Vanilla Beach reef. Four small Zodiacs packed full of men in camouflage uniforms were seen winding their way through the gap in the reef and motoring towards the beach. To Roger's amazement, there, on the beach, waving a torch, was Madame Largesse, also dressed in camouflage gear. There was no sign of Monsieur Vatinelle, nor any of the eight men who had recently arrived to occupy the four rooms ordered by Vatinelle in the dining room.

Roger looked on in amazement as the little army beached and the small squad of men quietly followed Largesse up the beach and through her room to a rickety and filthy truck, which Roger had never clapped eyes on before, parked in the hotel car park. Roger watched from the back of the hotel as the men, all of whom seemed armed with automatic rifles, clambered on to the lorry and chugged off down the hotel's winding driveway. The whole manoeuvre had been conducted quickly and quietly. Nobody spoke; everyone seemed to know what they had to do. This was a well-organised exercise.

The flabbergasted hotel manager, however, did not know what to do. It was still only 6.30 in the morning. Nobody in authority in Moroni would be up, and, in any case, he had no idea where the little army was headed or what they were going to do. Clearly, they were up to no good, so, at the very least, Roger thought he should alert the government and the police. By now Constance had appeared, bleary eyed but inquisitive.

"What the hell is going on?" she asked, as soon as she saw the shocked look on her husband's face. None of the phone numbers at the Palace nor any of the ministers nor the police were answering. Roger quickly related what he had seen to Constance and she joined in the futile effort to raise someone in Moroni. But they were too late. The damage had already been done. The President, Saif bin Sultan, was now in the custody of Monsieur Vatinelle and some of the eight men from the four extra rooms. They had, it appeared, hijacked the van that delivered bread to the Palace every morning at the crack of dawn. In this they had easily gained entry to the Palace, where, once in, they had headed straight for the gay President's quarters, awoken him from a deep sleep, and taken him prisoner.

During the time that Vatinelle and Largesse had been masquerading as artists in the hotel, they had apparently been out each day, studying the movements of Saif bin Sultan and his daily habits. They had somehow taken a trip round the Palace as tourists, and familiarised themselves with the layout of the building. They had observed the daily delivery schedule and selected the most regular, that of the daily bread.

Not only that, but they had also made a study of the radio station and the comings and goings of the personnel. To their delight, there was almost no security at all there, so it would be relatively easy for a few men to gain control. So the bread van carried Vatinelle and his fellow mercenaries into the Palace, much to the surprise of the baker, who allowed them on board, in place of the bread, and past the single guard at the gates of the Palace, who was used to waving in the baker's van at 7am each morning. He had long since stopped examining the cargo. Further up the coast, the boatload of extra soldiers was quickly able to secure the radio station, and so the Palace and the communications centre of the islands had been secured without a shot being fired.

The commander of the mercenaries was Emile Le Croix, who had, unbeknown to anyone of any importance in government, slipped into the country on the cattle truck flight from Paris a few days before. He had established himself in a cottage on the coast, just beyond Vanilla Beach, where he had already installed radio equipment that allowed him to monitor the progress of his men. Once he had received the all-clear that his men had captured not only the Presidential Palace, but also the President himself and the radio station, Emile proceeded to the station, where he announced to the astounded listeners that he was taking over control of the country, until such time as a democratically elected government could be formed. The word quickly spread through Moroni and the villages in the jungle.

Amazingly, the coup d'état had taken place without a shot being fired and by less than two dozen well-trained mercenaries. The only casualty, it turned out, was an astute journalist, who happened to be staying on holiday at the hotel. He had not been able to sleep and had been stretching on his balcony as the procession of uniformed men quietly made their way across the beach. His curiosity piqued, he quickly followed, witnessing them climbing into the old truck. A few minutes later a hotel worker arrived on his motorbike for his morning shift. A quick negotiation between the journalist and the hotel worker led to a loan of the bike on which the journalist set off in pursuit of the soldiers. Regrettably he was not a very good motorcyclist, and before catching up with the van, crashed on the potholed road and broke his neck.

The resistance from the local army and police force had been negligible and the general reaction from the public at large ranged from welcoming to disinterested. Hardly a soul, it seemed, objected to the downfall of their unpopular President with his greedy, self-serving ministers. Within a few hours of the "invasion" taking place, a large weather-beaten ship showed up at the harbour in Moroni, from which a further twenty well-armed mercenaries disgorged onto the rickety pier. Emile's little army had now increased to about forty men, just enough, in his judgement, to keep control of the entire nation.

Over the radio, Emile invited the Comoran armed forces and police to join with him in establishing a new democratic regime in the country and, within a day, their commander had instructed them to comply. A military coalition of mercenaries and local soldiers had soon established itself as an interim government with Emile as its head. All this without one shot. Not surprisingly, none of the greedy ministers of state were anywhere to be found.

Nobody in the country was more surprised at what had happened than Roger. The fact that his two innocent "artists" had actually been planning a coup was, to him, amazing. They had seemed such peaceful and compliant guests. Now, of course, he understood why they never behaved like normal resort tourists, and he could not help feeling a little foolish. He was also worried. The news of the coup would quickly spread around the world and there was no doubt that it would come as bad news to people who had booked vacations or were thinking about it. Roger knew that the travel industry would be putting a large question mark over travelling to the Comores. Holidaymakers would not want to risk coming to an unstable country.

"Damn it," said Roger to himself, but out loud. "If it's not one fucking thing, it's another. When will we get a free run at making this work?" In a state of despair, he called Dusty in South Africa to see if he could tell him what the hell was going on. Dusty seemed strangely unperturbed by the whole debacle. It was almost as if this invasion was par for the course. Even though Roger was depressed about the thought of further disruption to his business, he came off the phone vaguely heartened by Dusty's attitude.

"Maybe this was all part of a plan?" he mused. "I do hope they all know what they're doing."

It did not take long for Emile Le Croix to find the Vanilla Beach. What place could be better for Emile to take his breakfast? After all, it was a stone's throw from his heavily guarded cottage. Emile could practically run the country from the lounge of Roger's hotel. As a result, Roger and Constance, in a very short time, became quite close to the mercenary legend. Constance, of course, was particularly fascinated by him. Although no longer a young man, Emile had the personality of a swashbuckling cavalier. He was gruff, but he was also charming, particularly, it seemed, with pretty women. Probably in his sixties, the safari-suited mercenary's gnarled face bore the signs of a lifetime of adventures. His bushy eyebrows crowned mischievous dark brown eyes. A small, untidy, grey beard framed his face. When he smiled, which he did often, it was broad and generous. Emile was a man's man, but his appeal to Constance was instantaneous, and he knew it. It soon became apparent to Roger and his team that this was not Emile's first adventure as a mercenary, nor was it his first coup d'état. In fact, taking over malfunctioning and corrupt governments was his speciality. Roger wondered who financed his operations and why.

At the time of the coup, the Vanilla Beach had been full. Despite the publicity which inevitably flared up across the world after the word had got out about the coup, Roger's guests were not initially aware of any disruption. The sun was still shining, the water was still blue and warm and the hotel bar was still operating. However, as news of the coup spread around the world, Roger became concerned about the possibility of Emirates cancelling their weekly flight. If they did this, not only would he be unable to fly out his current hotel guests, but he would not be able to provide transport in the future. This could be the end of the Vanilla Beach.

Roger was, therefore, quite pleased that his new daily breakfast guest was Emile Le Croix, who now visited the hotel each morning before proceeding to the Palace. Roger needed to get Emile to somehow reassure the airline that their weekly flight would not be at risk. He explained the situation to the mercenary, who instantly understood. He offered to give his assurance to Emirates that their plane would be safe, and, at Roger's suggestion, also agreed to hold a telephone conversation with Dusty in South Africa to assure him that the airport was safe and secure. Unfortunately, due to poor communications within the fallen Comorian army at the time of the coup, there had been some disruption at the airport. Although there was no fighting, cautionary barriers had been erected to prevent an enemy aircraft from landing. Some minor damage had taken place to the runway, and the Emirates agent on the ground at the airport had reported this to the company. Constance's friend in Dubai had called to deliver a message from the Chairman of Emirates. The company would suspend all further commercial flights to and from the Comores until their engineers had ascertained that the runway was fit for purpose. They would be sending a small plane with engineers aboard to inspect the airport facilities, but first would need an assurance from Emile Le Croix that they would have safe passage. Roger began to feel that he had become the island's ambassador as he navigated the route to getting the airport open. In any event, it appeared that the weekly flight to deliver and collect Vanilla Beach guests would not be operating this week, so the current guests whose flights would be cancelled would have to be informed.

Roger spent a while composing a memorandum explaining to his full house of guests that they would not be returning to either Europe or South Africa as planned. Their departure could be delayed from a few days and, maybe, up to a week. They would not be charged for their accommodation and food for the period of the delay, no matter how many days this took. The note was slipped under the doors of all the hotel rooms in the middle of the night. Roger was braced for the inevitable negative reaction to his message. Even though the circumstances were beyond his control, his experience told him that this would not help him when it came to the inconvenience caused to his guests. Remarkably, the guests' reaction was far from negative. In fact, his offer to give free accommodation during the delayed period had turned out to be a major victory. Those guests whose work or circumstances required them to return on time knew that nobody could blame them if they could not, and those that were in no rush to return and were enjoying their stay on the island were absolutely delighted that they could continue enjoying the sunshine for free. In fact, at the height of the breakfast service, one rather brash South African man clinked his waterglass and stood up to make a speech of thanks to Roger and his tea, for their handling of the affair, which was followed by a spontaneous round of applause from all present.

Of course, there were a few who were not pleased. Lawsuits were threatened and other miscellaneous punitive actions against Roger and the hotel were promised, but these were from a small minority and Roger, buoyed by the reaction of the majority, stood his ground and refused to offer more in compensation. However, the whole affair had been extremely costly to the business, especially coming so soon after the disruption caused by the hijacked plane. "When," thought Roger, "will this nightmare of mishaps ever end?"

The mercenary invasion, with its incumbent excitement and drama, had, for a while, taken Constance's mind off her indignation about her husband's apparent attraction to the French housekeeper. Constance had no real evidence to support her suspicions about Roger and Brigitte, but her instincts told her that Roger was strongly attached to the little French bitch. At the same time, she was perturbed that she had caught herself being attracted to other men and that she was finding it difficult to extinguish her thoughts in this direction. Although she had resisted temptation at the time, she had found herself enormously attracted to the French actor, Alain Gabor. He, of course, had left the island, but she found herself hoping he would return. Then there was the band leader, Jean Pierre. She had begun deliberately wearing dresses in the evenings which she knew would appeal to the band leader. She just knew that JP found her attractive. She was certain she could have him and, more and more, found herself wanting to do just that. Constance found herself frequently fantasising about Alain and JP, even when she was in bed with her husband. Somehow, Roger, too, seemed distracted in their marital bed. It was hard for a young woman to be on an island, married to the boss. She had no female friends she could talk to, since they all worked for Roger – except one. During the air crash she had found herself working alongside Margaret Freeke, the engineer's wife. They got on well. The terrible task in the makeshift operating theatre had somehow brought them close. Maybe Margaret Freeke could be her friend. She really felt that she needed one. But was Margaret, who seemed to have such a solid relationship with her husband, the right person to talk to? What would Margaret know about her deviant sexual thoughts? Margaret did not seem the sort of person who would ever have any. Her husband, Colin, was such a steady person: such a rock.

Chapter Six
"Invasion"

The coup d'état had, at least, brought some benefits to the island and to Roger and Constance. For one thing, the publicity generated around the world, at least, put the little islands of Comoros on the front pages almost everywhere, and people that read newspapers or watched the television news had now heard of the Comoran islands. There had also been an influx of overseas journalists writing stories about the coup, Emile Le Croix and the island. All of them had stayed at the hotel, and contributed greatly to the room revenues, and especially those of the bar. The most useful message they had conveyed was that the island was peaceful and the hotel was great. Pictures of Vanilla Beach with its wonderful seawater expanse were appearing in magazines and newspaper supplements everywhere. Emirates had resumed the weekly flights and bookings for the future did not appear to have been affected negatively. "Maybe," thought Roger, "any news is good news."

The other good news was that the almost constant demand for kickbacks to greedy government ministers had stopped. Ibrahim's contacts and flow of information about what was going on at the Palace had, to some degree, slowed, but he still had enough friends on the Palace staff to keep him informed. As far as he could tell, progress was being made towards a democracy as arrangements were being put in place for an election in the future.

Despite seeing the new de facto ruler almost every morning at breakfast time, Roger could still not work out his guest's real role in the whole affair or what motivated him, or even rewarded him. "What," thought Roger, "does Emile get out of all of this, and who is paying for his gang of mercenaries?"

Roger was not alone in thinking about this. Despite the efforts of numerous journalists to interview the mercenary leader, he always declined, so information about his motives or even his sponsor remained pure speculation. Almost everybody saw him as an instrument for good, rather than a greedy mercenary, but nobody could quite understand why. Dusty and his pals in the South African foreign office could not, or would not, answer the question, nor could the government of France, from whom the Comores had gained independence some thirty years prior. It became known that, in between his previous swashbuckling adventures, Emile Le Croix lived quietly in a small town about fifteen miles from Versailles. There was, therefore, no doubt that, in some way, the French were behind this adventure in peacekeeping or state-building, but no one could prove it.

Even though, to most people, the takeover by Emile Le Croix appeared to have been a good thing, it was, nevertheless, illegal under international law. One is not allowed to simply invade a country and take it over, especially when the incumbent leader is in power by dint of legal means, which was clearly the case for Saif bin Sultan. In other words, Emile and his men had engaged in an illegal act of piracy and, despite all their good intentions, had overthrown a legally empowered government by force, even if the means of entry was only a bread van. Those in power in the United Nations Assembly were concerned that the events in the Comores, if allowed to continue, could give a green light to other adventurers who happened to fancy the idea of owning a country. The question was, of course, what could they do about it?

Roger soon found out. Once again, the management, staff and guests of the Vanilla Beach were awakened very early one morning by the sound of aircraft, this time, not one, but what appeared to be a whole squadron. As bleary eyes drew their bedroom curtains to see what the noise was all about, they witnessed an amazing and, for some, a never-to-be-forgotten sight. Hundreds of uniformed troops were swarming up the beach of the hotel. Offshore stood two warships flying the French flag. A fleet of small camouflage-painted Zodiacs were ferrying soldiers through the gap in the reef to the shore, where they were forming small but neat groups. Soon the whole beach was almost covered with uniforms. A helicopter from the ship hovered above making one hell of a clatter. The Vanilla Beach had been invaded. So, it seemed, had the Comores.

"What the fuck will happen next?" said a hastily dressed Roger. It was unusual for the calm-mannered hotel manager to swear, but after all that had transpired at his hotel in such a short time, he was almost ready to give up the ghost.

Emile Le Croix watched the whole show from his cottage at the far end of the beach. Any resistance from his small mercenary army would have been ridiculous. He called his men who were guarding Saif bin Sultan in town and told them not to resist when this French army reached Moroni, which it inevitably would.

"When they come for you, do not resist. Hand over the old gay and give yourselves up peacefully. I will look after you."

Such was the trust and admiration for their leader that all of Emile's men did as commanded. When the French army marched into town, the mercenaries came out of the radio station with their hands up, waving a white flag. At the Palace, they waited, as instructed, to hand over the President, before surrendering. There was no animosity between the liberators and the mercenaries. They were all Frenchmen, and most of those being now captured, had, at one time or another, served in the French forces. In less than two hours, the Palace, the airport and the radio station, were in the hands of the French military and, by extension, the French government.

As the troops were still landing, Roger had phoned Dusty to tell him what was transpiring. Dusty had told him not to worry. It was clear now to Roger that the South African government had been "in the know". Emile, the "trusted" mercenary had been used by the French to create a reason for them to end the independence of the Comores: to recapture it as part of the French Empire.

"Christ," thought Roger, "my hotel is just a political football." Somehow his life felt out of control. His hotel and his future seemed to be at constant risk and so did his marriage. He hoped this whole venture had not been a huge mistake.

Yet again, Roger found himself having to address and placate a hotel full of guests who had been looking for a sun-filled, relaxing holiday by the sea.

Once again, he realised that this was probably the most exciting thing that had happened to any of them, something to entertain their friends and dinner guests with for years to come. So, since this time the airlift by Emirates did not seem at risk, there might have been no harm done. Unfortunately, the pictures of troops flooding across the hotel's beach, which now appeared in magazines around the world, did influence future bookings. Suddenly, the desire to go to the Comores seemed to have cooled. For the next month the weekly aeroplane was only half full, or, as Roger saw it, half empty. The thriving business that had begun to emerge had suddenly evaporated. Soldiers and vacations do not mix.

As for Emile Le Croix, things worked out okay, almost as if they had been pre-arranged. Emile was eventually taken to court in Paris, charged with assault on a foreign nation. He had agreed to cooperate with the courts provided that his men were given very light sentences for their participation in the illegal invasion. Emile was found guilty and sentenced to ten years in jail. He was assigned to an open prison in the middle of France, near Lyons. It was so "open" that he simply walked out and went home. Nobody tried to stop him and nobody reported the event to the press. Nobody, it seemed, cared. The French had what they wanted; their colony was back where it belonged and ready for them to plot its future in their best interests.

But Roger now desperately needed to boost his flagging sales. The occupancy of the hotel had fallen from ninety percent, prior to the coup, to a measly forty percent. He figured his breakeven point was around fifty-five percent, so, somehow, he had to re-establish the business base. Fundamentally, recent history had shown there was nothing wrong with the Vanilla Beach itself. The site was wonderful and the hotel had performed well. He needed to get the word out that it was a safe place to have a holiday. Since the island was now under the control of the French, he decided to fish where the fish were. He would go to France, to see if he could work out a deal with a French tour operator to fill his hotel. Surely the French would not be scared to go to an island that was, in effect, a French province? At the same time, Roger planned to visit Hector in London to see how the casino training was going. Roger now really needed to open the little casino room to boost his revenue.

The question was, who would run the hotel while he was away? His department heads were all solid people but he could not put any one of them in charge of the others. There was, it seemed, only one choice: Constance. She had no formal training in hotel management but, by now, had considerable experience of watching her husband do it. After all, it was only for about three weeks that she needed to fill in. He knew she would be good with the guests and, since each department head knew what they were doing, she should not encounter too many problems or have too many difficulties to solve. Also, she would only be a phone call away. The only thing that really bothered him was Constance's obvious dislike of Brigitte. Roger could not afford to lose his housekeeper over a spat between two women, even if one was his wife. Having weighed up the options, Roger decided to take a chance.

And so it was that Constance found herself in charge of the hotel whilst her husband flew off to France in search of new customers to ensure their future. Rather than feel nervous of this new responsibility, Constance felt liberated. She was full of confidence, maybe a confidence born out of ignorance, but confidence nevertheless. For a few days things went well. The department heads, each of which could adequately cope with their own areas of responsibility, simply got on with the job, leaving Constance with the routine tasks of signing purchase orders and paying the bills. This gave Constance the opportunity to do what she most enjoyed: interacting with the guests. She had often complained about Roger spending more time with his hotel guests than with her, particularly in the evenings. He had always explained to her that it was important for a resort manager to be a good host, not just an invisible name on a welcome card. She was determined that what Roger did, she would do at least as well, if not better.

Two days after Roger's departure for Europe, a rather interesting group of guests checked in from the Dubai flight. Most guest arrivals to the resort brought little luggage. After all, how much did one really need for a week at a beach resort? This group, however, came with crates of equipment, multiple suitcases, and what looked interestingly like cameras and lights. From her office behind the front desk, Constance watched as this stuff was piled up in the lobby. She decided to investigate.

The group checking in seemed to be about ten strong. It included a few young scruffy-looking long-haired men and an older and rather Bohemian-looking bearded man, rather short and pudgy. "Pudge" appeared to be accompanied by a tall thin lady with lank hair and an exceptionally long nose. She rather seemed to tower over him. Among the arrivals, however, were four very good-looking young people who really stood out. They were not involved in the lifting of equipment at all, but were standing aside, talking and joking. Constance had seen a lot of beautiful people on the hotel beach during the first few months of the resort operation, but never any so strikingly attractive as the four arrivals chatting away in the lobby. Not just two men and two women, but two of the most handsome men that Constance had ever seen and two of the most amazingly beautiful women. "They have to be film stars," thought Constance. "How come Roger didn't warn me they were coming?"

Having quickly cast her eyes over the arriving group, Constance, conscious of how Roger would act, stepped forward with her broadest of smiles, and heading for Pudge with outstretched hand she welcomed him and his group to the hotel. Pudge responded with a smile and a deep Burton-like voice. "Well, thank you, ma'am. It's nice to be here finally." The voice was not that of a Welshman, but had twangs of North America. "Mr Charles Decouvert, at your service," he announced, with strong emphasis on the "Mr", as if he did not want to be perceived as French, "and this here," he said, gesturing to the tall long-nosed lady, "is Pip – Pip Dee."

Ms Dee nodded.

"Are you here to do some filming?" enquired Constance, without stopping for an answer, since she realised her question was rather silly. "If there's anything I can do to help, you only have to ask."

Pudge thanked her and then, together with Pip, proceeded

91

with the check-in procedure as Constance excused herself and reappeared behind the front desk to make sure the appropriate rooms were allocated. It seemed that Pudge and Pip had taken the two largest suites in the hotel, plus a whole bunch of double rooms. Several of the crew were doubled up but the four beautiful people had all been allocated separate rooms. "That's good," thought Constance as she grasped the idea that the beautiful people were not attached.

Constance saw to it that both male actors, Pierre Fontaine and Sacha DeCourcy, were given a couple of the best and most private rooms, well apart. She personally escorted Pierre to his room. The two beauties, Sophie Clarence, and Elizabeth Tangier, she placed in two adjoining rooms, which had the benefit of sharing a small walled private garden. The crew departed for their respective rooms. Nobody called to complain.

There was considerable speculation amongst the staff of the Vanilla Beach about the nature of the film to be shot. It was clearly a low budget affair, unless this was just a small part of a much bigger enterprise. Pudge had not offered any information, nor made any special requests, so, for a few days the hotel staff were only left to speculate. Meanwhile Pierre and Sacha relaxed on the beach or at the beach bar, whilst Sophie and Elizabeth took advantage of their little private garden to get an all-over body tan. Constance found herself almost unconsciously monitoring the customers at the bar, so it was not an accident that took her there when she spied the two hunks taking a cold beer. One of them, in his bathing shorts and sun glasses, Pierre, was all that a woman could want.

It transpired that Pudge and Pip had rented a villa in the foothills of the volcano that had once been the grand colonial home of a French billionaire. Roger and Constance were aware of the mini chateau, which they believed to have been shuttered, if not abandoned. Constance was, therefore, quite surprised to find that this seemingly deserted mansion was now being used as a film set.

Once production of the film had commenced, rumours about it quickly spread amongst the staff of the hotel and, after a few days, reached the ears of Constance. Mr Pudge was making an erotic movie. When Constance heard the news, she just wanted to laugh. "Who cares what they're doing?" she thought. "As long as they don't do anything to damage the reputation of the hotel, why should I care?" The thought of Sacha and Pierre cavorting in front of the cameras naked did, however, flash through her mind. She had witnessed the pair of them on the beach. They both displayed fantastic physiques, but for Constance, Pierre was the sexiest. It had been quite a while since Constance had enjoyed any sex.

Constance was not the only member of staff to fancy the two actors. Brigitte, the housekeeper, who was also feeling a little deprived since the break-up with Dinesh, began to make absolutely sure the two men were being properly serviced by the housekeeping department. This, of course, required frequent checks on their rooms. Of the two handsome men, Brigitte definitely preferred Sacha, who, in turn, welcomed her frequent "check-up" visits. It took precisely three days for Brigitte to find her way under Sacha's duvet. She was in heaven and Sacha was thrilled to have made a conquest of such a fresh young thing – such a change from the women he worked with.

The film crew had been at Vanilla Beach for a week when Constance received a special and unusual request. Sophie, one of the glamorous duo, had, it seemed, taken ill and was unable to shoot. Sacha had suggested to Pudge that he might be able to get Brigitte as a standby; after all, although not trained as an actress, she had a beautiful face and body, equal, if not better, than the experienced Sophie. Apparently, it would mean that Brigitte would need about a week off work and Pudge thought it better to seek Constance's permission before approaching Brigitte directly. In Pudge's opinion, Brigitte would bring a fresh young appeal to his film. However, if he had had his preference, he would have preferred Constance to be the stand-in. To Pudge, Constance on screen would be absolute dynamite, especially unclothed. But how could he ask her to do so? She was the hotel manager. Surely she would be insulted. Constance was a handsome woman, in Pudge's eyes, but not an accessible one, being a wife and hotel manager. But Pudge saw something smouldering beneath the efficient surface of Constance – something that might play out well on the screen. If Pudge could unleash her passion, he thought, she could put a real spark into his production. He knew she was a married woman, but where was her husband?

Pudge concealed his thoughts about Constance, and merely limited his request to asking that he "borrow" Brigitte for a few days, to replace the sick Sophie. Constance was instantly jealous of Brigitte. Constance would love to have been the one asked. She was irked that men seemed to go for Brigitte, rather than her. However, Pudge, of course, must not be aware of her feelings. "Of course, I don't mind – and thank you for asking. If Brigitte wishes to use up some of her vacation time filming, then it's up to her. She is a pretty little thing."

Pudge thanked her profusely.

"No, thank you for asking." Constance beamed, whilst sticking her chest out. "If you need any more help, just ask."

For the next day Constance could not get over the thought of Brigitte being asked to appear in the film. Despite the facts it was obviously a risqué movie and Constance was married and Brigitte not, Constance was still jealous. Being in a risqué film might be just the tonic that she and Roger needed: something different. In their first few years of marriage in England they had, from time to time, watched porn together before making love, but it was far from a habit or obsession. To discover his wife had actually been in one of these films might be the spark Roger needed to rekindle his passion. On top of that, Constance was convinced her body was just as toned and beautiful as the housekeeper's. Surely Pudge could see that. She decided to find out. She would start by inviting Pudge to dinner that night.

Before they reached the table, Constance had made sure Pudge had several glasses of the hotel's best champagne and, once at the table, the wine flowed freely. Pudge was clearly quite captivated by Constance. In his job he dealt with many attractive women, but, in his view, Constance was right up there with the best. Maybe he could not have her in his film, but, with her husband away, perhaps he could have her in another sense? Constance sensed that she had a fan. She decided to switch the conversation to Pudge's movie.

"Would you call your film an erotic movie?" she asked.

"I hope so," replied Pudge. "That's what I'm paid for."

"How is my little housekeeper doing?" she continued. "Is she erotic?"

"She's certainly very pretty," replied the little tubby man, "and, yes, I think one could say she is erotic, although it's the film itself that sets the tone."

Pudge was encouraged by the gist of the conversation. "Maybe," he mused, "this lady is more interested in what we do than I thought." Suddenly a thought struck him. He could invent a role for Constance in the movie. It needn't be a large one and she needn't take all her clothes off, just maybe the top.

"You know, Constance, we sort of make up the stories as we go along. The script is, shall we say, very fluid. I'm struggling to find an ending. But what if another beautiful lady, a more sophisticated lady than Brigitte is playing, were to come along and lure the stud away? She wouldn't necessarily need to strip. She could just hold out the hope and temptation that she might – just enough for the stud to leave the young lady he's been laying. I could write that part for you."

Constance's heart leaped. "How sweet would that be?" she thought. "To lure away the leading man from Brigitte." Of course, she would like to play that part, even if it did mean taking off some clothes.

"Sounds good to me," said Constance as she poured them both another glass of wine. "When do I start and what do I wear – or, maybe, not wear?"

When the effect of the champagne had worn off, later that night in her bedroom, Constance had cause to reflect. Was she really going to show up on the movie set? Was she really going to demonstrate to the housekeeper and the world what a sexy woman she could be? She was not sure. On the other hand, the thought of being on the set with a naked hunk had a lot of appeal.

Several thousand miles away in Paris, Roger Brown was unaware of the presence of the risqué film makers at the Vanilla Beach. He called Constance daily to check how things were going or to give advice if required. In regard to the film, Constance did not need any advice; in fact, she didn't even mention the film-making. Roger had signed a couple of very favourable marketing contracts with two major tour operators, one in Paris and the other in Frankfurt. Emirates was able to give airlift to Moroni from both cities, via Dubai. The potential from these solid operators was huge, so Roger soon left the continent well pleased with his efforts. In London he met up with Hector, who reported in detail about what he had learned at the Playboy casino and, together, the two men decided that they now had sufficient knowledge to open the Vanilla Beach gambling room. It was agreed that Hector would hand in his notice at Playboy and head "home" to the Vanilla Beach, this time, it seemed, with a bunny in tow.

To Hector, Peaches seemed like a very special girl. She was the mother bunny in the club. She had worked as a regular bunny for a couple of years before being promoted to over-see all the other girls. During that time, she had attended the dealers' training programme so understood how the games worked. She was a stunning brunette. She no longer had to dress in her bunny outfit but she had retained it as a souvenir and been happy to demonstrate to Hector how it still fitted her perfectly. Hector was entranced and Peaches, in turn, was smitten with him. When he came clean with her and announced that, as the accountant for the Vanilla Beach, he would soon be returning to the island, Peaches had decided she would go with him. Hector was thrilled. When Roger arrived in London, Hector was quick to introduce Peaches, with the recommendation that Peaches, once on the island, should be put in charge of the new gaming room. Roger was delighted; a pretty girl like Peaches was sure to draw the customers in and her knowledge would be invaluable. In addition to that, the opportunity to lodge two of his expat supervisors under one roof was a great benefit in regard to staff housing, even though, as the accountant and financial controller, Hector would need to audit Peaches' work, and it would, therefore, have the potential to be a compromised situation.

When Roger finally got back to the Comores, the filming crew had packed up and left. Nobody, including Constance, mentioned to Roger that they had even been there. Constance seemed pleased to see her husband again. To Roger she seemed very much like the Constance he loved. She had a lot to tell him about the operations of the resort in his absence and about how she had coped with everything. Roger was very happy with how she had managed and was very proud of her. Their romantic life seemed to be back on track and Constance's urge for sex seemed to have been rekindled. "Maybe," thought Roger, "absence really does make the heart grow fonder." After discussing their recent history, they agreed that maybe they had been too wedded to the hotel. After all, they were there morning noon and night. Roger suggested they move out of the premises to create their own life away from the Vanilla Beach, but close enough to be in constant touch. But, where would they go?

"What about Emile Le Croix's cottage?" said Constance one night. "Why don't we see if we can rent it – or even buy it? It's only a stone's throw from the hotel and it's even got its own little private beach cove." Constance had missed her swims; the thought of the thrill of skinny dipping off their own home really appealed to her, although she did not proffer this as a reason for citing the cottage. Roger thought this was a great suggestion. The little wooden beach house was completely detached from Vanilla Beach but within very easy reach and almost in sight. Thanks to Emile, it also had the benefit of being fully wired for communication purposes.

"That's a great idea. I'll see what I can do," said Roger who promptly set about tracing the owner. Not difficult. One discussion with Ibrahim and the relevant contacts were produced within a few days. Two discussions later, a lease was faxed through to the hotel and duly signed. Roger and Constance could move out and move in.

Roger now concentrated on getting the casino room finished. The slot machines had arrived, together with a fitter from the UK. They took up a lot of space and Roger, for a moment, thought he had over-ordered. But when the gaming tables arrived, he was thankful everything fitted in according to his plans. Peaches had also arrived with Hector and, together with Roger, they began to interview local maidens to train as croupiers. "Why are you only interviewing girls?" questioned Constance.

"Because they'll be more glamorous," replied Roger.

"Glamorous to who?" came back the retort.

Roger thought about it. Maybe Constance was right. Maybe a couple of handsome dudes might bring in the ladies?

As it turned out, finding sufficient applicants from the local villages who wanted to be croupiers was a sizeable challenge. In fact, it turned out to be an impossibility. The Muslim community did not take kindly to the sinful idea of a casino in their midst. Ibrahim had reported to Roger that, if the casino went ahead, there could be discontent amongst the hotel staff, but, at the very least, the word had gone out to the villages that their sons and, particularly, daughters, must not apply to work there. "Well, screw them," said Roger, in despair, "if the locals don't want the jobs, we'll just go back to Mauritius to recruit. After all, there are plenty there that already know how to do the job."

And so it was that, three weeks after her arrival in the Comores, Peaches was sent to Isle de Maurice on a recruitment trip and, when she returned two weeks later with photos of the attractive young ladies she had recruited, together with a couple of handsome young men to keep Constance happy, Roger was very pleased with her work. "At last," he thought, "something is going right." Peaches was turning out to be a great hire. Since she could now cut back on the training of the staff, because all her recruits knew how to deal, she was able to concentrate on the finer things, such as costume design and, together with Hector, the necessary control systems. Within weeks, the new casino was ready. It was an instant success with the hotel guests and a welcome addition to the facilities of the hotel. Peaches was a popular addition to the team and, because of her obvious attachment to Hector, posed no threat to the other resident beauties on the payroll. She was always smiling, at least to her customers. She rarely worked the tables, but she never stopped working the room. Her eyes were everywhere. She cut an attractive figure in her well-fitted dress.

Although the gaming licence specifically denied the right for any local national or any Muslim to gamble, it did not prevent the expatriate staff from so doing. A good number of locals also seemed to slip the net. At first this was not a problem. Roger saw it as a recreational facility for his team. However, when Peaches began to report that some of Roger's top team were losing a lot of their earnings on the machines and tables, Roger decided that this facility would have to be off limits for his staff. Some were not happy.

Chef Sparrowhawk was no exception. Although casino gambling is considered a social activity, being in a room with other people can be a singularly lonely experience. Sitting in front of a slot machine is not exactly a team activity. There is only one stool for each machine. Even at the tables, the gamblers' thoughts are often within themselves; there is no requirement, nor necessity, to talk to the other players. Sparrowhawk had nothing to spend his pay on. No family, not even any friends. For a short while, the casino became his second home. Initially he had ventured in because one of the installing mechanics had told him that a certain Australian manufactured slot machine was susceptible to liquid. He had maintained that if one took a straw full of coca cola and blew it into the coin slot, after a few spins, the coke would trigger the release of the jackpot. One night, shortly after the casino had opened, Sparrowhawk entered the slots area with several wraps of coins, a can of coca cola and a straw. When no one was looking, he would surreptitiously blow a little coke into the slot with a straw. He would then watch as he saw the black sticky liquid trickle over the drums of cherries and other symbols. He would then feed the coins into the machine, in between further spurts of coca cola. From time to time, he would have a small win, with wet sticky coins tumbling into the tray beneath the machine. After a while he had used up all of the coins. In frustration he checked that the number and make of the machine was the same as the mechanic had told him. It was. For three nights the chef went through the same process. Finally, he gave up. Just before he had to accept the boss's ban on employee gambling.

Roger and Hector soon calculated that, on average, each hotel guest lost about five hundred dollars in the casino during their week's holiday in the resort. That was almost the equivalent of adding a hundred dollars per night to the room rate. Roger was delighted but, as was the way in the Comores, his delight was short lived. Three months after the opening of the gambling room, Roger received a visit from a member of the quasi-French interim government, Monsieur DuMatin, who blandly enquired as to why the hotel seemed not to be paying the gaming tax. "There is no gaming tax," exclaimed an indignant Roger, not wishing to mention that he had previously been bribing a member of the toppled government to obtain the licence.

"I'm afraid to tell you that there is," insisted DuMatin. "Since the Comores is now a Département of France, the rules vis a vis gaming are the same as in France; slots to be taxed at forty percent of the revenue, and tables at twenty," he announced in a sombre tone. "I will be 'appy to leave you with the relevant forms which will need to submitted with the payment on a quarterly schedule."

Roger's jaw must have dropped at least a foot. Hector looked stunned.

"Well, gentlemen. I can see that you are not 'appy with the news, but the law is the law. I will bid you au revoir."

"Fuck," said Roger as soon as DuMatin had taken his leave. "Fuck, fuck and fuck!" His anger only subsided when Hector, after a minimum of research, unearthed that DuMatin had been wrong. There was no tax on slot machines in France because there were no slot machines there. DuMatin had mistakenly been referring to vending machines. It was with some delight that Hector pointed out the mistake to DuMatin, who eventually was forced to agree.

Chapter Seven
"The Grand Mariage"

Not long after the visit from the French tax official, the indigenous people of the island threw another curveball at Roger. Since the opening of the hotel, Roger had been very perturbed about the level of pilferage. The usage of all guest supplies had always seemed extremely high. According to Roger's calculations, every guest in the hotel would have to visit the toilet every thirty minutes to justify the amount of loo paper that was being consumed, and would have to wash their hands or face almost every hour. Roger knew that his supplies were being stolen, as did Brigitte and Chef Sparrowhawk. They had hired an army of security personnel, but the constant drain on supplies had not diminished. Roger remembered the clean-out that had taken place from the guest rooms while everyone was focused on the rescue operation for the hijacked plane passengers. Nice as they were, it seemed to Roger that all Comorans were a thieving bunch. He understood that they had very little in the way of personal possessions and that the wages were low, but, even so, stealing was stealing and he had to find a way of stopping it.

"Maybe I should get closer to the people," he mused. "Maybe I should take more interest in their lives and their customs. Maybe I should try to understand them better; get to know them; close the gap between them and us." Roger was, therefore, delighted when he and Constance received an invitation to the marriage of his head bartender, Coco, to a girl in his village. The invitation had come from Coco's fiancé's father, who, Roger learned, was an important man in his village – something like a mayor. A Grand Mariage is a big thing in the lives of Comorians. Despite this being a predominantly Muslim country, many French traditions had crept into the hearts and practices of the people. The marriage of a daughter is one of the biggest occasions in the lives of Comoran parents. From the day a girl is born, the family start to save up to pay for her marriage. When someone of importance is involved, thousands of dollars can be spent on lavish ceremonies and functions, which can sometimes last for days. Coco's prospective father-in-law, it seemed, was ready to spend a small fortune on his daughter's big day.

Constance fussed for days before about what she should wear. She certainly did not want to upstage the bride or her mother, but she did want to be smart. Ibrahim had told her that most of the women would be wearing traditional dress, akin to saris. He said it would probably be a blaze of colours, so Constance must not worry about the colour of her outfit. In the end, Constance opted for a fairly simple bright red dress with matching shoes. Roger decided to wear light blue slacks with a blazer and tie. Ibrahim, who was not from the bride's village and had not been invited, offered to drive his manager and his wife.

The route to the wedding followed a dirt road, several miles into the jungle. The road ranged from being hard and dusty to sections that were heavily rutted from earlier rains. It was not a comfortable ride since the suspension on the vehicle was not up to the horrendous bumps in the road. Also, the dust was flying around and creeping through every crack in the vehicle. Constance wondered why she had bothered to dress up at all. The air conditioning in the car did not seem to cope well with the heat and soon her red dress was showing distinct signs of creasing and little unwanted pockets of sandy dust began to cling to the bright red material. Roger began to regret wearing a tie; the sweat was trickling down his back. Sometimes the jungle of plants encroached on both sides of the road, forming a dark tunnel. At other points the road opened up, allowing the baking hot sun to fry the vehicle and choke the passengers with dust. The temperature gauge on the car hovered around boiling. Constance did not notice, but Roger, always on the lookout for things to go wrong, prayed that the vehicle would not suddenly overheat and stop.

Finally, the car reached the end of the track, which now opened out into an expansive clearing in the jungle. Roger and Constance were relieved to prise themselves out of the vehicle and dust themselves down. It was hot, unpleasantly so. Dotted around the large clearing and back into the trees and plants behind it were little houses, constructed from a mixture of black volcanic rock, tin and thatch made from the jungle plants. It was very primitive. However, what was not primitive at all was the huge table, or rows of tables, in the middle of the village clearing, long enough to seat at least a hundred people. It was ablaze with colour from flowers of all descriptions. Its sheer elegance and brilliance was a huge contrast to the paucity of luxury in the surrounding buildings. It certainly was an impressive sight, even more so because it was at the end of this rutted dirty road and several miles deep into the jungle. These long and colourful wedding banquet tables were set against a backdrop of multicoloured flags and bunting which adorned every little house in the village. The whole scene was so colourful and unexpected in its jungle setting that it took Roger and Constance completely by surprise.

But as Roger and Constance took in the sight, it soon became apparent to Roger that every single item, bar the flowers, on the wedding table was something that had been stolen from the hotel. The chairs surrounding the long tables were all from the conference room at the Vanilla Beach, as were the tablecloths, the cutlery and the crockery. Roger assumed that if he were to lift the tablecloths, he would find his own banqueting tables. He even recognised the vases holding the flowers.

"Christ," said Roger, almost under his breath to Constance. "Everything here has been stolen from the hotel. What a nerve these people have got: inviting us here to display their stolen goods. Have they no concept of right and wrong?"

"Please don't say anything," whispered Constance back. "You'll spoil the wedding."

"But it's all our stuff," grumbled Roger. "It's all stolen."

"Please, Roger, tackle it after the wedding. Don't spoil it for the bride."

Reluctantly, Roger took Constance's advice and decided to desist from raising the matter with the bride's father, their host, but he could not resist mumbling his complaint to Ibrahim.

"Oh no," whispered Ibrahim in reply, "they do own this stuff. They must have bought it in the market."

It took a while for Roger to accept that if you buy stolen goods in the market that it is okay, even though it is obvious from the logo and markings that the goods actually came from the hotel. But Ibrahim continued with his defence of the wedding host. "How does one know that the goods were not surplus to requirements at the hotel and sold off? That must be what he thought when he bought them."

"So," thought Roger, "even Ibrahim is willing to defend robbery."

Notwithstanding the one perspiring grumpy guest, the wedding was a great success and the celebrations went on for many hours. Much alcohol was consumed, even though alcoholic consumption was banned by their religion. Even Roger finally gave in. The alcohol, he assumed, had also been stolen from him anyway since the groom was head barman at the hotel. By the early evening Constance too was very well oiled indeed, and joined merrily with the local folk in dancing on the purloined tables. As she swung her hips and waved her arms, she was no longer anxious about the state of her little red dress and had long ago lost her shoes.

Roger decided it was time to go home, but Ibrahim, their driver for the evening, had disappeared. Luckily, he had left the keys in the vehicle, so after fifteen minutes of looking for him, Roger decided to head for home. He somehow managed to bundle Constance into the car and headed off down the rutted track in the dark. It was with considerable relief that Roger eventually came out of the jungle and located the tarred road. His annoyance about the stolen goods was, at least for the night, history. His annoyance at Constance's exhibition-ist behaviour was not.

The next day, still nursing a mild hangover, Roger decided to go to the market. Constance stayed in bed. Her head felt like a lump of lead. This was the first real hangover she had had since her party days back in London.

The market in the dusty town square in Moroni was much the same as any market in any poor country. Stall holders were showing their wares on little tables, which had been erected in two lines on one side of the square. Some had little ragged tents above them to keep the hot sun off their wares; some did not. The place was abuzz with chatter as the constant bargaining proceeded. It was no longer a surprise to Roger that most of the little tables, upon closer inspection, were hotel banqueting stock, which must have originated from the Vanilla Beach, possibly stolen from the previous operators. There was no way that, in the first year of Roger's manage-ment of the hotel, he had lost so many tables, so he could only conclude they had probably been stolen during the time the hotel was closed down, the time, in fact, when Ibrahim was the caretaker.

Careful inspection of other items, such as water glasses and linen, showed that they also were like the ones used in the hotel restaurant. One vendor specialised in lamps, which had certainly come from the Vanilla Beach. Each vendor claimed that he had bought the items from "somebody else" and it became more and more likely that that "somebody" had been Ibrahim.

Roger was now faced with a dilemma. Ibrahim had proven himself to be a very useful aide at the hotel. His ability to gain the confidence and trust of the old ruler had been extremely helpful, and even since the coup, his local knowledge and ongoing connections to the small civil service had continued to be useful. The fact he had been stealing from his employer, however, needed to be dealt with, even if almost all of it probably related to the period prior to the reopening.

When Roger returned from the market, Ibrahim was nowhere to be seen. He had failed to show up for his shift as concierge. Nobody, it seemed, had seen Ibrahim since Roger and Constance had left him in the village where the wedding party was still in full swing. Ibrahim, it would appear, had disappeared, at least for now.

Constance was still in bed, although her thumping headache had lessened considerably. When Roger came to see how she was faring, he was still fuming about what he had seen at the wedding and the market. "Don't blame the staff," Constance almost whispered in a husky voice. "Your security and controls are obviously inadequate. These are poor people. If you put temptation in their way, they'll take advantage. You're obviously making it too easy for them to steal. It's up to you and Hector to make it difficult."

Roger was surprised. Constance had obviously learned something being married to a hotelier. She was right. It was up to him to stop the rot; there was no point in blaming anyone else. His next meeting would be with his controller, Hector. One way or another they would figure out how to stop the bleeding. Maybe the invitation to the Grand Mariage had been a blessing in disguise.

It was Peaches' suggestion that really helped. Hector had shared the problem of lax security in the resort with her late one evening after the casino had closed. "Did you know that a couple of the French mercenaries who came with Emile Le Croix are still on the island?" she said as they were preparing for bed. "They might be more effective as security men than the locals. It's very hard for a local man to stop one of his neighbours or family from stealing. Someone from outside might have more clout."

"How do you know they're still here?" asked Hector as he brushed his teeth.

"Because they come to the casino – quite often," she replied. "I can tell from the way they gamble that they're pretty smart."

The idea was a good one. Four days later, Henri LeRoux, a short but heavily muscled Frenchman, dropped into the casino only to be confronted with a proposition from Peaches. The next day he was in Roger's office, being interviewed by Hector and Roger, and a week later was installed as the new security chief. It did not take long for the pilfering to stop. Henri was fearless in the pursuit of his job. Discipline at the back door and in the supply chain was quickly restored. The only downside was that, as an employee, Henri was no longer allowed to lose his money in the casino and his compatriot did not seem interested in gambling on his own.

The local employees naturally resented a foreigner in this position. This added to a groundswell of discontent that seemed to be growing amongst many of them, particularly the men. Comorians were not used to regular employment, nor to hard work. Those in the front line, with constant contact with the guests, seemed to enjoy their work, when they felt disposed to show up. Many others, with more mundane tasks like cleaning, gardening, or housekeeping, were less enamoured with the principle of appearing, day after day, for their routine jobs. Absenteeism was high, particularly amongst the men, and, because of the success of the resort, there was little respite from the constant pressure of servicing the guests. Roger's team had reported to him that there were rumours that the staff were being organised into a fledgling union, whose purpose was, like all unions, to improve the lot of their members. Roger did not want to have to deal with a union. He was, of course, keenly interested to understand what grievances the staff might have so that he could address them, but he did not want a gun to his head.

The appointment of LeRoux, a foreigner, seemed to bring things to a head, particularly after LeRoux had insisted on the firing of two junior cooks that he had caught stealing from the kitchen storerooms. The two men involved, it seemed, were very popular with their colleagues, who objected to the way they were being treated. Several members of the kitchen brigade laid down their tools and refused to work, staging a sit-in at the delivery dock of the hotel. Word spread quickly throughout the hotel and soon, without even knowing why they were there, many others had joined the "striking" few at the back door. There they sat, chanting and ranting.

Despite Chef Sparrowhawk demanding they return to work, they refused and their numbers grew. Roger, at the time, was in Moroni in a meeting with some government officials. Hector, having heard the rumpus at the back of the hotel from his office, hurried to the loading dock to appeal to the workers to stop the din and return to their jobs. Nobody was listening. There appeared to be no real leaders. Just a mob.

"This is when we need Ibrahim," mumbled Hector to Sparrowhawk, "someone that understands them."

Dinesh now joined the chef and accountant on the dock. "We need to understand their grievances," he observed. "I will try to get them to tell us. If we know what the problems are, we can address them."

Hector and Sparrowhawk nodded agreement. Dinesh now moved off the loading dock into the crowd below. A circle of demonstrators gathered around him. He tried to explain to them that they needed to form a small group to discuss their grievances with management in an orderly manner. He had no hope. The herd instinct had overtaken any reason. The circle that had formed around the food and beverage manager now threatened to crush him. The excitable crowd started to push him. The noise of excited voices reached fever pitch.

Just as Hector and the chef were fearing the worst for their colleague, Roger appeared on the loading dock, back from his trip to Moroni. On seeing the grave situation in front of him, Roger acted with pure instinct. Whereas his training in personnel management in London would have led him to a non- confrontational approach to solving the crises unfolding in front of him, his instincts were that this was not appropriate. The mob below him were used to strong leadership and a respect for authority which had been instilled into them by their local village chiefs. It was bred into them through their strong family relationships, respect for their elders and fear of their God.

Roger stood tall on the dock. Here, in front of the mob, he represented the ultimate authority, at least in their world of the resort, their workplace. There was a slight lowering of the noise as the mob looked at the boss in anticipation. Roger seized his moment. "I'm going to count to ten," he bellowed. "Go back to your work places. Anyone still standing here at the end of my count is fired. Do you understand? If you're still here when I finish counting, you'll no longer have a job in this hotel and no chance of earning any pay here in the future.

You will not be re-employed." Without waiting for a response, Roger immediately started to shout out the count. "One, two, three."

Nobody moved.

"Four, five, six," he counted on, in the strongest and most commanding voice he could muster. When he reached the number seven, a slight movement began. Some workers were leaving. By the time he reached "ten" the trickle had become a stampede. When he stopped counting there was no one left in the bay. Hector, Chef Sparrowhawk and Dinesh looked at their boss in amazement and with renewed admiration. Roger knew he had taken a chance, but, if he had learned anything in his first year or so in the Comores, it was that the people respect strong leadership. Now, with the mob dispersed, he would find ways to address whatever genuine grievances the employees had. But first, the two offending and pilfering chefs had to go.

A few days later, with normal service resumed, Roger and Constance moved to the cottage on the beach. There was still no sign of Ibrahim. Since the marriage in the village nobody had seen or heard of him. He had just vanished, it seemed, into the jungle.

Chapter Eight
"The Unravelling"

Moving from the suite in the hotel to the cottage seemed to be good for the relationship between Constance and Roger. Not that Roger was able to spend a huge amount of time away from the hotel, with its constant requirement for him to be on call to deal with staff and guests. Roger often reflected on the major difference between running a city hotel and managing a resort. People mainly stay in city hotels to conduct their business or explore the city itself. Their behaviour is mostly quite predictable. They use the hotel for sleeping and breakfast. After that, the city tends to take over. In a resort, the reason for them being there is often the resort itself. They have come to enjoy the hotel, not just to use it as a base for other activity. The demands, therefore, on management, are substantially more than they would be in a town setting. Managing a resort begins before dawn and ends when the last guest goes to bed. The result was that Roger inevitably spent more time in the resort than he did in the cottage. The benefit was that, in interacting with his guests, Roger got to meet, and in some cases, know, a vast number of interesting people.

Constance, however, seemed happy. Her renewed interest in sex certainly gave Roger a good reason to want to get away from the hotel. The cottage was basic but comfortable. Its situation right on a promontory provided it with fabulous views of the ocean and a very private little sandy beach. Where two bodies of seawater were conjoined at the promontory the azure water actually sparkled with colour. Constance enjoyed luring Roger onto the beach at night, where, from time to time they made love. Sex, in the open air and under the stars, seemed to be very erotic to Constance. Roger was a little more cautious, constantly worrying there might be prying eyes watching from the dark. If Constance felt the same it was more of a turn-on for her than a concern. In the day, whilst Roger was at work, Constance had renewed her habit of swimming naked. For her, this was the ultimate freedom. Despite all of this, there was no sign of babies. Constance assured Roger that she did not take precautions but she did not get pregnant. This seemed to disappoint Roger more than Constance.

Things at the resort were now going well. The reputation of the hotel was excellent in the travel trade and the occupancy was consistently high. Roger had begun design work on an extension of a hundred rooms on the second beach and was in negotiations with Dusty and the South African government to fund it. The only disappointment was that Brigitte had resigned and returned to France. Apparently, she had been spotted by a film producer who stayed at the Vanilla Beach whilst Roger had been on an earlier sales trip to Europe. She had, she explained to Roger on her departure, been offered a role in a film to be shot in France. She made no mention of her brief role in the erotic film that had been shot in Roger's absence. Nobody did.

Roger was extremely disappointed that Brigitte was leaving. He had worked hard to quell his physical attraction for her. He still remembered his reaction to hugging her before the aeroplane crash. He sometimes fantasised about what might have been, but, despite this, managed his relationship with her in a proper and professional manner. Her departure, of course, was a real blow to the efficiency of the hotel.

Constance agreed to stand in as acting housekeeper whilst Roger sought a replacement, but, for a few months, the agencies in Europe were unable to find a suitable candidate.

Since it was time for Roger to renew some of the travel wholesalers' contracts he decided to venture once more to Europe, where he would also take the opportunity of interviewing some replacement candidates for the housekeeping position. Because the recruitment agencies had failed him, Roger had been in contact with Molly Perkins at Sloane Towers. Molly had amassed a sizeable address book of young ladies who had worked with her and agreed to approach a few on Roger's behalf, so that Roger could meet them on his trip. He planned to be away from the Comores for a couple of weeks and, once again, asked Constance, to mind the store.

And so it was that life for Roger and Constance took a dramatic turn. Whilst Roger was in Paris visiting some of his main travel trade suppliers, he had cause to be walking down the Champs Elysées between appointments. There were several cinemas flanking the wide boulevard and, in passing, Roger found himself glancing at the promotional still photos from the movies, which were displayed in showcases on the street-facing walls of the cinema buildings, to lure patrons inside. Whilst passing one cinema, Roger was surprised to see in one of the photos a face that he recognised. He did a double take. The framed pictures on the side of the building clearly showed, amongst other half-naked men and women, several shots of his Brigitte, pouting at the camera and looking quite entrancing. On closer inspection, he was surprised to see that the furnishings in the background looked very familiar. Yes, he was sure, they were pieces of furniture from the Vanilla Beach. It looked as if the movie, whatever it was, had been shot at his hotel and that one of the girls in it was none other than his ex-housekeeper. Intrigued, notwithstanding the fact he had an appointment in an hour's time, he entered the building and bought a ticket for the film. He had never been to an erotic movie house in his life. The theatre, once inside, was surprisingly small. The air felt stale and, from what he could make out in the dim light, the whole place had a grubby feel about it. Roger fumbled his way to an empty seat, just as the film began.

Roger could not believe what he was watching. The film was a banal tale set on a tropical island. There were several pretty girls involved and a couple of handsome well-hung men, but, astoundingly the prettiest, freshest and sexiest of all was Brigitte. "No wonder," thought Roger, "that she has been offered a part in a mainstream film. Somebody must have seen her in this thing." Roger, of course, had never seen Brigitte naked before, although, since that time in his office when he was comforting her, he had often thought about her body, sometimes even as he made love to Constance. Now, in the dark privacy of a sleazy cinema in Paris, he was able to see what he had dreamed of, and he was not disappointed. Brigitte had a magnificent body. As Roger watched on, his appointment with the travel company was the last thing on his mind. He recognised the setting. It was for certain in the Comores and most of the furnishings in the sets included pieces of furniture from the Vanilla Beach. "When the hell did they shoot this?" Roger puzzled. Then the penny dropped. It must have been whilst he was off island, whilst Constance had been in charge. But why hadn't she mentioned it? Why had none of his staff said anything?

Then Roger found out why. As the movie drew towards its conclusion a new woman appeared in the story, equally beautiful and well stacked as the others. In fact, the new woman stole the show. At first, Roger could not believe his eyes. There, on the screen, in her full naked glory, was Constance, grinding away like the rest of the girls, but apparently having the time of her life. As the two male hunks played with her, whether she was acting or not, she seemed to be in a state of ecstasy. "Jesus Christ," uttered Roger. "How the fuck could I not have known about this? What a fool I am. The whole staff must have known about it." The shock was almost overwhelming and so was the anger. On the other hand, it was also amazingly erotic. But, putting aside his sexual reactions, Roger felt like a fool. A very big fool.

The film came to an end. Constance, it appeared, was its climax. Roger stared at the screen in incredulity. As the credits rolled, he was oblivious to what they were telling him. The handful of spectators, including, strangely, he thought, a few women, dribbled out of the theatre. Roger just sat there, staring at the blank screen, feeling numb. How could Constance do this to him? Is this why her interest in sex had perked up? When she had been making love to him, was she thinking of the hunks on the screen? Questions flooded into his brain – but no answers. He tried to rationalise it. "After all," he thought, "I've often thought of Brigitte whilst making love to Constance; what's wrong with her thinking about a hunk actor?" The rationale, however, did not sooth him. His emotions went from anger to despair. The cinema had emptied, but now a trickle of new customers began to find seats – men who had come to ogle his wife. He was tempted to watch the movie again, partly to see the naked Brigitte, but he was no longer in the mood. He levered himself out of this seat and made his way back onto the famous broad Parisienne avenue. He was still in a state of shock. When he phoned Constance later that evening, ostensibly, to check on things at the hotel, he did not mention his trip to the cinema. Constance was upbeat. Things were going well. She did not tell him that Alain Gabor was in the "house".

When Roger reached London a couple of days later, the shock of the movie had, to some extent, worn off. He had decided to avoid any confrontation with his wife until he got home. Now he had work to do. Firstly, to visit Mrs Perkins at the Sloane Towers to review any suggestions she had about a replacement for Brigitte, and second, to call on the various travel wholesalers who had been supporting Vanilla Beach. He could not, however, get the images of the erotic movie out of his head and this was not helped by the *Mail on Sunday* running a whole article about the "new" film sensation in Paris, his Brigitte, complete with pictures, carefully but teasingly selected from the movie shot in the Comores. The wretched story would just not go away. "Damn it," thought Roger, "when I select a new housekeeper, I am going to find the plainest 'Jane' that I can."

It was not a coincidence that the return of Alain Gabor to the Comores coincided with Roger's sales and recruitment trip to Europe. Although the actor had checked into the hotel, he spent most of his time at Constance and Roger's secluded cottage. On his first visit to Vanilla Beach, Constance had played hard to get – in fact Alain had failed in his attempts. This time things were different. Constance could not wait to bed him and seemed to have no conscience at all about doing so in her married quarters. For Alain, who enjoyed the chase, almost as much as the kill, this was a bit disconcerting, but who was he to complain?

On the third day of Alain's visit the two lovers were shocked to find Roger towering over them as they slept naked in the marital bed. Roger had returned four days earlier than sched-uled. Clearly, he had not alerted his wayward wife. Roger had intended to confront his wife about the movie. Now there was no need. Discovering his wife in his bed with another man was the straw which broke the camel's back. The marriage was over.

Chapter Nine
"A Burst of Sunshine"

Alain Gabor was anxious to leave; he did not want to be reading about his marriage-wrecking antics in the supermarket check-outs. But there were no flights out of Moroni for two days. Constance, although disappointed about his attitude, suggested he move to the little boarding house in Moroni where she, Roger and Dusty had stayed on their first visit to the island. Alain agreed. With Alain out of the way, Constance decided to reach out to Roger, who had moved back to a suite in the hotel. All the time, however, she was conscious that the whole hotel was watching, not just the employees, but also the guests, who had not been slow to pick up on the rumours of trouble in the managerial marriage. Roger was not listening. He had had enough. Constance's guest appearance in an erotic movie had been embarrassing, but her latest illicit tryst with the French actor was a blow too much. There was no way Roger could trust Constance ever again, not only as a wife, but also as his stand-in hotel manager. No, enough was enough. He would let the dust settle, then think through how to start divorce proceedings. Maybe time would make things a little easier. For the moment Roger was a shaken man, and also an angry one. But he knew that acting in anger could be stupid.

Constance now found herself on her own. The benefits of privacy at the cottage were now working against her. She saw nobody and nobody came to see her. JP, the bandleader, thought about it, as did Dinesh. Here was ripe fruit ready for picking, but the dangers were too great – at least for the moment. Constance had always been a social animal. Now she was on her own. The secluded cottage had become a jail and, at night, a very dark one. She thought about going to Cape Town to her family, but knew that running away would not solve anything. For the moment she decided to sit tight. Roger would have to make the next move.

Molly Perkins in London had done a great job in promoting the Vanilla Beach to prospective housekeepers and Roger had found himself almost spoiled for choice. He was undecided whether to offer the job to the fattest applicant or the plainest, but just could not bring himself to do either. To some extent he thought of the resort as a film set. Good-looking people add to the glamour. So, eventually, he went for the most glamourous. After all, he convinced himself, the Vanilla Beach had to be attractive in all aspects. Julie Jones was an English divorcee, around thirty-five years old. She had lost two children in a car accident whilst her ex-husband was driving. She needed to escape and what better place than the Comores? Julie was available at short notice, which appealed to Roger, and her arrival at the Vanilla Beach was imminent. As far as Roger was concerned, the sooner the better, because without Constance as a stand-in housekeeper, the standards of service in that department could rapidly deteriorate.

Despite the appalling tragedy of recently losing her family, Julie Jones put on a remarkable show of positivity. Her broad smile and attractive freckled face, beneath her striking red hair, were contagious. Roger liked her from the minute he set eyes on her; she had that effect on people. She had clearly been a good mother; it seemed to Roger that his Vanilla Beach needed a mother. He had no doubt in his mind she would be a good fit.

Political activity on the island had also gained traction. The provisional French government made possible by Emile Le Croix had now organised elections for a new President and members of parliament. Unlike in many countries, the people would be choosing the President as well as voting for their local representatives for parliament. The two leading candidates standing for the vacant Presidency seemed, to Roger, to be poles apart. Ikililou Abderellah, or LOU, as he was commonly known, was something of a firebrand – a "power to the people" candidate. He was also, religiously speaking, ultra-conservative and Roger feared, probably rightly, that if elected he would not be interested in tourism and would certainly force Roger to close his money-spinning casino. LOU was a member of the fledgling Al Qaeda; his name had been associated with the manufacture of bombs, one of which had been used to blow up the American Embassy in Kenya. But LOU was a rousing public speaker; Roger feared that his mob appeal might win him the day. He was, however, hopeful that the French, who were organising the elections, would make sure that Abderellah got less votes.

The other candidate was Ahmed Abdellaw Mohammed, an ex-military man. Younger than his Al Qaeda competitor, AAM came from a wealthy Comoran family with many solid local connections. Some women would regard Ahmed as handsome. He certainly knew how to charm them, and since, for the first time, women were to be allowed to vote, Ahmed seemed to have a good shot at winning the Presidency. AAM was also well travelled, with a keen knowledge of what was happening in the world beyond the Comores. He had been educated at a private school in Paris and later studied for his Masters at Cambridge in the UK. He already had two wives, but this, apparently, did not stop him from amorous adventures with many other women.

Roger, after several glasses of Bordeaux with French officials, was reasonably comfortable that AAM would win the election. However, without the insider information of Ibrahim, Roger did feel somewhat naked. "What on earth happened to Ibrahim?" Roger wondered. Nobody seemed to have any news from him; in fact, it was noticeable that nobody on the staff even spoke of him. Roger wondered if his employees knew something that he did not. "After all," he mused, "it wouldn't be the first time."

Without the need, nor the desire, to go home to his wife, Roger found himself more often at the bar than he usually would. Not that he was drinking to excess, but certainly more than normal. It was also a good spot to meet his guests and to hear, from the barmen, what else was going on in the country. Aware that Coco, the head bartender, had been the groom at the wedding where Ibrahim was last seen, Roger raised the subject of the missing man. Coco seemed a little reluctant to speak. This, indeed, was unusual for the garrulous bartender; Coco could talk to his customers about everything and anything. Roger pushed. "I'm really fearful for him," he continued with Coco. "If he's in trouble, I'd like to help him."

Coco smiled, knowingly. "He's not in trouble," he eventually volunteered. "He just causes it." Clearly Coco could not just stop there. He had merely tweaked Roger's interest even more. Roger waited. He knew Coco would just have to say more. "If you must know, Ibrahim is the cause of some scandal amongst the families. Some people are ashamed of his behaviour." Roger was even more intrigued. Coco stopped to prepare some drinks for a customer. When done, he returned to the subject. "Ibrahim has run off with my mother-in-law."

"What?" exclaimed Roger. "What happened?"

"After the wedding feast," continued Coco, "I was obviously otherwise occupied, but, according to some other guests, Ibrahim and my mother-in-law disappeared into one of the village houses. As you know it is uncommon for my people to take alcohol, but the wedding had been a special occasion where it was available for the guests. My father-in-law found the two of them and, in a rage, threw them out. Right out of the village. As far as we know they went to France."

"Wow," said Roger, "I'm sorry to hear that. Has your wife heard anything from her mother?"

"No, sir," said Coco, "nothing at all. Her dad wants nothing more to do with her. He is very angry."

"Well, thank you for telling me, young man. I will not discuss this with anyone. It is your family's private business."

With that astounding news, Roger moved away from the bar to allow Coco to continue with his work. Roger had been impressed with young Coco. He was one of the few Comorians who had really taken to the hospitality business. Under the guidance of Dinesh, Coco had turned into an excellent bartender, who could turn his hand to almost anything a guest might ask for. His buoyant and friendly personality had charmed many a guest. He was a good listener, but also a good talker. He seemed to like giving service and it was always with a cheerful smile. Above all, he was honest, which was saying a lot for a barman. He never diluted the bottles so that he could skim off the extra sales and he never introduced his own "private" stock to the bar. What he sold was the Vanilla Beach beverages, not his own, and the profits therefore all went to the hotel. He was a rarity amongst resort barmen and Roger knew it. All credit to his teacher, Dinesh.

Two days after Roger's chat with the barman, the new housekeeper, Julie Jones, arrived from London. Roger, understanding what a big step this would be for the young lady, decided to make the trip to the airport to greet her. As Julie Jones stepped off the plane, Roger wondered whether he had made the right choice. She clearly was not used to long-haul travel. Whereas most of the passengers emerged from the plane wearing the most casual and sloppy clothes, Julie appeared at the top of the steps like a visiting film star with a bright red off-the-shoulder sundress and enormous straw hat. Her lipstick matched her dress and her eyes were fully made up, as opposed to most of the other passengers who could hardly keep their eyes open. Her flamboyant appearance made Roger smile. She was like a burst of sunshine blasting through a cloudy sky.

Roger was on good terms with the airport management. After all, probably ninety percent of the customers coming through it were headed to or from the Vanilla Beach. As a result he more or less had the freedom of the place and was able to greet Julie at the door of the building and escort her through customs and immigration at great speed, whilst everyone else lined up to await their turn for the redundant questions, form filling and box ticking. The swiftness of the arrival process, however, was immediately negated by the wait for the luggage, specifically, Julie's luggage. Whereas most arrivals destined for the hotel carried bags just large enough to fit bikinis and toiletries, Julie, it seemed, had brought everything but the kitchen sink. As the sixth suitcase poked itself through the little rubber flaps onto the carousel, Roger began to have his doubts about his selection of housekeeper. On the other hand, one had to laugh, because Julie was like a gust of fresh air and, maybe, after four long years of establishing the hotel, fresh air was needed.

Julie's arrival had put Roger in a good mood. Lately he had been quite depressed about the situation with Constance. In no way was he forgiving Constance for her behaviour, but the lack of a companion and lover was leaving an empty space in his life. He was also looking forward to Monty from the Sloane Towers making a visit to the hotel. Whilst interviewing for the housekeeper in London, Roger had asked after the other three members of the Murder Club. Only one, it appeared, was still working at the Sloane Towers: Monty, the banqueting manager. Roger had touched base with his old friend and invited him and his wife on a free holiday in the Comores. They had not discussed the taboo subject of Mersky's death.

Back at the hotel, Roger escorted his new housekeeper to the bungalow Brigitte had vacated earlier. "The last inhabitant of this little house has become a film star," he said as he showed her around.

Julie giggled. "Lightning won't strike twice," she said, "and that's the last thing I would want."

"Me too," agreed Roger and then left her to rest.

When he reached his office, he was greeted by a couple of long faces, Dinesh and Colin Freeke. "I'm afraid we've received a cyclone warning," said Dinesh rather sombrely. "Due here in about twelve hours."

"But we never have cyclones here," started Roger. "They always go to Mauritius or the Seychelles. Never here."

"Well, according to the met office, this one, called Jane, is different. We'd better get prepared."

The only person on the management team who had experienced a cyclone was, of course, Dinesh. Cyclones in his home country were quite common. Roger turned to him. "Tell us what we have to do to prepare ourselves."

"Number one," started Dinesh, pleased he had been asked, "we tie all the palm trees together with strong rope. If one is weak and gets uprooted, it will bring down others or smash into something. If they are roped together, they will hold each other up.

"Number two. We must tape everything glass. The wind can be strong enough to blow in glass, or other flying objects might smash into it. If it has tape across it the glass will not shatter. It might crack, but it will not fly about the place.

"Number three. We must ask all the guests to fill the bathtubs in their rooms. We will almost certainly lose electrical power and that means we will lose our pumps. We will not be able to pump water around the place, so the taps in the kitchens and guest rooms will run dry. The full baths will be our water supply until the electricity is reconnected.

"Number four. We must put all the outdoor furniture into the swimming pool. If it is covered with water, it will not fly around and do damage..."

On and on droned Dinesh, enjoying his moment in charge. Both Roger and Colin listened in astonishment and admiration. They were impressed. Everything that Dinesh said made complete sense. Roger had less than twelve hours to make the prescribed tasks happen. He sprang into action, summoning his heads of department to the banquet room for an emergency planning session. Each department head was allocated a leadership job to oversee one or other of the contingency plans. Other issues were raised: Would the staff be allowed to go home to secure their own homesteads? How would they feed the guests and staff if they had no power for the kitchens? How would they prevent pilfering? Where would the guests be asked to stay for safekeeping?

There were, it seemed to Roger, often more questions than answers, but at least everyone seemed to be on the same side. Catering for a houseful without power, would obviously be a challenge for Chef Sparrowhawk. Given his propensity to break down in a crisis, Roger worried about him, but somehow or other, almost three hundred guests and even more staff would need to be fed. Pre-cooked cold food seemed to be the answer. The hotel did have a small oil-fuelled generator, designed to keep the cold room and kitchen fridges working, so Sparrowhawk was excused from the meeting whilst he set to work. Julie Jones, the newcomer, disturbed from her rest, pitched into the meeting as if she had been around for a year. To her, the whole thing was so much more exciting than Clapham. An atmosphere of nervous anticipation mixed with excitement hung over the resort as the skies got darker and darker.

As preparations were made, quite a few with the help of volunteering guests, the whole resort took on the air of a country waiting to be invaded. Little did they know that a cyclone can carry more punch than an army.

Chapter Ten
"The Cyclone"

It was midnight when the cyclone hit. Generally speaking, the hotel guests were spread about the resort during the day. The one time that they almost all congregated together was for the evening meal. Roger took full advantage of this mass feeding time to communicate with his guests. He had prepared a brief statement of explanation concerning the impending storm, copies of which were handed out to all diners as they entered the restaurant areas, and were also circulated to every room. In addition to this Roger and Dinesh, together with Peaches from the casino, moved amongst the tables answering questions from worried guests. Guests were asked to stay in their rooms until further notice once they had returned to them. Food, in the form of cold plates and sandwiches together with bottled water, would be distributed by hotel staff.

The news about the cyclone did not come as a surprise to the diners. For several hours before they had witnessed the staff engaged in a hive of activity. The pool area had been placed off limits and the sun loungers and other poolside furniture were carefully packed into the pool. Ladders were propped up against the swaying palm trees and thick ropes were looped around their trunks to lash them together. The housekeeping staff had been touring the hotel filling all the bathtubs, and posting instructions to guests about water usage during the impending storm. Sticky tape for application to glass was in short supply and nobody in Moroni had any more. The precious tape was therefore restricted to the large sliding windows and doors surrounding the public areas. Guests were asked to keep their bedroom windows tightly shut, even though the internal temperature might become uncomfortable.

Whilst carrying out these precautions, Roger and his team had underestimated the level of fear they might be causing. Cyclones and hurricanes were things that happened to other people in distant lands. They did not occur in civilised Europe. Many guests seemed to be looking forward to the adventure, but many more were, whether they admitted it or not, quite fearful. Almost all of them had seen images of destruction caused by storms in far off places. Would they now be part of these images?

At first the storm manifested itself simply as a very strong wind, whipping through the palm trees around the hotel. Although it was dark the sea appeared to be quite calm, though the normal moonlight had been obliterated by the dense cloud. Gradually, however, the winds strengthened, until they were howling through the gardens and the arched gaps in the architecture between the hotel buildings. Then the lights went out. The power supply to the hotel had been interrupted. The rains started. Not just heavy rain, but the most vicious rain anyone in the hotel had ever heard, smashing like stones against the bedroom windows. The noise was so loud it was truly frightening, not just the torrential rain beating on the windows or the whistling howling wind, but also the crashing and banging of items outside or on the roof that had not been properly secured. Most guests later swore they had seen the glass in their bedroom windows actually bend. Most admitted later that this had been the most frightening night they had ever spent. In the public areas the larger expanses of glass bent and cracked. Only the sticky tape suggested by

Dinesh stopped the shards flying all over the place and causing even more damage.

As the storm raged, there was no form of communication between management and the holed-up guests. There was no feasible way of communicating. Nobody slept. Most were scared out of their wits. Even the adventurers did not venture outside; the winds were just too strong and the rain stung the body.

For five hours the storm raged. Then, suddenly, it went quiet. Although the hotel management had, earlier in the dining room, explained that there could be a dip in the rough weather in the eye of the storm, and that nobody should be fooled into thinking the worst was over, some people had not listened. All the written and verbal instructions to guests had stressed that the calm time as the eye passed would be temporary and they must stay inside with doors and windows closed tight. As the eerie quiet fell on the resort, hotel guests flooded in relief from their cages. Doors and windows were flung open in relief. Arguments broke out. Those that had read or listened to the instructions started to explain before berating their neighbours for not following the rules. Fear had turned a little nasty.

Normally, first light at the resort would come at 5am, but there was no such thing. Had there been, those guests at the far end of the hotel would have realised what some of the banging and crashing was about. The wooden boathouse had been demolished in the wind. Planks of ripped-out sidings had scattered all over the beach and the unprotected boats had been thrown, like balloons, all over the place. Two fourteen-foot dinghies were now lodged on the roof of the hotel, and several surf boards and windsurfers were dotted in the trees like Christmas decorations. Most of the planting in the garden had been ripped from the soil and blown away. Salt spray from the ocean was covering everything.

Nobody could be sure how long the lull in the storm would last. Roger, breaking his own rules, did a quick tour of the battered public areas. To his relief most things seemed intact. Although many of the windows had cracked under the strain of bent glass, there did not seem to be any severe damage. The chairs and tables that had been stacked and tied together had resisted the force of the wind. There was water everywhere, but this could be easily dealt with in the morning. As far as he could see, there were no fallen trees, at least around the public areas and the pool. Roger wondered about Constance. In the hours leading up to the storm he had had no time to consider the fate of his wife in the secluded cottage. Now, in the lull, he thought of her. "Fuck," he said to himself, "I should have warned her. Christ knows how she'll be getting on." What, however, Roger had not done, Dinesh, had.

When the cyclone resumed it came back twice as hard. It was now ferocious. Roger once again sought shelter with a few of his top team. The casino had been designated as the safest place to be. It was a box with no windows. Peaches was playing host. She had stocked up with plenty of coffee and tea. Roger had forbidden anything stronger because he wanted clear heads in case of emergencies. Whilst the storm raged outside there was nothing any of the management could do. Peaches gave lessons in casino games, whilst all hell broke loose outside. Julie Jones, the new recruit, was hilarious. She could not get a handle on the rules of the games: any of them. But her infectious laugh kept everyone in a good mood and took their minds off the dangers outside. Roger could not sit still. He constantly ventured outside of the box, despite his own instructions, to gauge the ferocity of the storm.

On one of his sorties Roger caught sight of a young man running from the room block into the public areas. He appeared to be calling for help. Roger yelled back, trying to make his voice heard above the din of the wind and rain. The man stopped running and Roger approached. Immediately Roger knew there was something seriously wrong; the man's eyes were full of fear. "It's my wife," the man screamed, "she's having a baby."

Roger stayed calm. "What room is she in?" he shouted out over the din.

"329," came the reply, "please help. She's not due for three months."

"Go back to her now," yelled Roger. "I'll send help immediately," he lied in an attempt to calm down the young man.

The man ran off, back from where he had appeared. Roger rushed back to the casino. He was clearly panicked as he burst into the room. "A guest is having a premature baby, room 329. Anyone know anything about delivering babies?" he blurted out, more in hope than expectation.

"Me," said Julie, suddenly serious, "I've had two children. I know about childbirth!"

"Come with me," yelled Roger, forgetting he did not need to shout. Then, as an afterthought, added, "What do you need?"

"Clean hot water, towels, a large bowl and plenty of luck," said Julie. "Just show me where the mother is – then get the things."

Julie Jones was the star of the night. Forty-five minutes after her arrival in room 329, a four-pound little girl was born. She was small, but perfectly healthy. They called her Julie Jane.

Finally, at about 8am, in the first gloomy light, Roger thought the storm was abating, albeit only slightly. The gaming instruction stopped. Dinesh and Chef Sparrowhawk made their way to the kitchen, Colin Freeke, the engineer, and Roger set off for a tour of the property.

What Roger had not realised in the night was the extent of the water damage, caused by the strong winds blasting water across the site. Despite the protection of the reef, the water in the bay had been whipped up into waves, which, at some point had sent salty spray flying towards the hotel buildings that were now looking completely discoloured by ugly patterns of brown and grey. Five palm trees had been uprooted, but, as projected by Dinesh, they had been held up by their neighbours. They saw the boats and surfboards that had been thrown onto the roof before being faced with the destroyed boathouse. Worst of all, Roger had declined to take out insurance against cyclones, having been assured they did not represent a risk. "There's always something," Roger mumbled to himself. He was in negotiations with the South African government to buy out their share of the hotel. "Thank God I haven't bought them out. Better to let them pay for their share of the clean-up," he thought, as he trudged around the depressing site. Vanilla Beach was looking very sad and Roger wondered if it was all worth it. So many things seemed to go wrong.

Roger was still worried about Constance. He found it hard to admit, after all her bad behaviour, but he did not wish her ill. She must have had to endure the brunt of the storm on her own in the cottage, which sat on an unprotected promontory. He needed to know she was alright. He knew that Mrs Freeke was quite close to her. Maybe he could ask her to go and check. He could not spare any of his heads of department to do so, because they were badly needed at their own stations. Mrs Freeke agreed, much to Roger's relief, and he now put the matter behind him, at least until he heard back.

His priority was to get the power back on. His hotel guests might be thankful for a cold breakfast and lunch but would certainly be complaining by dinner time if Chef Sparrowhawk was unable to cook or they were unable to have their baths and showers. He headed straight to the plant room where Colin was pondering the damage. "Any news on when the power might be back on?" asked Roger, rather half-heartedly, since he felt that he knew the answer.

"None, whatsoever, I'm afraid. They have no idea of just how many places the lines have come down in, and they certainly do not have the men to fix them. If you have any pull at all with government, tell them they need to bring in the army."

Luckily, in Moroni, the temporary French government was still in place. The elections were due in only a week's time. Those in power knew exactly what to do and within twenty-four hours a planeload of army engineers had been flown in from the South of France. Armed with this news, Roger and Sparrowhawk set about how to feed over three hundred people without any power. The first evening was a barbeque on the beach at which the resident band gave an "unplugged" concert. It was so successful that most of the guests asked for it to be repeated. Soon, Sparrowhawk had devised a whole series of "bakes on the beach". The guests were hugely thankful for his innovation and, in any event, seemed to enjoy the alfresco environment as much as the restaurant. Roger was relieved. And thankful for his chef.

However, his relief was tempered by the report he had received from Margaret Freeke. The cottage had been severely damaged. The wall facing the ocean had been ripped off as well as part of the roof. Decorative items and pieces of furniture were strewn all over the place. There was no sign of Constance. In many ways this was a good sign, but, on the other hand, where the hell was she? She had not headed for the hotel and her little car was still parked near the damaged cottage. Roger knew everyone had far too much on their plate to start searching for his wife, but he needed to register with the authorities that she was missing. At the hotel, he located LeRoux, his newly hired security chief. "Monsieur LeRoux, if you do nothing else, find my wife!"

This was not hard. It turned out that Alain Gabor had never left the island. Temporarily despatched to the boarding house next to the Presidential Palace, whilst awaiting the next flight out, Gabor had time for reflection. He was infatuated with Constance. Just because he had been caught with his trousers down by her husband had not, in his view, changed anything. She clearly did not love her husband anymore and Alain could simply not get her out of his head. If he left the island now, he knew it would be all over. He could not leave in these circumstances. He had to know if they could make it work, irrespective of their marital encumbrances. He decided to stay. He soon got a message to Constance that he was still in Moroni in the horrible little guest house. She was alarmed but flattered. She had already been caught with him once, so the damage had been done. What had she got to lose by seeing him again? And so, she had. They decided that the guest house was too public, especially slap next to the government offices. Constance then remembered the house that the filming had taken place in. How could she forget? A nice secluded place and, presumably, still up for rent. There was no Ibrahim around to do the deal, but Constance now knew how to get in touch with the owner, which she did. Soon the grand house in the jungle became their secret. With news of the cyclone approaching, Alain and Constance had rapidly brought forward their plan to move into the old dilapidated house.

At first, the Chief of Security was stumped but it did not take him long to follow the clues to the mansion in the jungle. He did not need to go in. The battered rental car in the drive and the laughter from inside told him all he needed to know. Now he needed to tell Roger.

Chapter Eleven
"Old Friends and Bomb Damage"

Three months after the cyclone, Roger was taking stock of his life. The mess left behind by the storm had been cleared up, the buildings were freshly painted and, by and large, the lush landscaping, which had been so badly battered during the storm, had been re-established – all thanks to Colin Freeke and his well-drilled team. Business at the resort had remained strong. The elections had taken place and, as expected, AAM had won and been installed as the new President. This did not mean, however, that LOU had gone away. Instead, he had gone into the bush, where, every day, more Al Qaeda recruits joined him. From there, he and his followers were a constant threat to AAM's new democracy. For Roger, this political unrest was worrying. His plans for the hundred-room extension were ready as was his deal to buy out the South African government' shares. He needed to be sure he really wanted to do these things; he needed to be sure he really wanted to tie his life to this island in the Indian Ocean with its potentially dangerous political instability, especially now he was not with Constance. Although he was constantly surrounded by the "family" of his management team and the ever-changing parade of guests, there were times when he was lonely, severely lonely. He was also drinking too much, and he knew it.

As he sat in his suite pondering what he should do, he

found himself looking back on the last few years. They had not been easy; he had been through a lifetime of unexpected incidents. "Surely," he thought, "the worst is over?" Surely all the hard work and overcoming of obstacles should now pay off? In five short years he had taken a wreck of a hotel and turned it into a profitable business: one that had survived a barracuda attack, an airline crash, a coup d'état, a military invasion, governmental corruption, robbery, a cyclone and, worst of all, the breakdown of his marriage. Of all those things, the last was absolutely the worst. Without Constance, what was the point of being there? He sometimes had dreams about a life with Brigitte, but she was now out of his reach. After two hit movies in France, Brigitte was the new darling of the European movie business. She was now the biggest film star in Europe and Hollywood had beckoned. Brigitte was now in a different league and, anyway, after only one short hug, was she ever really in his?

Constance, strangely, had not left the island. Alain Gabor had. Their hot romance, cloistered in the rental mansion in the jungle, soon cooled. Their lives were just too different. The only thing that bound them together was passion but passion can wear thin cooped up in a crumbling old house with no air conditioning and no other social life. Alain, after the conquest, missed the city life: the buzz of the cafes, the constant recognition that he received in the streets and his circle of friends. Constance missed the bustle of the hotel and wondered if she did not actually miss the steadiness and love of her estranged husband. Roger had made sure that the cottage on the promontory had been repaired and so, not long after Alain's departure, Constance moved back and her morning swims off the private beach once again attracted hidden onlookers. Roger kept away from her and she did not feel welcome at the Vanilla Beach. Dinesh, on the other hand, had not been shy. Finally, he had found that his advances were welcomed, as were the band leader's. It appeared that Constance was as active as ever, but, notwithstanding this, there was no real love left in her life and, in the case of the two suitors from the hotel, their interest was more in the chase than the capture.

In order to conclude his buying the South African government out of the hotel, Roger would need signatures from Constance, who, at the very beginning, he had set up as a co-owner of his share of the property. Should he decide to move forward with the purchase of their shares and the financing of a new wing to the hotel, he would need a sign-off from Constance. This, again, was something that gave Roger cause to prevaricate.

As he sat alone in his suite, nursing a full glass of Talisker, with the ice clinking on the cut glass, his musings were interrupted by the phone. "It's Monty here, from the Sloane," a buoyant voice proclaimed. "Jill and I are coming to see you in your island paradise. We'd like to take you up on your offer. We'd really like to come in ten days' time. Any use to you? Will you be there?"

"Of course, Monty. That would be great. It will be fantastic to see you. Give me the dates and so on and I will meet you at the airport."

"You don't have to do that, mate," protested Monty. "I'm a big boy."

"Never mind that. I want to make sure they let you in!!"

Monty laughed, as only Monty could. "Okay, I'll send you the details and see you soon. And I can't wait to see that gorgeous wife of yours!"

"That's great, my friend. It will be smashing to see you – and don't bring your traveller's cheques; this one's on me."

The call from his old friend jolted Roger out of his depressed mood. The chance to renew his friendship with Monty would be great. Clearly Monty knew nothing about his split from

Constance; he would tackle that subject after Monty had arrived, although the fact he was bringing his wife, Jill, might just complicate things.

Now there were two pretexts to see Constance. First, he needed to explain to her his plan to buy out the SA government and expand the hotel, and second, to alert her to the fact that Monty and Jill were arriving the following week.

Roger decided to walk to the cottage. After all, it was only the length of the sandy beach in front of the hotel bedrooms and then less than four hundred yards down a footpath along the promontory. If he went by car, he had to go inland for half a mile to get there. When he reached the cottage, Constance was sitting on the porch, reading a book. She was wearing blue shorts and a tank top. Her tanned legs were curled up under her body. She looked stunning. As a woman in her early thirties, she was physically in the prime of her life. "How," thought Roger, "have I managed to lose such a beautiful woman? What did I do wrong?"

Constance neither heard nor saw Roger until he was almost at the veranda. "Oh," she said in surprise, when she finally heard his steps, "you should have warned me you were coming. I would have put some make-up on."

The image of the last time Roger had disturbed her, in bed with Alain, flashed across his brain. He tried to erase it.

Constance was still talking. "It's nice to see you, Roger; it's been a long time. What can I do for you? Can I get you a cup of tea, or a beer?"

Roger declined. "May I?" he enquired, as he pulled up a wooden chair on the deck. "I have some things I need to discuss with you."

Constance beckoned for him to sit down. She assumed he wanted to talk about divorce. But no, Roger began to pour out his thoughts about the business: his plans for expansion, his plans for refinancing and his need for Constance to sign off. Constance listened intently, only interrupting him from time to time for clarification. Finally, when through with the proposals, he took a deep breath and said, "I've missed you." Tears welled up in his eyes.

Constance unwound herself from the pile of cushions she was perched on and slowly moved towards him. She was not wearing a bra; her breasts swayed slightly as she walked. Through his wet eyes Roger noticed. Oh, how he had missed her! She wrapped her arms around his seated body and hugged him. "I've missed you too, my love. I'm so sorry. And I'm so proud of how successful you've been. I didn't deserve you."

They stayed hugging for almost a minute. Roger raised himself off the little chair and held her tightly to his chest. They did not speak.

Images of Constance with Alain flashed through Roger's brain, as did the humiliation of seeing the film on the Champs Elysées. "What am I doing?" he suddenly asked himself. He wanted to push her away, but he couldn't. He felt comforted pressed against her body. He felt he was where he belonged.

Finally, Constance spoke, "Why don't you move back to the cottage? You look all-in. The bachelor life obviously doesn't suit."

She was right. Roger did not like living alone. But, how could he just wipe out her behaviour? Wouldn't it always be there to haunt their relationship? He needed time to think. He didn't answer. Instead, he changed the subject. "Monty and Jill are coming to stay next week. They don't know we are split up. Maybe we should try not to be whilst they're here? Maybe I should move back for the week. Then we can see..."

Constance did not take this as a ringing endorsement that they could rekindle their relationship, but she did not push the issue. She had to accept she had been the wayward wife, but Roger would also have to accept that life with him could be dull. "Yes," she thought to herself, "that's the word – dull. The hotel is his life – not mine!"

Later that afternoon, Roger loaded up a few items into his car and took them round to the cottage. This time, Constance was fully made up and looking absolutely gorgeous. He wanted to stay there but was required at the hotel. He asked her to meet him later in the restaurant for dinner. She smiled and agreed.

By the time Monty and Jill arrived the next week, to all appearances, Roger and Constance were as happily married as they had ever been. Roger did his best to let his team run the hotel, whilst he and Constance relaxed with their old friends. One evening, after a lovely dinner fuelled by at least three bottles of wine, the two men found themselves alone on the bar chairs alongside the pool. The ladies had taken themselves off to the casino, where Constance, although not allowed under the house rules as a relative of a staff member, was gaming heavily. For the first time since Monty arrived, the subject of the death of Mersky in London came up in their conversation.

"You know, after all this time," started Monty, "the police have not closed the case. You really do have to wonder why. After all, the man did drop dead on a tennis court, not over a bowl of soup in our restaurant."

"Yes, it's strange, isn't it? Do you think that one of our four ever said anything?"

"I have no idea, but there has to be a reason why the cops are still asking questions."

"They've never been in contact with me," said Roger, "how about you?"

"Yes, they did interview me, but, apart from saying he deserved to die, I told them nothing. After all, I haven't the first clue how he died. I didn't draw a killer card."

"Monty, I shall pretend I did not hear that. You know we agreed we'd never tell anyone which card we drew."

"Well, sod that. What does it matter now?" said Monty. "Anyway, it was just a slip of the tongue. Too much vino."

Roger thought for a moment. "Since you've told me about your card, I might as well tell you I also didn't draw a killer card."

"Wow," exclaimed Monty. "That means, if he was murdered, it had to have been Christian or Bruno. Who'd have thought?"

"But he wasn't murdered, Monty," said Roger. "He had a heart attack."

There was silence whilst both men took in what they had just learned.

"We'd better go and find the girls, before they break the bank," said Roger, snapping the silence.

That night, back at the cottage, as Roger reflected on the conversation at the bar, he smiled to himself, imagining how Christian and Bruno must have felt when they had drawn the killer cards. He knew how relieved he had felt when he had not.

The subject was not raised again during the rest of Monty's stay. Roger and Constance continued to play host and hostess to the couple from London as if there had been no interruption in their marriage. It was fun to be with old friends and, as far as Roger was concerned, having Jill and Monty in the house was almost part of a healing process in his relationship with Constance. Maybe, he thought, there was a chance they could put the misadventures of the past behind them. On the island there were new beginnings. Maybe there was also a chance of a fresh start in the marriage.

The newly elected President of the Comores was an impressive and handsome man. Well educated and well travelled, he had a clear idea of what he could do for his people. The poverty which enveloped most of the population, and the inbred backward-thinking religious zealots that they looked up to, made the challenge of governing exceptionally difficult and, sometimes, even dangerous. AAM knew he had to energise the economy by harnessing the natural blessings of the islands. Vanilla was available in abundance, but was mainly wasted. Sugar could grow like a weed, and there were multiple mineral extraction opportunities. The Vanilla Beach had proven that tourism could also be a major source of income, but their tourism infrastructure needed updating. Major investment would be required from abroad, but, first, Comorians would need to show they knew how to work. The government would also need to wipe out the culture of corruption, starting, of course, within its own ranks. This would not be easy.

AAM was a hard worker, but he played hard too. The example he set with his own luxurious lifestyle was meat and gravy to his opponents, who championed simple living and frugality. Pre-election, AAM lived in probably the finest house in the Comores with his two wives and five children. He had cleared many acres of jungle and created a modern sugar plantation and several horse paddocks. He loved to ride and was an expert horseman. On a few occasions he had ridden a large stallion right into the lobby of the Vanilla Beach, much to the astonishment of the guests. His steed would clatter down the tiled floor of the lobby towards the bar. He would dismount with a flourish, and tether his mount to a pillar at the restaurant door, from which the horse could reach, with a stretch, the landscaped garden for a snack. AAM, with the clattering of spurs, would approach the bar, order a large brandy, and call for the manager. The whole place knew when AAM had arrived.

Roger was not brave enough to ask the President to leave his horse outside, instead, preferring to use the opportunity to discuss economics and tourism. Sometimes, Constance would be with Roger. It was obvious to Roger that AAM was interested in his wife. It made him uncomfortable. The question was, what did Constance think about it? Was she playing up to him because he was the President, or was she actually flirting? Luckily, these instances of horseback invasion were few and far between. AAM had too much to do; he could not spend every day at a beach resort.

His political opponent, LOU, had not been idle either, and was gathering swathes of support from the ultra-poor, the lazy, and religious fanatics. He had to be neutralised. The military had been monitoring, as best they could, the activities of LOU and his men through a network of implanted spies. They had been made aware of hidden portable bomb-making stations in the jungle and rumour had it that the bomb which had recently obliterated the US embassy in Nairobi had actually been manufactured at LOU's bomb "factory". If true, such a finding could be hugely negative in terms of the Comores' relationship with the Western world, from which AAM was seeking financial investment support. AAM had decided to invite the CIA to help him establish the extent of the bomb "factory" facilities and their history. Unfortunately, this decision had backfired badly. The CIA were able to prove, at least to the satisfaction of the US government, that the Comores had been the source of the bomb which did so much damage to American lives and property. Once this news had become "public", albeit in a very limited form, various national security organisations around the world were notified, one being the United Arab Emirates.

When Roger received the call from the managing director of Emirates Airlines to say they had no option but to cancel their flights to Moroni, he was devastated. Without this lifeline of the weekly flights from Dubai (and by extension, Europe) and South Africa, the Vanilla Beach's blood supply would be cut off. This was a partnership that had, for several years now, been highly profitable for both parties, the resort and the airline. It would be a disaster for Vanilla Beach if this lifeline were to be severed. The news of this impending catastrophe hit Roger like an ice-cold shower. The discussion with Emirates on the phone got Roger nowhere. He had effectively been notified that all flights to Moroni on Emirates would be cancelled from two weeks henceforth. Panicked, Roger decided to board the next plane to Dubai. He needed to get to the chairman of Emirates, the MD's boss, to plead his case.

Both the Sheikh and the managing director showed the utmost courtesy to Roger upon his arrival in Dubai, but they were stubbornly resistant in their view. "Look," reasoned the Sheikh over a cup of sweet tea in his surprisingly spartan office at Dubai airport, "once we have been advised by a reliable and recognised intelligence agency that bomb-making terrorists are operating near one of our user airports, we have no option but to discontinue flights. Can you imagine the uproar that would occur should we ignore this warning, and an incident resulting in harm or death were to take place? It could wipe out our airline. We have no choice. We have had a wonderful and productive partnership with you, but it is small in the overall picture of our business. We have much enjoyed working with you, but, as I have said, we have no choice now but to stop." He smiled a sympathetic smile, which was the royal signal that the interview was over.

Roger offered to pay for extra security at the airport. He offered to build a ten-foot-high fence around the whole airport facility. But it was all to no avail. The ownership and management of Emirates were adamant. They would not take the risk of flying to Moroni, however small that might be. End of story. Roger desperately tried to negotiate a charter deal but he was wasting his time. There was little point in him flying back to Moroni. He had to find an alternative means of getting his guests to the island. In the meantime, a cloud of gloom descended on Roger.

Sitting in a hotel room in Dubai, he racked his brain for a solution. Could he lease a plane? Could he buy a plane? Could he find someone who already owned a plane who would have an interest in flying to Moroni? There had to be a solution. And there was. Roger had been dealing with travel wholesalers in Europe, who had been booking the seats on Emirates, for several years. There were, however, a whole slew of other integrated travel firms which not only sold vacations but also owned aircraft. They tended to be more at the low-cost end of the vacation business, but they did move millions of passengers a year. Maybe one or more of these travel companies would be interested in supplying airlift to the Vanilla Beach? That might take care of traffic from the north. He would have to find another solution for the South African business.

It took Roger another two weeks in Europe to secure a deal. It was not ideal, but, at least, could keep the resort afloat for another year. Eurotours, a huge integrated travel company based in Frankfurt, owned a fleet of customised jets and a network of travel agencies spread across Europe. They were the ideal company to provide passengers but they drove a hard bargain. The price they were willing to pay per hotel guest was one-third less than the average rate the Vanilla Beach was already realising, and the mark up that Eurotours added to this rate was never less than fifty percent. Roger, very reluctantly, signed a deal for a year, with the promise of a renewed higher room rate in a year's time. At least this would help Roger keep afloat and give him time to figure out a more profitable arrangement. And Eurotours was willing to start sending passengers immediately, so there would be no empty period when Emirates stopped flying.

Relieved, but unhappy, Roger flew back to Dubai to catch the last weekly Emirates flight home. He was not pleased, when he got back to the hotel, to learn, amongst other things, that the man with the horse had made several visits to the property. "Why doesn't he get on with finding the bomb-makers, instead of poncing around on a horse?" he asked himself as the jet lag and general problem-solving weariness kicked in. On the bright side, Constance welcomed him home with open arms; she seemed genuinely happy to see him.

Chapter Twelve
"Death and Salvation"

For almost six years now Chef Sparrowhawk had consistently delivered high standards of cuisine. From time to time Roger worried that the sheer drudgery of turning out interesting and high-quality fare, week after week, to the ever-changing group of residents would become so boring that Sparrowhawk's attention to detail and high standards would slip. Sparrowhawk had done an excellent job in training local cooks to prepare food that was completely alien to their local custom. They, in turn, had introduced a local flavour to the chef's menus which he had enhanced and the result was both interesting to the guests but familiar enough that they would be prepared to sample and, then, enjoy. Roger was constantly amazed that the standard of food emanating from Sparrowhawk's kitchen remained so high. He was also grateful. Although the chef and the manager were never friends, they had a healthy respect for each other and a very solid relationship. If Roger needed to see Sparrowhawk, he would never, ever, ask him to come to the manager's office. He would always do him the courtesy of asking if he could come to the kitchen. Also, Roger would make a point, at least once per week, of stepping into the kitchen, after the evening service, and enjoying a glass of brandy with the chef when they would chew the fat for at least an hour and sometimes into the early hours of the morning. But, during all these weekly rendezvous, Roger never really got to know the man. Chef Sparrowhawk's private life was a closed book.

Here was a man who Roger perceived as having no friends, no particular interests, and no history. His whole life seemed to orientate around the kitchen at the Vanilla Beach. Roger often used to worry that one day his chef would simply say he had had enough; that he was bored or lonely or whatever, but that never happened. Frightened that Sparrowhawk would burn out or just go island-crazy, Roger would encourage him to take annual leave. This was often a struggle, but when Roger forced the issue, the chef always went to the same place: the Easter Islands. To Roger and Constance this was unfathomable. If you lived and worked on a remote island such as the Comores, why would you take your annual leave at another remote island on the other side of the world? It made no sense. In fact, it seemed incredibly sad.

Sparrowhawk lived in one of the staff bungalows. He had made almost no attempt to personalise the place, even after six years of residence. The walls were as bare as when he first moved in. He appeared to have no friends, certainly no lady friends and not even any little boy friends. The only books he had were cookery books. There was no memorabilia at all. He did not appear to follow any religion. He never seemed to receive any mail. Whenever, during their brandied chats, Roger tried to probe about anything personal, the shutters came down. Not that he did not have opinions about what was going on in the world, either in politics or sport. He did, during their late-night chats, but none of these were ever, it seemed, translated into any possessions. To Roger, Sparrowhawk was an enigma. But he was a great chef and a good teacher – even, in a weird way, a good team member.

Roger liked to be able to read the mood of his key employees. He was always looking for clues or hints about their stability, at least in terms of their commitment to their jobs. On an island, you needed to be ahead of the game, should anyone be planning to jump ship. Chef Sparrowhawk gave no clues.

Until it was too late. One morning Sparrowhawk did not show up to work. His well-trained sous chefs were not too alarmed. They proceeded with the preparation of the lunch as they had many times before. But, when lunchtime arrived and the chef had still not appeared, something that had never happened before, the first sous chef alerted Dinesh that he was missing. Dinesh sent his assistant to Sparrowhawk's bungalow to investigate. What he found was horrifying. Sparrowhawk's limp body was hanging from a rope fixed to the light-fitting in the living room, a chair kicked aside on its back against the wall. He was dead. This loneliest of men had taken the ultimate lonely step. Chef Sparrowhawk had not left the Vanilla Beach team as Roger feared he might one day; he had left the world. The limp and lifeless body hanging from the ceiling seemed to sum up his sad and lonely life.

When Dinesh reported his man's horrific findings to Roger, who, at the time was in his office, he could hardly get the words out of his mouth. Dinesh had worked with Sparrowhawk for six years. In all that time they had never had an argument. Although they were not close, they were colleagues who had worked in harmony. The potential for conflict could never be higher than between a head chef and a head waiter, but this had never occurred during all the stressful service times. Dinesh had no idea the chef was so emotionally unstable; he seemed to be the most stable man he had ever met.

Roger was horrified. He rushed to the scene with Dinesh. He could not control his tears. Somehow, he felt he had failed the man. He was the only person on the island, as far as he knew, that had any sort of personal relationship with him and here he was – dead, still hanging from the ceiling, his head tipping gruesomely to one side. It was just not possible; and yet it was. There, before his eyes, was the chef, dangling from the ceiling.

"Fuck," said Roger, quite quietly to himself, "this fucking place is spooked."

For weeks Roger was downcast. He blamed himself for the tragedy. Constance did her best to comfort her husband, constantly assuring him that what had happened was not his fault, but the healing process for Roger took many weeks. Roger and Constance discussed the funeral. As far as they knew the chef had no living relations. There was no one to tell. In the end they decided the Vanilla Beach was actually the chef's home and the supervisors and staff his family, so a simple funeral service was arranged to take place on the beach with a burial thereafter near the little vegetable garden Sparrowhawk had nurtured with love. Apart from a skeleton staff of volunteers, almost everyone who worked at the hotel came to pay their last respects. Of all the mourners, Roger was probably the saddest.

For some time, Roger could not bring himself to contemplate replacing the chef, but, little by little, he realised that the locally trained young men in the kitchen could not cope. Roger would have to set to and find a replacement. Once again, he found himself briefing the employment agency and a few weeks later Roger was back in Paris. There was no way he was going to hire a chef for his hotel without first meeting him. The cooking was important, but so was the calibre of the man. Island life was not for sissies. Roger would need to find a man who could not only cook, but also cope. This had to be done personally.

In Paris, there were posters all over the place, advertising Brigitte's latest movie. Her pouting lips and come-hither eyes were everywhere, reminding Roger of what he had missed. "It would be nice to catch up with Brigitte," he began to think.

"Maybe I should give her a call?" The thought nagged away at him for a couple of days. Whilst interviewing prospective chefs, Roger found his thoughts continuously straying to Brigitte. She was like a magnet, pulling him closer and closer, and her face was everywhere. Only a sharp tug in the other direction could save him. Sitting alone in his hotel room after a full day of interviews he suddenly decided. "Hell, I'm going to call her. After all, no harm in making a phone call." Deep in his heart, he knew there probably was.

Brigitte sounded really pleased to hear from Roger. It did not take one simple phone call to get to her. Various studio personnel seemed to have taken over her life. It appeared that she had many "old friends" who pestered her and Roger had to work his way through a barricade of assistants before word reached her that this was the real Roger calling. "You're just the man I need," said Brigitte, after some preliminary small talk. "I need to get away. I need to get to a place I can have some peace and quiet for a while. I'm really exhausted. The studio – they keep me going like a dog. I must have a break, somewhere where no one will find me. No press. No pictures. Can I come to Vanilla?"

Roger's heart almost stopped. He could not believe his good fortune. The hottest French film star was asking if she could come to his hotel, to his home. This was a dream come true.

"Of course, you can come," Roger replied, trying to not show the excitement in his voice. "You can have the suite I used to stay in. It's really private. Or Constance and I can move out of the cottage for a while into the hotel, and you can use our little home. It has a private beach."

At the mention of Constance, Roger caught a slight hesitation before the film star replied, "Oh, Constance. How is she?"

Roger was not sure now whether he should have offered his home to Brigitte without first asking his wife. Surely

Constance would realise the publicity from a trip to Vanilla Beach by a famous film star would be worth its weight in gold. Or would she?

"Constance is fine," he finally replied, "but no babies yet."

After a few minutes more of small talk, Brigitte had to go, but not before giving her assistant's details to Roger, with instructions to liaise with her regarding the trip to the Comores. Brigitte seemed certain that she would come. Roger immediately called Constance to alert her. There must be no misunderstandings. This was strictly in the interests of the hotel. Having a famous film star choose the Vanilla Beach for a quiet vacation could only be good for the hotel. Constance would certainly recognise that.

Constance did. Roger was nervous to mention his suggestion that Brigitte should take over his and Constance's home, but Constance's sixth sense was functioning well when she heard the news of Brigitte's potential visit. "Why don't we let her use the cottage?" she said. "She wouldn't get pestered by anyone there."

Roger was floored. There was no need to be the person responsible for this decision. "That's a great idea," he said. "Are you sure you'd want her to do that?"

Of course, Constance hated the idea. She was deeply suspicious of the fact that Roger had actually contacted Brigitte. She had waited for Roger to object, but no, he did not. In Constance's mind, she would have to be on high alert.

The next couple of months were frustrating for Roger. He really wanted to proceed with the outright purchase of the hotel and the plan to add rooms, but had decided to play for time in this regard until he could see the effect of the new deal with Eurotours. Despite delivering a steady flow of hotel guests from Europe, the room rate he was getting was considerably lower than what he had been able to secure from the

Emirates flights. The calibre of the clients had also fallen drastically with the result that their daily spend in the hotel was much lower than before. In addition to this, the new travel company did not fly on to South Africa and back, so the entire South African market had been cut off from Moroni. The net result was that the hotel was now barely profitable. Then came the heaviest blow. Eurotours, now aware that they were the sole lifeline to the Comores from Europe, advised Roger that from the end of the year they would be reducing the price they would pay per room by thirty percent. They did not intend, he discovered, to reduce their asking price in their brochure to the public; they had just determined that they would take a bigger cut. They had him, in Roger's view, "by the balls". Before committing himself to the acquisition of the shares and new construction, Roger knew that he had to get back to the days of a better clientele. His problem was that he did not know how to do this and nor did Constance.

His salvation came from a very strange place. Barely a few weeks after Roger's recruiting trip to France the call came from Brigitte; this time not through an army of studio personnel but directly from the film star herself, using a cell phone whose number Roger did not recognise. He did, however, instantly recognise the voice of his ex-housekeeper turned superstar. His heart leaped. "Roger," she began, purring now, like the actress not the housekeeper, "I want to take up your offer. I'm coming to see you. I need a total rest. I'm coming on my own. Nobody here knows. I'm coming on a private plane. Can you make all the arrangements for the landing and a room – or, if you can, like you say, the cottage?" One long sentence and a question that was music to Roger's ears. "But, Roger," she continued, "no publicity, no photos – this is just a visit, a very private visit."

"Of course," replied the manager, "of course, my dear, no one outside of the Comores will know you are here."

A date was set for the following week. Roger promised to make arrangements for the jet to land and, once again, confirmed that the cottage could be Brigitte's for as long as she needed. Roger was tingling with excitement. But he was also worried. Since the Eurotours deal, the standards of the hotel had dropped considerably, as had the nature of its clientele. Also, the absence of Jimmy Sparrowhawk had badly affected the quality of the product. Roger was frightened that Brigitte would be disappointed and not want to stay. After all, she was used to the fancy hotels and restaurants of Paris. "What a blessing," he thought to himself, "that I suggested the cottage."

When a smiling Brigitte stepped off the Bombardier jet ten days after the call, she looked as beautiful as ever, but tired. More tired than a journey in a comfortable private plan could cause; tired, it would seem, from the constant pressures and demands of the studio. Even so, Roger's heart skipped a beat as he hugged her at the bottom of the aeroplane steps. Constance was not there.

As Roger drove his Landcruiser through the untidy, litter-strewn outskirts of Moroni, past the ugly radio station, then into the bush, Brigitte could feel herself relaxing. The fresh air and the scent of vanilla now reached her. It was good to be out of the noise and dirt of Paris. It was good not to be followed by screeching motorcades of paparazzi. It was just plain good to be back. As the Vanilla Beach came into view, Brigitte asked Roger to stop the car. The two of them stood in silence for fully three minutes just taking in the view and the nature, something that Roger rarely did. Finally, Roger put his arm around her and escorted her back to the car. The touch of her body was thrilling.

Roger drove straight to the cottage, which Constance had made a real effort to dolly up, making it more of a guest suite than an untidy domestic residence. For the sake of peace, and her own intense curiosity, Constance was there to greet their film star guest. Small courtesies were exchanged, even an unconvincing hug of welcome, and then both Constance and Roger took their leave. Roger had provided Brigitte with the services of a cook and a housekeeper who he had arranged to be on call with the press of a button. Otherwise, Brigitte, they said, would be left alone. She was, of course, welcome at any time to use the guest facilities at the resort, but if it was privacy that she wanted, then she should have it. When all was clear, Brigitte took off her clothes and walked gingerly into the clear blue sea. It was heaven. It was another gift from Allah to the hidden crowd in the jungle.

After a full two days of isolation, Brigitte was keen to rejoin the world. She called Roger to ask him if he could escort her on a tour of the hotel. Of course Roger would be willing to do that, but he was somewhat nervous that his famous guest would notice the lowering of the standard of the rest of the clientele and, even the commensurate reduction in the standards of service on offer. It was agreed that Brigitte would walk to the boathouse from the cottage, where Roger would meet her. From there they could walk the length of the beach and even venture into the rooms, should Brigitte be interested to inspect her old territory. Brigitte was keen to meet her successor, Julie. She thought it would be fun. She was not wrong. Julie was always fun and not the least bit intimidated by Brigitte, either as her predecessor or a film star. "Maybe I can become a film star too, after training in this job. If you hear of any parts for a middle-aged plump mother going, please let me know," she quipped almost as soon as they had met. Just as everybody else did, Brigitte immediately liked Julie.

It was not long, however, before Brigitte noticed a slippage of standards. Over lunch, Roger explained. "The drop-off in standards is almost entirely due to the low room rate that we are able to achieve, and that's due to the gouging of the tour operator who owns the aircraft." Brigitte was interested, so Roger went on to explain the whole story, about the bomb-making and the refusal of Emirates or any other airline to offer scheduled services. "If you can't get the airlift, you can't get the people," bemoaned Roger. "It's a pity, because we had proven that Vanilla Beach can be a paradise for a wealthy clientele."

"I think the French have some culpability here," said Brigitte finally, after some thought and a good cup of coffee. "After all, the French think they own the place; they should be made to look after..." She suddenly stopped in mid-sentence. Dinesh, who had been keeping out of the way under Roger's instructions, had appeared. Dinesh, looking handsome as ever, was walking towards their table, hand outstretched for a greeting. He got one, but not what he was expecting. "Had any good screws this morning?" came in crude French from the mouth of the film star. "I don't want to talk to you. You can fuck off!"

Dinesh looked stunned. Roger was embarrassed. Brigitte had certainly hardened up during her brief stay at the top. A somewhat flustered Roger indicated with his eyes that Dinesh should retreat – and he did.

"Sorry about that, Roger," said Brigitte, her voice now returned to its previous lovely tone. "He needs to know where he stands." Dinesh's bad treatment of Brigitte had clearly hurt.

The day after the lunch, and the little tour of the hotel, Brigitte, once again, contacted Roger. She had a plan, she told him, about how to revive quality airlift to Moroni. It turned out that one of her many admirers in Paris was none other than the State President. In fact, he had famously been spotted one night by the paparazzi visiting Brigitte's accommodation on his pop-pop motorbike, although they had both denied any sexual relationship. Brigitte felt strongly that France had a duty to the Comores, with whom it happily interfered with when it suited, to provide air service, especially, as Roger had proven, since it could be done profitably. It would be her mission, she advised Roger, to see to it that Air France resumed a quality flight service from Paris to Moroni, once per week, with onward service to Johannesburg. After all, that only required one of the existing scheduled flights to South Africa to make a detour. Brigitte told Roger she had no doubt that the President of her country would move heaven and earth to accomplish this small favour.

To Roger's amazement, it only took ten days from the time of Brigitte's call to the State President until he received a call from the operations manager of Air France, with the good news that his company would be initiating a regular flight from Paris to Johannesburg via Moroni twice per week. Roger was overjoyed. Then, as a bonus, Brigitte announced to Roger that she intended to throw a party at the Vanilla Beach for all her new-found friends in the movie business. Remarkably, after a short period of isolation in the cottage, Brigitte was already missing the hurly burly life she now lived in Paris. The party could coincide with the rescheduling of Air France and could be a promotion for the airline as well as the hotel. "Tell your Eurotours people they can get stuffed! After my party, everyone in France will know where the Comores is and how to get there."

Luckily for Brigitte, this conversation took place on the phone between the cottage and his office at the hotel. If it had not, Brigitte would have been crushed by his hug of joy, relief, and gratefulness. Roger felt as if the clouds had parted. What was beginning to be a drudge would now turn out to be something worth doing, something worth all the effort. "Thank God for Brigitte," said Roger out loud, then added in his head, "she really cares about this place. Did she really care about me too?"

Constance, in the adjacent office at the time, overheard most of the conversation with Brigitte. She did not like the little hussy, but had to admit her alliance with the business might turn out to be really useful. She was still not convinced her husband was not enraptured by the housekeeper-turned-superstar, although he had certainly played by the rules during her stay. Nevertheless, when she and Roger had sex, she had the strong intuition that his mind was on the glamorous film star, not her. Constance would have loved to have known just why. After all, her body was just as beautiful as Brigitte's: a fact she could justify, having both been naked in the same movie. In fact, if anything, Constance was more fully endowed than the little French bitch. But Brigitte was now the superstar, and Constance the hotel manager's wife. That, to Constance, said it all. Despite these feelings it was in Constance's best interest to keep them tightly buttoned up. For whatever reasons, Brigitte was about to lend a helping hand. If her husband's infatuation with the French girl was good for business, then who was Constance to get in the way? Maybe it was time for Constance to use her charms to advance her own agenda.

Chapter Thirteen
"The Renaissance"

State President Ahmed's horseback visits to Vanilla Beach seemed to have stopped, but his interest in the wife of the hotelkeeper had not. In his private collection of dubious films, Ahmed had a copy of the film that had kickstarted Brigitte's movie career and had featured Constance: the very film that had surprised and shocked Roger on the Champs Elysées. He looked at the film quite often and the more he did the more he thought about the idea of making love to this gorgeous woman. It mattered not a whit to Ahmed that she was married to the man who produced more foreign revenue for his country than any other resident. His last horseback arrival at the hotel had, it seemed, coincided with Roger's recruiting trip for a chef in France. Constance had been temporarily in charge of the hotel. Naturally, on hearing the clatter of hoofs on tiles from her office, she had gone to the lobby to greet her illustrious guest. After all, he was the President of the country and, quite rightly, she needed, as the hotel manager at the time, to do him the courtesy of a personal greeting. She also thought he was a hunk. Sitting in a quiet corner of the bar terrace with a pot of lemongrass tea, Ahmed had quite openly enthused about her beauty, and, dressed in her trim white linen (resort manager) suit, she did truly look fantastic. He had made no bones about the fact he desired her and, with infinite charm, assured her that he was used to getting what he desired. He had suggested they meet at the cottage but, despite her body urging her otherwise, she had declined. Ahmed, dressed in leather pants and a rough but expensive denim jacket was truly a fine specimen of a man. Constance envied his two wives. The image of the three of them having sex together flashed across her mind. But she still said "no." This was the last time Ahmed and his horse appeared at the hotel.

Since that meeting, Constance had thought often of Ahmed. She had been puzzled and disappointed that his interest in her had dissipated. She knew that she had not given into his advances, but, at the time, she had really been trying to make things work with Roger. Roger had been away at the time and she was in charge of the hotel. Much as her body desired otherwise, she really was making an effort to behave as the good wife. Now, however, with Brigitte back on the scene, things seemed different. She realised that Brigitte's notoriety might indeed be the saviour of the Vanilla Beach, but she could also see that her husband was besotted. He did his best, of course, to disguise this, and she had no way of knowing whether the feeling was reciprocated by Brigitte, but the idea that her husband was so much in the French film star's thrall, really, and quite naturally, rankled with Constance. On top of that, as much as Constance loved her husband, she still found him totally boring. His life was the Vanilla Beach. She was just part of the furniture. But, actually, she knew that she could have been Brigitte; she had seen the film.

Because Ahmed had not appeared again at the hotel, Constance decided to go to him. On a flimsy excuse of giving aid to the local hospital, Constance obtained an official appointment at the Palace of government, the same place where she had first met the now-deposed gay President with Dusty and Roger. Constance wondered how she would be received. After all, she had turned down the advances of the most powerful man in the country. Ahmed, however, was more than happy to receive her. Further meetings had followed. Unlike many of his conquests, who were brushed aside or discarded after the first sexual encounters, Ahmed's fascination and interest in Constance did not subside. The early signs of this liaison seemed to indicate that more than physical attraction was bringing them together. Constance now found herself making all sorts of excuses to "go into town". Roger did not seem to really notice, such was his intensity in trying to get the Vanilla Beach back on its feet. This entailed many meetings with his star guest, Brigitte, who, from the privacy of the cottage, was busy rounding up all of her film star contacts to travel on the inaugural Air France flight in a few weeks' time. Despite pressure from the studio chiefs in Paris, Brigitte refused to return to work. She had made up her mind that first she would throw the biggest party anyone had ever attended on a tropical island.

On Brigitte's advice, Roger set up a "feet in the sand" night club on the second beach, just like those she frequented at Juan les Pins. Brigitte also required a stage and VIP dining area to be built. She had managed to persuade no less than three of the most established and popular French singers to appear together at the party. They were all far too "important" to share a stage with others, but Brigitte had worked her magic and got them to agree to put on a show – and all for nothing other than a few free days of beachfront wining and dining. Roger, for his part, had contracted the most experienced firework firm from the UK to design a display that would be talked about throughout the world. What they suggested was a programme that appeared to burn down the hotel to the sound of Ravel's *Bolero*. Roger, with his new chef, also set about designing a three-day gastronomic journey that would equal anything his worldly guests could get in Paris or New York.

Brigitte and Roger worked as a team. For a couple of weeks, they were constantly together, talking together, planning together, brainstorming together and, from time to time, touching. Roger so wanted to hold Brigitte. He was obsessed with her charm, her effervescence and her delicate beauty. Of course, she knew it, and so did Constance. However, to her credit, Brigitte kept her distance – just!

When the Air France jet carrying the first passengers on the route arrived, they were met at the little airport with a charming local choir in colourful island costumes and Jean Pierre's hotel band, supported by scores of local musicians who had been primed by the bandleader. Everyone had a smile on their faces. It was a happy welcome and the weary passengers were entranced.

The special gastronomic and water sports activities entertained Brigitte's famous guests in a light-touch fashion that made them feel they were on vacation, but the tempo finally built as they reached the climax of the visit, the gala evening and show. The night club on the sand was a big hit and the casino tables and slots were humming. Peaches revelled in the company of her famous guests and much money flowed over the tables for two great nights. The casino "win" broke all records.

Much to Constance's increasing annoyance, it was Brigitte who acted as hostess, not herself, the manager's wife – and it was Roger who was constantly at the film star's side. For the first couple of days Constance kept a very low profile. Despite her loathing of Brigitte, she knew how important this public relations event was to the financial health of the Vanilla Beach and, after all, she did own a large slice of it. But by day four, Constance had had enough of playing second fiddle to the ex-housekeeper and decided to attend the party in the tightest and sexiest outfit she possessed. She would show Brigitte's friends who was really the glamorous one.

Up until the gala evening, the participants in the events were the visitors on Brigitte's guest list, but for the gala evening, with the French singers and the fireworks, Roger had felt it prudent to invite the President of the country and a few other local VIPs. Despite the fact he had been having his way with Constance almost every week of Brigitte's stay, Ahmed had decided to show up at the party with his two wives in tow, both dressed up in wonderful local costumes, rich in colour and texture. In comparison, Constance looked like a tart, but she knew by now that Ahmed was partial to tarts. She also knew that some of Brigitte's adoring fan club might welcome a distraction. Maybe a few photos of the hotel manager's wife in *Paris Match* might help the hotel occupancy? Plus, she still liked to tease JP, the band leader.

All Brigitte and Roger's plans for the gala event went splendidly. The dinner was special and much wine was imbibed. The after-dinner show of a trio of the most famous French popular singers ever assembled was superb, each one vying to outperform the other, and the firework display drew gasps of astonishment and awe from the onlookers, who, by now, were truly well oiled. The star of the show, however, was Constance. She looked so stunning that most of the men could not keep their eyes off her as she moved freely from one group of admirers to the next. Ahmed, handicapped to a degree by his formal position, but also by the presence of his two wives, looked on with a mixture of lust and envy. He liked to control Constance and found seeing her flirt outrageously with so many others to be a new and unwanted experience. Roger, at first, was a little embarrassed, but in fact he didn't really care. What he cared about was the success of the party, and hence his hotel, and, unsurprisingly, the happiness of Brigitte. As the evening raced on and the after-firework-show dancing began, Roger realised that the party was a great success and, for the first time in the evening, he began to relax. He asked Brigitte to dance. She agreed. He held her tightly in his arms, his body pressed against hers. She did not move away. This time, nothing came between them.

Constance was not around to see the pair. Ahmed, having asked his drivers to take his wives home, had stayed on at the party. It did not take him long to locate Constance, now wrapping herself around one of the French singers in the casino. His look to her was almost a command. Through her alcohol-induced glaze, she saw him. She unwrapped herself from the entertainer and swayed into the arms of Ahmed. The two disappeared into the darkness of the hotel car park. It was clear to anyone watching that the marriage of the hotel manager and his wife was now well and truly over.

Brigitte slept with Roger that night. Neither was drunk or even close to it. They were, however, drunk on their own happiness. Roger could not believe that his dream of making love to the most famous film star in Europe had actually come true. This, finally, was not a dream.

Chapter Fourteen
"A Surprise Package"

The divorce was reasonably amicable. Both parties had an interest in getting it over with. Ahmed was pretty insistent that Constance leave the hotel; he was so enamoured with her that he wanted exclusive access whenever he so desired. Constance also wanted a quick break from Roger; life promised to be so much more exciting with Ahmed. About one thing, however, Constance was adamant; she would not be wife number three. Either Ahmed would have to divorce numbers one and two, or he would have to put up with Constance as his "kept woman", but with all the financial protections of a wife. Ahmed had no options, at least for the moment. It would be political dynamite for him to divorce the wives because they both came from eminent local families, whose support he needed as a politician. Apart from which, in his mind, he had never promised to be monogamous to Constance; that was just an assumption Constance had made.

Ahmed had explained to Constance that wife number three is really wife number one, but the huge leap to become part of a harem was just too much for Constance to take. As it happened Ahmed had installed the first two wives, with their offspring, in a rambling house within the grounds of the Palace buildings, whilst he lived almost permanently in the state apartment within the main building. It was into this apartment that Constance moved, and it was this apartment that she shared with Ahmed on a nightly basis or, at least, on the nights he was available.

As President of the country, Ahmed obviously had plenty to occupy his days. Staying on top was a full-time job. There were constant meetings and, from time to time, trips around the country, some of which caused him to be away overnight. Although Constance was entranced with her new lover, she found herself with little to do during many days and, especially, when Ahmed was travelling. The courtiers at the Palace and the visiting politicians regarded her as an ornament; they did not take her seriously and assumed that her tenure as number one lady would not last long. The other two wives treated her with a certain amount of disdain. Strangely, they did not seem to be jealous at all. To them, the fact their husband had a new mistress was not an issue. As far as they were concerned, they were secure. They also accepted each other and their relevant status. It was forbidden for them to take lovers. Should they do so they could risk their secure status, which would not be good politically for their families or their own economic welfare. As a result, the two women had become close. They were both in the same boat.

After a few weeks of daytime loneliness, Constance decided the best course of action would be to make friends with her "rivals". After all, she was now the Queen Bee. The best way to pre-empt any attack on her privileged position from within would be to know and understand her enemies. Through a member of staff, Constance sent word that she would like to visit the wives. Their reply was immediate; she would be most welcome. Venturing into the wives' quarters was an eye-opener for Constance. Up until then she had only seen the two women in traditional Arabesque clothing, which completely covered their bodies and eliminated any possibility of displaying their shape. To her surprise she was greeted by the elder wife, "number one", who was wearing a pretty silk sleeveless blouse and a very short skirt. She introduced herself, with a rather timid smile, as Fatima. She was probably no more than twenty-five years old. The second wife, Lula, could not have been more than eighteen. She was dressed in jeans and a tank top. She wore no shoes. Around them was evidence of children, but none could be seen or heard. Tea was offered and taken. Everyone was polite and gracious. Fatima made it clear that Constance was welcome to visit at any time. When Constance left, after about an hour of small talk, she was truly puzzled. These two young ladies had shown neither jealousy nor hard feelings towards her, the women who had stolen their children's' father and who had, presumably, interfered with their love life.

During her first month in the Palace with Ahmed, the two made love almost every night Ahmed was at home. His appetite for sex was insatiable. He had a large collection of semi-pornographic videos which he often insisted on watching with Constance before making love. He particularly seemed to like the erotic movie featuring Brigitte, the housekeeper, and, of course, Constance herself. At first, Constance found this unnerving, particularly "sharing" with Brigitte, but then decided to let the sexiness of it to get into her own head. In all her life with Roger she had never experienced such heights of eroticism – and she liked it.

Meanwhile, things had not gone so well for Roger. His first night with Brigitte was all that he had hoped for. It was everything that he had dreamed of so many times. But it was not to last. There could be no lounging in bed for Roger and Brigitte on the night after the party. Roger had a hotel to run and Brigitte, as the hostess, had multiple guests she had to mingle with before they set off back to Paris over the next two days. Brigitte was sweet, loving and charming to Roger, but, clearly, she was not going to become his partner. She was grateful for the safe haven Roger had offered her at a time of burnout, but now she yearned to get back to work in Paris. The visit of so many friends and associates in the film business had reignited her energy and the idea of settling down as a hotel manager's partner held no appeal whatsoever. To her, one loving night with Roger had been her way of saying "thank you" to a good friend. She did not want to lead him on. She loved him, but not to the extent that she wanted to spend her life with him. There were far more exciting and interesting men in Paris. Roger was devastated. He thought that he really loved Brigitte. What he loved was the thought of loving her. It seemed to Roger that he had lost a wife and a lover. He had nobody.

But he did have a hotel and a business to run. It was clear that Constance wanted no part of his life; somehow, he had failed to satisfy her as well. So the sooner he could take her out of the business the better, and he determined that this must be done as part of the divorce settlement. Constance also wanted out, so agreement was quickly reached. A value of Constance's share of the business was rapidly agreed, based upon a multiple of recent earnings. Constance did not seem to focus on the fact that, since business had been bad, the price she agreed to was a "steal" for Roger. Constance's mind, it seemed, was elsewhere and she sought no advice, either from her lover or a professional. Roger, with nothing to focus on except his business, quickly produced the paperwork required to buy out his wife and a local court sealed the sale and the divorce at the same time. The whole process took less than a month. Roger was now free, even if he was lonely. However, the grand opening party had produced huge positive interest in Vanilla Beach from France and South Africa, and the regular air service provided by Air France promised to enable the resort to re-establish itself as a premier vacation destination. So Roger's despondency was at least tempered with the prospect of good earnings.

Constance had resisted all requests by her new lover to marry. She would only do so, she said, if he divorced Fatima and Lula, which, of course, he could not do. On the other hand, she wanted him to provide the financial security blanket that she would have got as a wife. Whilst the two existed in the world of sexual utopia, this disagreement did not seem to intrude, but, nevertheless, it existed. Then, everything changed. After just over two months of living with Ahmed, Constance discovered she was pregnant. After all those years of trying for a baby with Roger, it had only taken two months with her new lover to become impregnated. It had been so long since Constance had even thought of having a baby that this news came as a complete surprise, even a shock. Now, Constance had not just herself to think about. Ahmed had already sired five children with number one and number two, so, to him, this news would not be too significant, but Constance suddenly realised she now needed the security being married to Ahmed would produce. She decided to change tack. After all, "being wife number three is, in fact, actually being wife number one," she rationalised. But a tiny voice in the back of her mind said, "until wife number four comes along."

Ahmed was thrilled with the news. And he was delighted that Constance would now marry him. He promised her that she would not be relegated to the wives' compound; that, with her, things would be different. She could stay with their baby in the Palace apartments, or with him on the family ranch, should he lose the Presidency. "You will always be my number one," he announced, "my very special wife." For Ahmed, to marry a white girl and for her to produce an heir was something to be really proud of. Ahmed could not keep the news to himself and, so, it was not long before it found its way to Roger who did not take the discovery of Constance's pregnancy well. To him, it was so depressing. For years he had been longing for her to have their child, and for years he had been disappointed. For Constance to fall pregnant so soon after their split was an insult to his manhood. He felt a complete failure. However, other matters were also troubling him. His acquisition of Constance's shares had put him in a position to proceed with buying out the South African shareholding, giving him a hundred percent ownership of the resort, but to do so he needed to borrow a substantial amount in addition, to enlarge the hotel. What caused him to pause was the constant news filtering through from the jungle that LOU, the opposition party leader, had been gaining political ground throughout the country. Like all previous leaders in the Comores, Ahmed's inability to curb the excesses of his personal lifestyle, in the face of widespread poverty amongst the general public, had led to a large element of dissatisfaction amongst the electorate. Ahmed had governed sensibly, compared to his autocratic predecessors, and avoided the pitfalls and temptations of corruption that engulfed other leaders. But, despite this, he had been unable to eliminate widespread poverty. It was this poverty that was the feeding ground of his rival LOU, and he had quietly been gathering followers in the race for potential votes. Although the next general election was scheduled in only two years' time, the possibility of a communist government was not attractive to the resort hotel owner. Furthermore, LOU proposed a policy of nationalising private enterprises in the country and his published plans for the "luxury" Vanilla Beach was to convert part of it into a hospital and the rest into housing units for workers. The prospect of LOU gaining political control in the Comores would be the end of Roger's potentially lucrative business. It appeared that Ahmed still had the support of the majority of voters, especially the women, who seemed to universally adore him, but there was no question that LOU was gaining ground. Maybe Roger's best possibility would be to "take out" rather than "put in". Maybe he should place on hold any thoughts of further acquisition or extension until he knew that LOU would be defeated once and for all.

A few months went by. Business at the resort was excellent. Brigitte resumed her celebrity life in Paris. Her new film, which was extremely risqué, was a smash hit in Europe and the heavily edited version was a big success in the USA. Brigitte had become a global star; more than that, she had become a global sex symbol. The pouting French actress's photograph was everywhere, a constant reminder to Roger of what he had had and what he was now missing. Nevertheless, Brigitte had proven to be a good friend to Vanilla Beach. Beneath it all, she had not forgotten her background and Roger appreciated it, even if she never rang him anymore.

Constance's term of pregnancy progressed. She was now officially wife number three, but, as her body changed shape with Ahmed's child, his interest in sex with her diminished and, to her chagrin, his trips around the countryside increased. When she discovered that wife number two, young Lula, was also pregnant, Constance was absolutely livid. For her new husband to have the odd fling with an admirer when he travelled on business was one thing, but to slip off into the courtyard of their home, to impregnate the young girl, right under her bedroom window, was a step too far. After an initial flaming row with her husband, she refused to talk to him for several days, but it was not long before his charm worked and she forgave him. Notwithstanding that, Constance absolutely hated being pregnant.

When the baby was born, apparently seven weeks early, everything changed. Everything. What emerged from Constance's womb was a little boy, not the swarthy little chap that one would expect as the offspring of an Arab, but a pale, blue-eyed little fellow with the beginnings of curly blond locks. This was not Ahmed's child. It could only be Roger's.

Constance did the maths. It was true that, up until the time of Brigitte's party at the hotel, she had still been sharing a bed with Roger; it was mathematically possible this was Roger's child after all those years of trying. It was highly unlikely that it was, but one only had to look at the little baby to know that this, indeed, was Roger's son. "Jesus," thought Constance, "what the fuck do I do now?"

Chapter Fifteen
"Damage Control"

When Ahmed first clapped eyes on the tiny baby, nestled into Constance's bosom, he immediately saw the problem. He wanted to scream with anger. He wanted to rant and rave and throw things around the room. His anger was at boiling point. He knew instantly that this was not his son. He had no idea whose it was. All he knew was that Constance, even at the very beginning of their relationship, must have been two-timing him. That was alright for a man, but not for a wife. It did not occur to him that this little baby could be the product of the dying relationship between Constance and Roger. Ahmed was too angry to count. He did not give a fuck whose baby it was; he just knew it was not his. Without a word, he stormed out of the room. Constance had no chance to explain. Outside the door, Ahmed took several deep breaths. His mind was racing. What were his options? Get mad and throw out mother and child? But he was legally married to her. Not that that mattered. Under his laws, by repeating "I divorce thee" three times he could end the marriage, but there would be consequences, both political and financial. Screaming and shouting, he knew, would not get him anywhere. It might ease his feelings and tension, but it would not solve anything. The truth was that the woman he loved had just had a baby that was sired by someone else. He could look like a fool when word got out. On the other hand, he had just admitted that he actually loved Constance. She was not like all the local women he had had, nor the prostitutes in Paris. She was a special woman, very special. So how could she have done this to him? Maybe she didn't know? Maybe she too had been surprised? Maybe she genuinely thought the baby was really his? But how could this happen? Ahmed's mind raced. What should he do?

After several minutes of mental turmoil, he made a decision. He would re-enter the room where Constance was lying with her baby and see what she had to say. Whatever happened they were in this thing together. The local press would soon be clamouring for a birth announcement and the inevitable photographs. They would have to take some decisions together, however painful they might be.

When he opened the door to the bedchamber, Constance was crying. Still clutching the little blond baby, she looked up at Ahmed with a mixture of fear and dependency. She desperately needed him to understand the surprise he had had was no greater than hers. She had genuinely believed, until an hour or so ago, that the baby she was carrying was the product of Ahmed's exceptional lovemaking. Clearly that had not been the case, so the maths told her there were only two other possibilities, either Roger or JP, the bandleader. Looking at the babe in her arms, there could, however, only be one father: Roger. "Best keep quiet about JP," she decided.

Ahmed attempted a smile. "How are you feeling, my love?" He did not expect an answer. He looked again at the innocent baby, snuggled against his mother.

"Well, one thing's for sure," he continued. "It's not his fault."

Constance, relieved that he was not going to shout and scream as she had expected, decided to speak. "He is as much a surprise to me as he was to you, my love. I've done the maths.

This baby was conceived before I came to you; before I left the Vanilla Beach. The numbers work. I've gone full term with the baby, which means it was conceived whilst I was still with Roger. It's sod's law. I was with him for ten years and could never get pregnant. Suddenly, as I'm on the verge of leaving him, I do. I would never have believed it was possible, but when I look at this little thing, I believe in the impossible. I'm so sorry, my love. I was sure this was our doing; I so much wanted it to be our doing. I love you. And now I don't know what to do." She burst into tears again.

Ahmed held her. He looked at the little white boy snuggled against her. She was right. It was not the baby's fault. He was an accident. Clearly Constance would need to look after him – at least for the moment, but he could be the laughing stock of the country if it appeared he had been cuckolded. No, nobody must see this baby. He must "die" in the birthing process.

"This is what we are going to do, my love," announced Ahmed suddenly. "We are going to tell the world that the baby was premature and only just clinging on to life. We will say that there was an urgent need to get the baby to hospital in France for life-saving support. We will charter a plane for the purpose. That bit will be true. No one in the Comores will get to see the baby. Once he is in France I can, through my channels, get him immediately adopted. He will start a new life with nice new parents. No one will ever know where he came from, especially him. He will have a new mother. He will grow up never knowing the circumstances he was born into. He will leave here today under the strictest of security. All those involved will be sworn to secrecy on pain of death. You will be allowed, naturally, a period of grieving. Then life will go on. We will try for our own." Ahmed held his stricken wife tightly. She was sobbing. Then, as an afterthought, he said, "You know what, my love, once he gets to France, we will announce that the poor little soul passed away on the flight; that we were unable to save him. That will put a closure to the issue and he can genuinely start a new life." Ahmed seemed pleased with his solution. "Yes," he said, "that's what we will do."

Constance, however, was beside herself with grief. As weak as she was, she wrestled herself away from him. This was her baby, not his. Why should he have the right to say what was to become of the child? Also, what right did she have to deny Roger the opportunity to know his only son? But, the more she thought about it, as she calmed down, the more sense there seemed to be in Ahmed's hasty plan. After all, Roger did not even know he had a child. After all these years of trying, why would he even consider this a possibility? To bring up the baby as a member of the Presidential household would not only harm Ahmed's position, but would always put the child in the position of the unwanted, the bastard baby. The more she thought about it the more she could see the sense in Ahmed's quickly considered solution. Maybe this would be the best for everyone, including the baby. And yet, as rational as the plan seemed, every time, as a new mother, she looked down at the babe, her resolve to let him go melted. It was something she just could not do.

However, when you are married to the most powerful man in the country and weak from childbirth, there is only just so much you can do. Ahmed had moved quickly to alert the medical team who were present at the childbirth that their complete complicity and silence in regard to the adoption plan was required. He made it quite clear what the results of loose talk would be. Farming the little white baby out to a local family could not work. The baby must be moved to France and adopted as soon as possible, before Constance could interfere, and before the local rumour mill could start to churn. Through his contacts in Paris, Ahmed quickly made the necessary arrangements. Baby Roger would be going to a good family, desperate for a baby boy. A charter flight would be organised immediately and no one in the Comores would know the truth, especially Roger. Ahmed and Constance would resume their life of marital and sexual bliss and, maybe, a new baby would soon be on the way. Constance was too weak to fight. So, within three days of childbirth, she had lost her baby to an unknown destination and faked his loss. The faking was not difficult. She really had lost a child.

Over the next few months Constance was deeply distressed. Observers, of course, put this down as the natural result of losing a baby at birth, so she was allowed her period of misery. Ahmed understood this too, but only up to a point. Constance made no effort to get back into shape. She was now a mature woman in her thirties and, at that age, the body takes longer to heal after childbirth. The brain takes longer too. The fantastic taut body that Ahmed had lusted after, was, at least for the time being, no longer available. He was not a patient man. He loved her, but he also loved sex and Constance was just not interested. She also brooded on the fact he had been with wife number two whilst she was pregnant. For some reason this really galled Constance. She kept thinking of her husband caressing the young girl in their own backyard, literally as she slept in the room above. She would have been happy at the time to have engaged in a threesome with Lula and Ahmed, but his covert dalliance with the girl really troubled her. She had to face it, there was no way he was going to change. She either had to accept it and take what she could out of the situation, or leave. Neither option really appealed. Despite all of these irritations, nothing had caused her distress more than the loss of her child. Constance was stuck in a deep depression.

Back at the Vanilla Beach, Roger had, like everybody else, heard of the miscarriage and death of Ahmed and Constance's baby. His anger at learning of the pregnancy was now tempered by the sadness of the news. He had come to accept that the failure of his marriage to Constance had been as much his fault as hers, but he would not have wished such sadness on her. He realised there had been a third person in their marriage, but that was his fault rather than Constance or Brigitte's. When Constance received Roger's little note of commiseration over the loss of her baby, she sobbed uncontrollably. How could she possibly have misled the man she had loved for so many years? How could he ever forgive her? He must never find out. Never. She would have to carry the guilt forever.

Roger, now really concerned about the political situation on the island, was busy stashing the proceeds from the renewed level of business, since Brigitte's intervention, away in a UK bank. He also had started to look for a business partner who might buy a piece of the action. He reckoned he could sell off Constance's ex-shares for a considerable profit. Maybe, he thought, one of the international hotel groups might be interested; perhaps such a group would also be interested to take over the management. Roger was feeling tired.

Chapter Sixteen
"Mount Karthala"

When volcanoes erupt, they normally give fair warning. As the red-hot lava builds up under the summit of the volcano, the rumblings of the monsters are normally heard and the underground vibrations from the mountain are detected, often days and sometimes weeks in advance. Local residents, although unable to prevent a quake, at least have a window of time in which to prepare for it. Not so in the case of the Comores' Mount Karthala. On the morning of July 15th, at 3am, without any warning of any sort, the mountain suddenly exploded, sending plumes of red flames and molten lava several hundred feet into the air. It was a spectacular sight. It was also frightening. Like everyone else in the resort Roger, who was back in the beach cottage, was awakened by the noise from the explosion. One glance into the reddened sky told him what had happened. Mount Karthala, after fifty years of sleep, had awoken. Of all the disasters that could have and had affected the Vanilla Beach, this was not one Roger had planned for. He had been assured by Dusty and many other experts that this volcano was dormant. Even his insurance company had accepted the volcano was no risk. Risk or no risk, Roger knew his resort guests would not know the history of the mountain; they would not know the direction of lava flow, from previous eruptions, had never been in the direction of the hotel; they would not know they were safe. They must all be in a state of complete panic, which he would need to address. Roger was fully dressed and heading towards the resort within less than five minutes. His mind was racing. He needed to calm down if he had any hope of calming everyone else. Taking a deep breath, he entered the lobby of the hotel, where he was greeted by the ever-alert Colin Freeke, Dinesh, and Julie, the bubbly housekeeper. Several frightened, hastily dressed guests had also appeared, clearly worried out of their minds.

"Open the meeting room," Roger barked at Colin. "Make sure the mic is working. You, Dinesh, stay here and direct guests to the banquet room. We will address them there. We need to explain that any lava flow will not head in this direction. We need to tell them they will all be safe at the hotel, but they must not venture near the mountain." As he finished speaking, a sleepy-looking Hector appeared with his wife, Peaches, who had only just gone to bed having closed down a late night in the casino. "Hector," said Roger. "You get on the phone to find out what's happening, if you can find anyone, and I'll deal with the guests." The explosions from the mountain were getting worse, sending plumes of flame and molten rock higher and higher into the sky. From the beach the occupants of the hotel had a spectacular view. They could also see brush fires starting in the mountainside jungle as hot flaming rocks fell. Nobody wanted to be in the meeting room; everyone wanted to be outside watching the show. So Colin quickly rigged up a loudspeaker function using the band's equipment so Roger could address the guests on the beach. As more and more gathered out there, Roger was able to explain the history of the mountain and the previous patterns of lava flow. "The hotel will be safe," he announced, several times, as more worried guests gathered. "The path of the flow will not come near the hotel. Please do not venture from the property."

Most of the guests were thrilled to witness such a spectacular event and a good deal of high spirits and drinking carried on through the night. Some, however, were frightened. Some of the children were really scared and clung to their parents' pyjamas or shorts. Some, much to the annoyance of many, would just not stop crying. There were also those that were praying. This, more than anything else, was a sign of God's strength and power. A volcanic eruption to them meant that God was angry.

For several hours, until dawn, the massive and noisy firework display continued. As with most firework displays, however, once you have seen the most spectacular and stunning elements, its continuation can become boring. As the mountain produced more of the same exploding lava, some hotel guests trooped off back to bed, as if the eruption was nothing more than a violent thunderstorm. Roger and his team set about providing refreshments for those that remained. As he crisscrossed through the crowd, handing out teas and coffees, the firework display continued. Sometimes there were lulls in volcano activity, leading people to think it was all over, but then, suddenly, another large explosion would signal a giant plume of flame leaping into the early morning sky. As far as Roger was concerned, it was far from over. He did not know for sure, but he was certain the road to Moroni would be cut off, and he began to worry about how his supplies would get through in the following days. Whilst others were oohing and aahing at the lava display, Roger was already chartering helicopters and boats in his head to circumvent the closed roads. This might be a wonderful display for his guests, but Roger was already worrying about the disruption to the logistics of running an almost-full hotel. He knew too, and understood, that almost all his staff lived in the foothills of the volcano. Could he blame them if they did not show up to work? No, Roger quickly realised that the next few days could be very difficult. He also worried about how the closure of the only road to the airport would affect him.

At 6am everything changed again. In the dim early morning light, the volcano-watchers now saw something different. As flames continued to leap from the well-formed crater at the top of the mountain, a huge bulge in its side facing the hotel seemed to be forming. The mountain was actually reshaping as people watched from the hotel. The leaping lava from the crater crackled and roared, but now there was a deeper, almost groaning sound, coming from the direction of the mountain. Literally one side of it seemed to be moving, the one that faced Vanilla Beach. Then, at exactly 7am, on July 29th, the side of the mountain blew off. The pressure from within had found a weak spot in the hillside. Suddenly, rocks, soil and flaming lava were bursting from a massive crack in the mountain facing the Vanilla Beach. A new and larger stream of red-hot lava was pouring down the side of the mountain, not, like the original stream, in the direction of the sea between the resort and Moroni, but this time, straight towards the hotel. Its movement was not quick, but it was, without question, heading in the direction of Roger's hotel. It was only a matter of time before it reached it. Roger, who had thought that after all the disasters he had coped with at Vanilla Beach there could be no more, was now faced with the biggest one of all. Within a few days, maybe even hours, his hotel could be destroyed and there was nothing, absolutely nothing, that either he, or his staff, could do about it. Worse though, in his thinking, would be the fate of the villagers, many of whom were his staff, who had built their homes on the safe side of the volcano – the side that was, it seemed, now in peril. "What the fuck will happen to them?"

It did, in fact, take almost two days for the slow, but unstoppable, flow of red lava to reach Vanilla Beach. By then, however, there were five flows, the main stream having been divided by the natural formation of the mountain as the molten lava gushed, at first quickly, and then more slowly, down the mountain side. The scalding hot rivers crushed and devoured everything in their paths. Villages and villagers' belongings were swallowed up. Vanilla plantations caught fire and the jungle crumbled as the molten rock rolled by. The largest lava flow was the first to reach the resort. Luckily it narrowly missed the main buildings and dropped hissing into the sea on the beach earmarked for the hotel extension. The acrid smoke that filled the air as the hot rock hit the water blanketed the whole resort, causing people to cough and splutter.

However, two of the following breakaway flows slowly and inexorably ploughed their way through the heart of the hotel's public areas, setting fire to the buildings as they did. There was no point trying to resist. There was nothing Roger, nor anyone else, could do. As the buildings that Roger had so painstakingly restored and maintained withered and fell in the heat, there were tears in his eyes. All he could say was "Fuck!" But there was little time for self-pity. There was work to be done: hotelier's work.

Luckily, the bulk of the rooms at the boathouse end of the site were saved and Roger, still the consummate hotelier, applied himself to reallocating the guests to these rooms. There was no way he could evacuate his guests to the safety of Moroni, except by helicopter, but since there was no immediate threat to life, this was not necessary. Roger's biggest problem was feeding his guests, since one of the lava streams had decimated his storerooms and kitchens. The team had had enough warning to remove all the goods from the stores and fridges to safer ground, but there was no way to refrigerate them, so, in the tropical heat of the island, he knew that supplies would not last long. Numerous guests were constantly stopping Roger to ask questions that he could not answer: "How are you going to get us out of here? When will the volcano stop spewing lava? Can we have our money back; our holiday has been spoiled?" and so on. Roger, normally a pillar of patience and understanding, began to be impatient with them. Telephone contact with Moroni was impossible. All cables along the road had been destroyed. There was no way anyone could answer their irritating questions. So, it was with great relief that, after three days of scrambling to look after his guests and keep them safe, help finally arrived in the form of the international Red Cross, with helicopters, food supplies and communications equipment, but, above all, the experience to deal with such emergencies. Soon the Vanilla Beach looked like a scene from a disaster area on the television news.

In Moroni, President Ahmed had quickly enlisted the help of the French state and the French had responded with alacrity. Air France had despatched two jet liners, full of emergency supplies and the capability to airlift all foreigners, including Roger's guests, out of the country. It became quite an exercise to get the hotel guests to the airport, using helicopters and boats, but eventually a complete evacuation was achieved.

The mountain had destroyed the Vanilla Beach; in the process it seemed to have destroyed Roger's will to carry on. Roger was a broken man. There was no way he could see a future for either himself or his team at the hotel. After so many attempts to bring down the hotel, fate had now won in the form of a power beyond the control of a mere hotel manager. Roger realised that this was truly the end of his resort. There was now nothing to sell. His only hope was the insurance policy he had shrewdly negotiated. He was covered for a volcanic eruption but not, strangely, for an act of God. In Roger's view, he had had so much bad luck at Vanilla Beach that he no longer believed in God. He was just worried the insurance company might not think likewise.

Roger's management team had stuck with him through thick and thin. The last few months of trading had been excellent, so there was some money in the bank. Roger knew it would be an uphill battle to collect on the insurance policy and that this might take a long time. He now needed to address the problem of paying off his loyal management team. However, just when he thought that nothing else could go awry at Vanilla Beach, he was, once again, proved wrong. As the dust settled in the surrounding villages, those that were homeless started to look elsewhere for temporary accommodation until they could resettle. Where better to stay than the remaining wing of the Vanilla Beach? At first, they came as a trickle of destitute families, clutching the few possessions they had rescued from the approaching red river of lava. Then, they came as a flood, and within two days every room of the still-standing part of the beach hotel was jam-packed with refugees from the stricken villages. Roger's luxury hotel was now a refugee camp. It had not taken LOU's rabble rousing to occupy the hotel; the volcano had done it for him.

Luckily for Roger, the cottage was untouched. However, the supervisory accommodation, which had been home to Dinesh and his colleagues, was unusable, so Roger's team had been taken by the Red Cross crews to temporary accommodation in Moroni. They all realised that the game was up. They knew it was not Roger's fault, but were hopeful Roger would do the decent thing and pay them out properly. They would all need time to find new work. The phone system was now up and running, so it was possible for Roger's team to communicate. A meeting was arranged in Moroni, and Roger was able to hire a chopper to attend. He had previously worked out with Hector that he could afford to pay all the remaining supervisors six months' salary in lieu of staying on. He thought that was fair and so too did Hector. Nobody complained. Everybody was in a state of shock. Roger, now all on his own, was clearly very depressed. As he made his farewells to his loyal team, he found it difficult to hold back the tears.

.

Julie, the housekeeper, put her arms around him. Dinesh called for the group to offer Roger three cheers and, one by one, his loyal management team expressed their thanks and appreciation for their now ex-boss. For Roger, it was an emotional end to life at Vanilla Beach. He wished Constance had been there. She had not produced a baby for him, but she had helped him with the birth of Vanilla Beach. It would have been fitting for her to be at its death.

Chapter Seventeen
"The Chips are Down"

It took two years for the insurance company to pay Roger for his lost shareholding in the Vanilla Beach. There was no question that Roger had insured against the risk of volcano damage. The insurance company had been remiss in allowing Roger to do so, but since Mount Karthala had not erupted for over fifty years it had gone off the radar of the clerk who vetted the policy. The company tried to avoid payment by claiming it was an act of God, but Roger argued that almost everything is, for those that believe in God. Although the South African government had not been as cautious with their insurance, and therefore were not entitled to compensation, they did, through Dusty, lend considerable support to Roger's claim, going as far as to threaten to cancel all insurance they had with the company unless Roger was paid out.

During the first year following Roger's departure from the Comores, he had stayed in Paris. Brigitte, upon learning of the closure of Vanilla Beach, had immediately contacted Roger with her sympathy; news and pictures of the spectacular eruption had been published across the world, even in the special world of Hollywood. She was now a resident of Beverly Hills in California, since her rocket to stardom had taken her to the West Coast. She still owned the apartment in Paris, which was outstandingly and sumptuously decorated, with a striking but slightly risqué portrait of Brigitte above the mantelpiece as a constant reminder of the owner. "You can stay there as long as you like, my darling," she purred to Roger. "It is empty." Roger was not penniless, but nevertheless he had taken up her kind offer, in the hope that she might become a frequent visitor. During the year Brigitte did visit Paris several times but treated Roger like a friend, not a lover. Brigitte, now in her mid-thirties, was looking wonderful. Despite the hard work that stardom was, Brigitte remained as fresh and beautiful as ever. However, amazingly, she was still single and, for Roger, all hope had not gone. Despite her move to Hollywood, Brigitte was still the queen of Paris, and her circle of friends were leaders, trend setters and celebrities of the highest order. When in Paris, Brigitte entertained the rich and famous, and Roger was always included in the list of invitees. In fact, Roger, with his multiple tales of disaster in the Comores, had become a very entertaining dinner guest.

Before leaving the island, Roger had visited Constance, now the third of four captive wives, to say goodbye. Constance had put on a lot of weight. She seemed pleased to see him. She was tight lipped about her new status as a secondary wife. The fact she could accept such status mystified Roger. His Constance would not play second fiddle to anyone. He could not imagine what had changed. Roger gave her a brief hug; very brief, since he was conscious he might be under observation. As they parted, he felt her hand linger on his. He could tell she was sad. What he did not know was that she desperately wanted to tell him about his son, but knew she could not. Keeping a secret of this magnitude was a terrible burden.

After a year at Brigitte's, Roger moved out into a rented apartment in Rue Verdun, a stone's throw from the Arc de Triomphe. He had considered returning to London, but his circle of friends was now in Paris. One by one he was working his way through Brigitte's unattached female friends; he was having plenty of fun and enjoying the fact he did not have to deal with the daily routines and shocks of running the Vanilla Beach. Gradually, however, boredom set in and the absolute lack of challenges, apart from his ongoing tussle with the insurance company, had left him feeling lacklustre. He started to look for a business to run, something he could get his teeth into with his savings and the money that was coming to him from the insurance.

At a dinner party one night in Paris, Brigitte introduced him to a friend of hers, Monsieur Blancpain, the Minister of the Interior. Blancpain and Roger hit it off well and, over a couple of glasses of Dom Perignon, Roger learned that the Ministry was in the process of seeking a buyer for the casino in Nice. Apparently, the casino had been recently closed by the Ministry for continuous flouting of French casino laws and tax evasion. Blancpain explained that the government needed a new operator to buy out the current owners, who, he explained, were a front for the Italian Mafia. Since it would be something of a forced sale, Blancpain explained, with a sly wink, his Ministry could probably help the buyer pick up the casino for below market price, because only an approved buyer would be allowed to operate. "I understand, from Brigitte, that you operated a casino in the Comores," said Blancpain with a slight smile. "Maybe you would consider operating this one in Nice?"

Roger realised why Brigitte had set him up to talk to the Minister. Brigitte was, once again, working her magic with Roger's interests at heart. "Maybe she still does love me?" he wondered.

Within days of the dinner party at Brigitte's apartment, Roger was in the Minister's office. This time the meeting was rather formal. Several of Blancpain's civil servants, all with dark suits and shiny shoes, were in attendance, nodding and smiling on cue. The meeting room was lined with books and history. An aide to the Minister described the scope of the casino, which apparently was housed in a magnificent Romanesque building on the Promenade des Anglaise in Nice, right on the seafront and at the heart of the city's upmarket shopping district. The gaming room comprised twenty gaming tables. There were no slot machines, since slots were still not licensed in France. There was a parking garage beneath the property with access from the palm-lined seafront drive. For some years, it was explained, the Ministry had been eyeing the activities of the casino and its current owners. The last mayor of Nice and a previous Minister of the Interior had granted the gaming licence to these owners several years prior. As the Minister had implied, the business was actually a front for the Mafia, who had been using it to launder their ill-gotten gains. The mayor had lost his position and the newly elected mayor had decided, with the help of the Ministry, to clean house. All Roger had to do, according to the Ministry, was reach an agreement with the men from the Mob for the purchase of the property, and the issue of a new gaming licence would be almost automatic. Roger, apparently, would qualify to own the casino on the basis of his unblemished record of operating a casino in the "French" Comores and having paid his casino taxes in full and on time. Due to the unusual circumstances, it had been decided there would be no need for any sort of tender to award the new licence; this would merely be an extension of the existing one. "Finally," thought Roger, "a benefit from those cursed taxes."

Roger agreed to meet the seller's representative to see if he could conclude a deal. He also agreed to travel to Nice to inspect the property. A private word with Minister Blancpain, hastily arranged by Brigitte, was sufficient to elicit a guide price that Roger should consider offering for the lease on the property. Brigitte was also able to convey to Roger, separately, how Blancpain could be personally rewarded for setting the whole thing up. Roger, now happy that the price was well below the payout he was about to receive from the insurance, set off to Nice. A closed casino in the heart of the city was of no interest to the new mayor, who was delighted to meet with Roger upon his arrival, and to offer his assistance in any way. The sooner one of the city's star attractions could be reopened, the better it would be for everyone concerned. The mayor escorted Roger to the shuttered casino, now heavily guarded and locked to keep out the banned owners. Roger was pleased with the size and condition of the place. The main gaming room was impressively grand, its ornate ceiling held aloft by massive round faux marble pillars. Several smaller "private" gaming rooms flowed off the main room and the normal grilled cashier and enquiry booths nestled into the back of the gilded room. This stuffy palace was about as far removed from the cosy casino at Vanilla Beach as it possibly could be. "Christ," thought Roger, "I thought gambling should be fun. Not intimidating."

"You'd feel you needed to dress up before coming in here," he exclaimed to the mayor.

"Mais, bien sur, you need to wear a tuxedo to enter. That is only proper," said the mayor, missing completely Roger's point. Roger decided to refrain from further comment. He could see that the norms of casino gaming in Nice would need to be changed.

"No slot machines then?" asked Roger, almost nonchalantly, since he already knew the answer.

"Of course not," replied the mayor, "slot machines are for children. A Frenchman would never gamble on a slot machine."

Roger kept silent. He knew full well it was the slot machines that had produced most of his casino revenue at Vanilla Beach, and the majority of his guests had been French. It was necessary to have the tables, to help create a casino atmosphere and add life to the proceedings, but the margins in favour of the bank were so small on the tables, and the labour cost of operating them so high, that the profits were far slimmer than those from the slots. It slowly occurred to Roger that the fact slot machines were not licensed in France was not because they were evil or anti-social, but simply because the French government thought they would be "beneath" Frenchmen. France, or, at least, Monte Carlo, was the spiritual home of casino gambling. It was not to be sullied by mere toys and gadgets, like slot machines. "What," Roger thought to himself, "if I could get permission from the government to operate slot machines in France? This could be a huge opportunity. There's no way that Frenchmen, and particularly Frenchwomen, would not take to slot machines less than any other nation of men and women."

Excited by the prospect of being the first to operate slots in France, Roger realised he would need more than just the Casino de Nice for premises. He would need to acquire as many of France's sleepy stuffy casinos as he could, in a great hurry, before anyone else cottoned on. Brigitte might need to work her charms on Blancpain more often than she had bargained for.

Roger looked at the casino building with new interest. If the Minister could be persuaded to allow slot machines on the premises, where could he house them? The formal gaming room was far too grand; it might be able to house a few machines, but rows of the garish noisy things would completely change its character and be detrimental to the existing business, whilst being too grand and overwhelming to the average slots player. The answer was the basement: a vast space across the entire footprint of the building, currently being used as a store room. By Roger's quick mental calculation, the space could accommodate at least three hundred machines. "If each machine could produce a hundred Francs profit per day (roughly the average win per machine in Vegas)," he figured, "that would work out at eleven million Francs per year. Christ, God bless Brigitte!"

The next step was to meet the Italians. In preparation, the mayor provided Roger with the few sets of accounts he had wrestled from the casino owners. Clearly the accounts were useless because for tax reasons the real revenue and potential of the casino had been hidden. What was interesting to Roger, however, were the "other" lines of revenue that from time to time fed into the books. Upon enquiry with the mayor's office, it turned out these were management fees from four smaller casinos the company owned in other provincial French cities in the South. "Christ," muttered Roger, on discovery of this, "if I could roll these other casinos into my deal for Nice, I could have a much broader platform for the slots." With that in mind, when he finally set off for the meeting with the owners, Roger's goal was clear. He needed to buy all their casino interests in France. If he could do that, he then needed Brigitte to persuade Blancpain that he should be given a licence for these "childish" slots. This could be the most productive "conquest" Brigitte would ever make.

The meeting with the men from the Mob, in the presence of the mayor, was short and sweet. Dottore Guido Garda was their "representative", accompanied by Salvo Marini. Garda looked and spoke like a lawyer. Marini did not speak, other than to offer the odd grunt. His stare and his silence were, however, intimidating. A price was quickly agreed for the casino in Nice, but Garda was somewhat taken aback when Roger announced that the deal would be contingent on him buying the other small provincial properties. Marini's face gave nothing away. Roger was gambling on the fact that if they lost control of the crown jewel in Nice, the smaller places would not be worth the effort of managing. Garda asked for a moment in private with Marini. After ten minutes or so, the pair returned. "Yes." The price for the smaller four casinos would be equal to the agreed price for Nice. With smiles and handshakes all round a deal was struck. This had been the easiest deal Roger had ever made and the whole price was still under his insurance payout for Vanilla Beach. Everything was, of course, subject to the approval of the Minister of the Interior, Monsieur Blancpain, and on Roger coming up with the full amount of the money within twenty days.

There were more handshakes and an agreement to meet in two weeks' time to close. As Roger, Garda and Marini stood up to leave, Salvo Marini spoke for the first time, "May we have a moment with you, Monsieur Roger, without the mayor?"

"Of course," replied Roger, "if the mayor doesn't mind."

The mayor graciously offered the use of an adjacent meeting room and bade farewell. No sooner had the door closed then Marini spoke again. "Congratulations, Mr Brown. You've done a good deal. We've all done a good deal – and we look forward to a long and fruitful partnership with you." Roger was immediately nervous. He had no intention of partnering with the Italian Mafia. Marini did not stop. "You understand that when you are the owner of the business, you will need our protection. The gambling business is a rough one. You'll need to make sure you're left alone. We can help you of course. You'll need to budget for security. I would say, roughly ten percent of your casino win, yes, that should be enough to make sure your premises are safe, but, more importantly, that you and your French film star are also safe. We need to make sure you're around to run the business."

Then, without stopping for an answer, the two men got up to leave. "Arrivederci, Mr Brown," said Garda, as he closed the door. "We'll see you in two weeks."

Roger sat in stunned silence for a good few minutes, alone in the little glass-walled meeting room. He had considered bringing someone with him to the original meeting, like a lawyer or accountant, but decided against doing so. Now he was pleased with his decision. Whatever happened he would not want anyone to know he might be about to do a deal with the devil.

When Roger returned to Paris and announced he would buy all the Mob's casinos in France, Blancpain was as impressed as he was pleased. Getting the Mob out of this business would mean huge brownie points for the Minister, along with the rest of his cabinet. The proviso that Roger put on the deal, however, was puzzling, but also a problem for the Minister. Amending the gambling rules to allow casinos to operate slot machines might not be as simple as it seemed to Roger. Getting a change to laws in France, which had been in place for many years, would be difficult. But Roger had made it clear that were he not allowed to place an unlimited number of slot machines in the five casinos he was buying, then the purchase would not go through. It was time for Blancpain to cut his boss into the deal.

Neither Blancpain nor his President had the first idea what revenue a slot machine could produce if it were conveniently placed in the centre of a French city. They were both firmly of the view that the effect on the casino business would be small and likewise the antisocial effect on the population of the city itself. The two men were powerful enough to quickly amend the national gaming regulations to allow slot machines on licensed casino premises. They did receive some opposition from the Minister of Justice, but this was quickly squashed. Better still, from Roger's point of view, the tax on winnings from slot machines was set at a ridiculously low rate of ten percent, simply because the ministers concerned thought it would be ten percent of almost nothing. Nobody in authority believed a Frenchman would stoop to using a slot machine. No thought seemed to have been given to Frenchwomen!

Even though the whole process of amending casino licences had been achieved with indecent haste, it still could not be accomplished within the two-week closing date set for Roger to acquire the Mob's casinos. In order to secure and finalise the deal with the Italians, Roger had to force Blancpain to organise a line of credit for him until the new licensing rules were completed. This had been enormously difficult to pull off, but, once again, Brigitte's charms at the Ministry seemed to pay off. Roger also needed time to think about the Mafia's insurance proposition. He might be able to shield the revenues from the slot machines for a while, but he knew the Mafia would soon figure out that ten percent from the machines should also be included in the insurance premium – and who was to say they would stop at "ten"? Roger decided to cross each bridge as he reached it. As far as he was concerned, there ought to be enough honey in this deal to keep everybody sweet, including his old employees, Hector and Peaches, who had reluctantly returned to London after the demise of the Vanilla Beach.

When the couple heard Roger was in the process of acquiring a gaming business in France, they were practically on the next ferry. Hector had landed a good job in the City but Peaches could not find a place in the closed masculine shop of casinos in London. Having run her own casino, albeit a small one, she did not wish to return to the ranks of employee at one of the male-dominated London clubs. Hector went off to the City every morning; Peaches was bored. Roger's impending transaction in France was not only offering a solution, it was also offering a lifestyle change. They would be based on the glamorous French Riviera and would both have jobs – Hector as company controller and Peaches as gaming manager. But, best of all, Roger had offered them a ten percent share in the business. Their decision to leave England and join Roger's new company was not hard, especially since they had picked up more than a smattering of the French language during their time in the Comores. They were delighted to be reunited with their old boss and excited by the potential of the clanging slot machines.

As soon as Roger had concluded the acquisition of the casinos, the basement of the casino in Nice was converted into a slot palace, housing, initially, a hundred and fifty colourful and noisy machines. In their paranoia that slot machines would bring down the tone of the casinos in France, the ministers had insisted that any such machines should not be allowed in the same room as the gaming tables. This, of course, was music to Roger's ears, he would have paid money to site them away from the stuffy atmosphere of the gaming tables. As for the building in Nice, the newly decorated basement, with its separate entrance from the street and no regulations about producing ID or anything else, meant visitors could enter the casino as easily as going to the supermarket. Roger could not have hoped for more. In the first six months of operating the slots room in Nice, each of his hundred and fifty machines was producing an average daily win of five hundred Francs per day, or over two million per month. The dingy basement had been transformed into a sparkling, garish, noisy space, with flashing lights and electronic noise. The musical donging as the coins were swallowed by the greedy machines, frequently drowned by the crashing of cash into the winning trays, made this the noisiest and most frenetic room in the city. The housewives and shoppers of Nice flooded into the room which operated day and night. It did not take long for Roger to add another hundred and fifty machines, which had the effect of almost doubling his revenue. Roger quickly added fifty machines to each of the four other provincial casinos, which, although the daily win achieved far less than in Nice, at a hundred and fifty Francs per day per machine, still netted revenue of close to one million Francs per month.

The provision of the slots also had a positive effect on the gaming tables, since, some of the new footfall to the casino found itself in the casino proper and almost none of the table-gamers descended to the slots. Roger and his associates were soon rolling in money. The slot machines alone produced over sixty million Francs in the first year, of which only ten percent needed to be paid in casino tax. The gaming tables and ancillary revenues produced another ten million. Surely, they would not need to give ten percent of everything to the Mob? Hector would just have to figure out how to keep two sets of books: one for the government and the Mob, and one for Roger, himself and Peaches.

Chapter Eighteen
"Brigitte"

Exactly one year from the date the casino in Nice reopened, lightning struck. Not from the sky but from the vicious hands of the Mafia. A group of men, armed with crowbars and other metal implements, walked into the casino gaming room. They did not stop to present their passports and ID. Within minutes every stick of furniture in the room had been smashed. The gaming tables were overturned and the beige ripped from them. The roulette wheels were trashed, the chandeliers shattered and the cages at the desks bent out of shape. What staff were on duty simply stood back and watched. The slot machines in the basement were untouched. At the same time, whilst the main gaming room of the Nice casino was being substantially trashed, similar groups of masked thugs walked into four other provincial casinos and ripped them apart, again without damaging the slots. No messages or clues were left as to the identity of the perpetrators, but nobody, especially Roger and Hector, had any doubt as to who they were. The difference between Roger, Hector and the gendarmerie and public was that Roger and Hector knew why. The insurance premium had been paid regularly to the collection man, but neither Roger nor Hector realised that information concerning the real daily win had been freely flowing to the "insurance company" since the reopening of the casinos and the installation of the slots. Either Marini and his mob had worked out they were being short changed, or members of Roger's staff were informers – or both.

It took Roger eight weeks to repair the damage and replace the gaming tables, during which time he was forced to keep on the trained staff and pay them. It did not take Roger more than a week to admit his "mistake" to Dottore Garda, and offer the full ten percent of win as the insurance premium. The only difficulty was that Garda explained that, "due to increased costs of insurance", the premium had now been raised to fifteen percent. "I also have a message for you from Salvo Marini," said Garda. "If you try to cheat us again, that pretty little film star friend of yours will have scars on her face for life. Do you understand?" Roger understood; the thought of Brigitte being disfigured was horrific. It seemed he had no choice but to continue with the insurance company and accept its conditions of doing business. Roger began to realise that although he had bought a business, he did not own it.

From that moment on, Roger's interest in the business waned. His initial excitement about how rich it would make him had taken a hit. But he continued to make excellent profits which he also continued to share. However, the shadow of the Italians blanketed the business and somehow seemed to weaken his hand in dealing with all the other petty mobsters around him. There were ongoing problems in operating. The staff were constantly on strike, although they adamantly refused to officially call a "strike", thereby circumventing the labour laws that controlled the behaviour of striking workers in France. In other words, Roger had to pay them, even though they had withdrawn their labour. On top of this the armed vehicle which carried his cash to the bank was frequently hijacked, never, it seemed, within the boundaries patrolled by the local police, but always in "someone else's" pitch. Nor could Roger ever win a case in the local courts. Whether the case involved a member of staff or even his gaming customers, the local courts always found in favour of Roger's opponent if they were French. In short, although still very profitable, Roger found himself operating in a hostile and unpleasant environment. If that was not abundantly clear it certainly was on the day a small incendiary device was posted through the letter box of Roger's rented apartment in Nice. Fortunately, the device malfunctioned and no damage was done. Needless to say, the local police showed no interest in seeking the perpetrator, so, reluctantly, Roger just shrugged and wrote the experience off to the cost of doing business in France.

Despite all of these problems, Roger's scheme to introduce slot machines to the casinos of France was paying handsome dividends. Even after the ten percent tax on the machines and the fifteen percent insurance payments to the Mafia, Roger's little business was netting well over thirty million Francs per year for Roger and his "partners", Brigitte, Hector and Peaches. In enlisting Brigitte's help initially with Minister Blancpain, Roger had gifted the film star ten percent of the business. How much she had needed to pass on to the Minister and, in turn, the President, he had no idea, but it was certainly enough to ensure that Blancpain did his level best to maintain the tax rate at ten percent, despite pressure from other ministers that slot machine taxation should be raised as high as fifty. Whilst the current government was in power, Roger's revenue stream seemed safe, so he decided that, despite the pain of doing business, he might as well continue with the fair wind. Sooner or later, he realised, the wind would change and Blancpain and his allies would be blown away.

Since opening the doors of the casino in Nice, Roger had invested in a spectacular property along the coast towards Monte Carlo. His house in Eze, Bord de la Mer, had been owned by a middle eastern prince, who wanted to sell because one of his sons had been killed in a high-speed motorboating accident nearby. The house had been built clinging to the rocks on the sea side of the lower corniche between Beaulieu and Monaco. It was one of the few properties on the Cote D'Azur on the sea side of the road. The building consisted of a series of spaces, piled one above the other, clinging to the rock face and cantilevered over the Med. From the main living quarters, with their amazing and unimpeded view across the Mediterranean towards Cap Ferrat, one could proceed via an elevator and through a short tunnel to a pool deck, boathouse and dock, where the Prince had kept his own super yacht. The buildings were surrounded by lush planting which effectively hid them from the sea. The house that Roger bought was, in fact, one of the finest private homes in the South of France. Roger's only problem was that he had no one to share it with. Not that he lived like a monk. Clearly, he was a prime target for the pretty single, and sometimes not so single, young ladies of the Cote D'Azur, but his dreams were still in the direction of Brigitte. In fact, despite the ongoing attention he received from the young ladies of the Cote D'Azur, and despite the multiple evenings he spent at the beach clubs of Juan les Pins or Regines in Monaco, Roger was actually very lonely. He needed someone to share his life, but nobody he met measured up to Brigitte. Sometimes he thought of the fun he had had with Constance, but the difference was that he had "owned" Constance, whereas, he had only tasted Brigitte. To Roger, Brigitte was still out of his league, but, nevertheless, he still hoped for promotion. For a man who had it all, Roger felt that he had nothing. In his life he had tackled all the challenges that had been thrown at him and won. The challenge of loneliness was not so easy.

Roger named his new house "Vanilla". Thrilled as he was with his acquisition, he was about to be even more so, when he discovered it was on the cusp of leaping up in value. One day, upon returning home from Nice, Roger noticed a strange-looking truck parked around the bend from Vanilla. Upon investigation it appeared that the truck was a part of some rock-drilling equipment. Unknown to Roger, the local authorities had decided to drill a road tunnel through the mountainside to shortcut the corniche road that wound its way around the cliff face and, as luck would have it, Roger's house. When completed, this would mean the main road would no longer pass by Roger's front door, but proceed through the tunnel, leaving the original road as a private driveway up to and past Roger's property, controlled by traffic lights at each end. The Gods must have been with Roger because this huge expenditure by the provincial government was about to increase the value of Vanilla by several million Francs. It seemed that from a financial perspective, Roger could do no wrong.

Little by little the film roles available for Brigitte in Hollywood were drying up. She still had offers from French studios, but almost all of them involved taking her clothes off at some point in the film. Although in her mid-to-late thirties Brigitte was still a very beautiful women, she was far from stupid, and knew that her days as a sex symbol would soon be over. She also missed her native France and spent more and more of her time in the Parisienne apartment. It took a few months for her to visit Roger in Eze, but when she did, she was blown away with the villa's beauty and ambiance. Her visits became more frequent. She was proud of Roger. Proud that he had been so successful in his business ventures and pleased that she had, through her contacts, been able to help. Roger had proved to be a good friend, from the time he had hired her as housekeeper to the present day. She knew that he loved her. She remembered, as if it were yesterday, the night they had made love, but she also knew that she was not "in love" with the man. She valued him as a friend. She did not want to lose his friendship by falling in love. In fact, Brigitte wondered at time if she would ever fall "in love". As France's leading sex symbol, she had lived through many affairs, including with many of the world's sexiest men, but she had never been in love with any of them. Despite her misgivings about Roger, the more she visited him at Vanilla, the more she realised her feelings for him were far deeper than any she had experienced with her numerous "lovers", but were they feelings of real love or just friendship? Maybe Brigitte's failure to find real love had something to do with her upbringing as an orphan? Maybe, deep in her heart, she did not feel worthy of love? Brigitte's idea of love seemed to be somewhere between sexual appeal and friendship, including large measures of both. If she was really honest with herself, as far as Roger was concerned the balance was tilted to friendship. The truth was that Roger did not set her on fire with his sexual appeal, not in the same way several other men had. She knew she could have sex with Roger at the drop of a hat, but she also feared this would mean the end of their friendship. She valued it too much to risk losing it.

Roger, however, took a different view and it was hard for him to do otherwise. Despite Brigitte's intentions to keep their relationship platonic, she did little in her behaviour about Roger's house to dampen his lust. She would casually move about his house scantily clad and, whilst at his cantilevered pool deck, would always sunbathe topless. In treating him like a friend, or even brother, she did nothing to cool his sexual ardour. In fact, Roger often had to leave the house on the pretext of "going to the office", just to cool down. He decided that things had to change. One night, upon returning to Vanilla after a drinks party with friends in Monaco, Roger effectively raped her. Brigitte, who rarely had too much to drink, put up little resistance. In fact she found his new-found forcefulness extremely sexy. This was a Roger she did not recognise. This was a Roger she actually quite liked.

Much to the intrigue and amusement of the staff at the house, the next day, Brigitte moved from the guest suite into the master bedroom. The relationship between the boss and the film star had taken a dramatic turn. The boss, for the first time since they had moved into Vanilla, seemed happy. The next two weeks the new lovers, but old friends, did not leave each other's sides. Nor did they step outside of Vanilla. The staff of the house, whom the film star had always treated with respect, were delighted at this turn of events. To have France's hottest film star as the mistress of their house was something to be proud of, something to boast about to their children and grandchildren. They were pleased too for their boss, who had suddenly sprung to life. For several glorious weeks the house was a happy one.

Happiness, however, can be fleeting. Less than a month after their coming together Roger and Brigitte had to part. Brigitte's presence was required in Paris at the film studio. A wealthy neighbour in Eze had offered her a seat on his private jet to Paris, where he needed to attend a business meeting, and Brigitte accepted. Less than fifteen minutes into the flight, tragedy struck. The plane crashed into the Alpes Maritime and Roger and Brigitte's happiness with it. The pilot and crew were all killed, as was the owner of the plane. The only survivor was Brigitte, but she was so badly injured she would have been better off dead. She was, in fact, brain dead and taken to hospital in Grenoble in a comatose state, where she was pronounced stable but without hope of recovery. The crash and Brigitte's condition made headlines across the world. The queen of Hollywood and the darling of France would never grace the screen again, although her great beauty, of course, would live on film forever. The fact that Brigitte might also live for a long time, whilst not living at all, was horrifying to the world, but to Roger this was the greatest tragedy of his life. No sooner had he found happiness than it had been whipped away from him, but, more importantly, his lover's whole life had been suddenly stolen from her. She was still alive, but not living. Roger was heartbroken. Now, he had no one.

Brigitte's comatose body was moved to a clinic in Nice. She was still breathing but none of her other body functions were working. Nobody could tell Roger if Brigitte's cognitive abilities were still functioning, since she could not or did not respond to any requests, instructions or stimulation. She was just a body, lying there, completely immobile and unresponsive. Her face, by some miracle, had not been touched by the accident. Although it was drained of colour her features were as beautiful as ever. For days, and then weeks, Roger sat by her bedside, hoping for a sign of life, but there was none. He knew that there was no hope for his lover; he knew that, even if she could regain consciousness, she would live the rest of her life as a vegetable. He began to ask the medics to put an end to her life, but, under French law, they were not allowed to do so. And, in any case, Roger had no rights in the matter. He was not her kin. She was an orphan. There was nobody to legally make decisions on her behalf. She just lay there, without motion, and there was nothing Roger could do. After several weeks of vigil, he had no idea whether Brigitte even knew he was there. However, he came to her bedside day every day, just in case it gave her comfort. Eventually, after a few months, he realised it was useless to be there. He needed to attend to his business. He cut his visits back to twice per week, but may just as well not be there at all; there was zero reaction from the body lying in the clinic bed. Each time Roger climbed into his car after leaving the clinic, he cried. Nobody else knew the mental pain he was suffering.

Roger tried to concentrate on other things. He decided to expand the business by acquiring other underutilised casino licences in France, but immediately discovered that the comatose body of Brigitte still had a hold over him. The terms he had agreed, or, at least signed, when Brigitte was gifted her share of the casinos, stated that any sale or acquisition of or to the business would need to be signed off by Brigitte. Apparently Blancpain had insisted on this to protect himself. Brigitte was still alive, but, clearly, could not sign anything. Until she passed away, whenever that might be, Roger could neither grow nor sell the business. He was completely stymied. Amazingly, Brigitte had exercised control over Roger's life since the day he had hugged her in his office in the Comores, even if she did not know it. Roger did not hope she would die, but began to resent the fact she was kept cruelly alive. Even, he often mused, if she were to recover, her disfigured body would be forever a problem. No, it was better that she die, and the sooner for her and everyone else, the better.

The ghastly situation did not change for two years. The press began to lose interest and so, too, did the public. For over a year the studio which made Brigitte's last movie left it in the can. But there was too much money tied up in the production for it to stay unshown for long. And, besides, the publicity created by the plane crash, was a perfect platform from which to launch Brigitte's last movie. Everyone in France, and many others around the world, would want to catch a last glimpse of the sexiest lady on screen. Keeping the film in the can would be criminal. But it was Brigitte who had the last laugh. On the day the film was released worldwide with great fanfare and publicity, Brigitte died. She quietly slipped away in the night and, as she did, her facial muscles moved for the first time in over two years. They moved into a smile. The studio did the right thing. They postponed the worldwide launch of the film for a month, during which time, of course, many more people decided they must watch it. In death, Brigitte was a worldwide box office hit.

Roger was relieved, but also devastated. His own will to carry on was shattered. He did not see a lot of point in his now-lonely existence. He had nobody in his life, but worse, he did not want anybody.

Brigitte's will was straightforward. She left all of her estate to the orphanage in France which had cared for her as a child, with the exception of her shares in Roger's casino business, which she returned to him. In due course the orphanage received over twenty million Francs. Roger was now free to sell the casino business. He had had enough of France. He decided to sell Vanilla and move back to England, where he had no plans at all. As the days went by, taken up with interminable form-filling relating to the sale of the business and his home, Roger fell into a deep state of depression. His marriage had been a failure, and, just as he thought he had found happiness it had been cruelly snatched from him. Apart from his parents in the UK he had no dependents: nobody to love and nobody to love him. He had money, but, alas, no happiness. He was lonely and reclusive and retreated within the walls of Vanilla, awaiting its sale with a succession of large whiskies throughout the day and night.

Chapter Nineteen
"Prison"

When Roger stepped off the plane at London's Heathrow air-port, having left Nice two hours earlier, he was met by two uniformed police officers and one detective. He was asked to step aside to let the other passengers pass. "Roger Brown," said the detective, "I am arresting you for the murder of Antoine Mersky. I must warn you that—" Roger did not hear the rest of the sentence. He was stunned. However, he did nothing to resist, meekly offering his hands to be cuffed, as he had seen others do a hundred times in the movies. "After all this time," he thought, "how the fuck did they reach this conclusion? What do they actually know? Or are they just guessing?"

The news of Roger's arrest was soon in the headlines, not only in England where the alleged crime had taken place, but also in France, where he had spent so many years. The news even reached the Comores. When Constance read about her ex-husband's arrest, she was shocked. She knew that Roger could not have killed Mersky; it was not possible. She did not understand what was going on in England; she needed to find out. Her marriage to Ahmed had, amazingly, worked out quite well. Even during the period after the loss of her son, when she had done little to get back into the shape Ahmed lusted for, he continued to be supportive and understanding. Although, for a while, he clearly sought sexual gratification elsewhere, he continued to be kind to her and, to the best of his ability, give her loving support. She was different from his other wives. She was not just an object or a political necessity; she was someone that he genuinely loved. He was so sorry that he had hurt her. He knew that taking away a mother's child was possibly the cruellest thing that one could do to a woman, but he had no choice. He was a politician. He knew what he had to do to survive. Nevertheless, even though, for many months, Constance refused to lose weight or make herself look attractive in any sense, he still loved her. He decided to give her time, to give her space. And his strategy worked. Little by little Constance began to realise that life must go on. She looked at herself in the mirror one day and did not like what she saw. She determined to lose weight and reclaim her glamour. She missed Ahmed's lovemaking; it had always been edgy and different from her European lovers. It was something that made him special. He knew how to please a woman.

The news of Roger's imprisonment came several months after Constance had achieved her goal of luring Ahmed back to her bed. She was in a happy place. But, the awful news from London had shocked her to the core. "He can't have done it," she shared with Ahmed. "This has to be wrong. I must find a way to help him. Please, my love, please help me. I must go to London. I must see what I can do."

Ahmed understood. He was well aware that his harsh decision to remove her child had been especially hard for her; now he had a chance to make things better. "Of course, if you are so sure he could not have done this, then it is your duty to help. Of course, you should go to London. I will come with you, my love. We will do this together."

Ahmed knew he could not go to London for long; he had a country to run. But he could, at least, accompany Constance for a short while to make sure that she had all she needed to help her ex-husband, or, at least, for long enough for her to ascertain what exactly was going on. "The police must have some reason for arresting Roger; they must have some evidence," he thought, but did not voice it to his wife. "At least," he thought, "I can set her up with a legal team to look into the whole matter. Enough to get her mind clear."

Through a team of lawyers hired by Ahmed, he and Constance were able to ascertain that the police had reason to believe Roger had exchanged a bottle of water in Mersky's tennis bag for a spiked one. This alleged swap had taken place when Mersky left his bag in his office in the Sloane Towers whilst he went to the bathroom, before proceeding to the adjacent gardens to play tennis. It was not clear what the alleged spiked liquid contained. The source of this information was, apparently, Gorgeous George, who had been sufficiently convincing that the police believed him. Why he had waited so many years to produce this evidence no one could explain. Unfortunately, the story had also been confirmed by the hunchbacked elevator operator, who had been coming on duty at the time, although why he had been in the vicinity of the executive offices remained a mystery. What the police had not shared with anyone was that, out of the blue, new evidence had emerged causing them to reopen the murder file. Bruno, the ebullient restaurant manager and erstwhile member of the Saturday night drinking club, had been suffering from early dementia. This had become so difficult for his family that he had been removed to a care centre in Ealing. One day, in a state of agitation, Bruno had related the story of the four playing cards to his carer. At first, she thought it was just one of his ramblings, but he kept insisting the police should be told. The more his carer and others at the home ignored his story, the more agitated he had become, until, one day, the supervisor of the home decided Bruno might calm down if his story was relayed to the police. At the request of the home, an officer from Ealing Police Station attended the bedside of the sick man, who seemed relieved to relate his story to the man in uniform. Of course, it would be hard for the police to use this "evidence" in court since its source was a confused patient in a care home, but, nevertheless, it cast a dark shadow on the other three members of the murder club. That, combined with the evidence of Gorgeous George and the hunchback lift operator, was enough to reopen the murder case and cast a suspicious shadow across Roger. It also seemed odd that Roger had fled the country and gone to live in an almost-unheard-of island off the coast of Africa. Although there was no hard evidence against Roger, it was certainly worth bringing him in for questioning and also enough for a judge to decide that he should not be released until a trial could be held. He appeared rich enough to qualify as a "flight" risk.

What Ahmed's lawyers did not understand was why Roger was not putting up any evidence or effort to repudiate these claims. Roger did not want visitors in jail and refused to brief a lawyer. He had simply clammed up. Constance, of course, attempted to visit him, but he refused to leave his cell. According to the prison authorities, Roger seemed to be in a deep state of depression. He did not want to see anyone. It would be several months before his case would come to trial. Until then he would not be allowed his freedom, nor would he be offered any psychiatric help.

The news of Roger's arrest and imprisonment had also reached Julie, the housekeeper, who, upon returning to the UK, had been employed at a hotel in Torquay. Julie was also deeply shocked. In her short employment at the Vanilla Beach, she had become very fond of Roger. He had been nothing but kind and appreciative of her work and particularly helpful when it all came to a crashing end with the volcanic eruption. The Vanilla Beach had helped her over the period of despair after the death of her husband and children. She too, simply could not believe that Roger was capable of murder. So, on her days off, she had taken to going up to London to see him. For the first few weeks, he refused to meet her, but she was persistent and, after a month, he reluctantly let her in. What she found was a completely different person from the man who had been in charge of the Vanilla Beach. Roger had always carried an air of complete control; he always knew what to do. Now she found a shrivelled little man, deeply depressed. She could hardly get a word out of him. Each time she left, she cried. But the prison authorities encouraged her to return, as did Roger's court-appointed lawyer, Brian Green. "At least he sees you," they all told her. "You're the only one."

When Constance found out about Julie's visits, she contacted her. She was really grateful and offered to pay for Julie's expenses in making the weekly journey. Julie, who had little time for Constance based on her limited experience of her in the Comores, refused, but she did recognise they were both on the same side; they both wanted to help him. In his depressed state in prison, Roger was doing nothing to help himself, or his case. He would not have cared if they had brought back the death penalty, just for him. In fact, he would welcome it. Since the trauma of Brigitte's long coma and eventual death, something in Roger had died too. He saw no reason to be alive. The only thing that lifted his gloom was Julie's visits. They did not speak much, but her mere presence was, at least, a comfort. Julie was not complicated; she was just kind. However, even Julie's concern for him was not enough. Roger had no will to live. So, why bother to defend himself? The police were, in effect, cooperating with his desire to leave this world.

With the refusal of Roger to hire a lawyer, the court appointed one; Brian Green, a newly promoted barrister, had been handed the case. He was soon to find out that representing a prisoner who refuses to cooperate is difficult and frustrating. The evidence, such as it was, seemed fairly flimsy, but unless the prisoner actively denied his guilt, there was little Green could do. Roger, so far, had stopped short of pleading "guilty", but also refused to defend himself against the charges. In Green's view, the evidence against him was either thin or inadmissible, but to be certain of winning his client's freedom he needed his cooperation. It did not take long after Green's appointment for Constance's lawyers to join forces with him. They had also concluded that the evidence was insufficient for a conviction, especially since it emerged that their client, Constance, had been with Roger on the night before the alleged "spiking" of the water. Roger, apparently, had been on weekend duty and, as a special treat, had allowed Constance to stay in the hotel with him. At the time, they had not known this was a weekend when Mersky would choose to stay in London and not go to the Cotswolds. Nevertheless, they had stuck to their plan to spend the night together in the hotel, since this would be the first time Roger would allow it. Constance might not be able to recall every movement of her husband on the fateful morning of the death, but the fact she had not detected anything odd about her husband's behaviour would be fairly convincing testimony. In the opinion of Roger's legal team, the evidence against him was so inconsequential it was almost ludicrous, but unless Roger was prepared to defend himself, they were worried he might condemn himself instead. Unless he spoke up to deny it, there was always the possibility he was, in fact, guilty or that a jury would see it that way. What Constance had never known, because Roger had chosen not to tell her at the time, was that Mersky, upon discovering Constance had stayed the night with Roger whilst he was on duty, had severely admonished him and screamed and shouted at him as never before. In fact, this had been the first time Mersky had actually reprimanded Roger, and Roger had been quite shaken, embarrassed and actually angry about the incident.

What Roger had not known, because Constance had never told him, was that Mersky, equipped with a master key, upon discovering that Constance was staying in the hotel, had let himself into the suite occupied by Roger and his wife. Constance had just stepped out of the shower when her husband's boss entered the room. She was caught naked, but her screams of abuse at the intruder, whom, of course, she recognised, caused him to retreat before any physical contact had taken place. Constance had been shocked and shaken by this unwanted intrusion, but, rather than put Roger's job at risk, she had decided to keep "mum". She was so angry, though, that she could have killed him.

When Ahmed returned to the Comores, having set Constance up with the lawyers and advisers, Constance decided to follow her other goal; to find her and Roger's son. For this goal, she did not need Ahmed's help; in fact, she did not even want him to know about her mission. Maybe, thought Constance, just maybe, the knowledge that Roger had a son would jolt him out of his current state. At the moment it was clear to Constance that Roger had no desire to live. Being confronted by an heir might just change that. Using her own financial resources from the sale of her shares in the hotel, Constance set about interviewing detective agencies, honing in on those that claimed to be able to trace missing persons. All the information she could give them was the date her son had been whisked away to Paris and, of course, a picture of his father. She quickly realised the detective work would need to be carried out in France, with French-speaking agents, so it was not difficult to settle on an international agency with a branch in Paris. Soon Constance found herself briefing a young French private detective, Guillaume Martin, who had travelled from Paris to meet her in London. The young man obviously wanted the date of the flight to Paris with the newborn, the make and number of the plane, where it had landed, and a list of Ahmed's contacts, including lawyers and bankers, in Paris. It took Constance a few weeks to assemble all of the information, so she drip fed it to Paris, whilst she ostensibly remained in London to help her ex-husband in jail.

Weeks turned into months. Julie reported that Roger's depression seemed to be deepening, not lessening. Constance heard very little from Paris. Ahmed began to insist that his wife return. A sense of gloom spread across all involved. A trial date had been set, but it was five months away. At Ahmed's insistence, Constance agreed to make plans to return to the Comores. After several months in London, she had not been allowed to see Roger once, and seemed to be no closer to discovering the whereabouts of her son. It was with a heavy heart that she booked a ticket to fly back to her husband. Three days before she was due to fly, Detective Guillaume called. "I 'ave good news," he started. "We 'ave found your son." Constance's heart missed a beat. She was shaking with excitement. "He is living in Versailles, with 'is new mother and father. He is at school there. His father is a doctor of medicine. His mother stays at home. They are Arabs. The boy's name is Ahmed."

"Jesus Christ," said Constance, shaking with the shock, "how the heck do you know all of this?"

"We 'ave tracked down the plane arrival to the small airport in Beauvais, north of Paris. We found the people who were on duty at the airport. Two of them remembered the flight with the baby. The airport CCTV had a photo of the car that took the baby away..." Constance was no longer listening. She knew now that they had done their job. But panic set in. What on earth could she do with the information without Ahmed finding out what she had been up to? He would be furious that the well-kept secret had been uncovered. It might have disastrous consequences for his political position. Now the genie was out of the bottle, how could she use the information to help her first husband without seriously jeopardising her position with her second? For the first time in her life, Constance was panicking. "Are you okay, Mrs Constance?" said the young private detective. "It must be a shock to you. I understand. When you are ready, please call me back and tell me what we should do with this information. Thank you." Click. He had gone.

Constance had three days before flying back to her husband. "Calm down," she told herself, "you must make a plan."

Constance wrestled with her dilemma all night. Nobody knew the true story about her baby, except Ahmed and herself. She had promised Ahmed that she would never disclose the truth to anyone, especially Roger. But she felt it was important for Roger to know. It might give him the will to live. The only person Roger appeared to be listening to was the bubbly housekeeper, Julie, but if she shared her secret with Julie, who knew where that might lead? It was imperative no one should uncover Ahmed's secret. This would be political dynamite. But what was her alternative? If she wanted to shake Roger out of his depression this was, perhaps, her only hope. By the morning she had decided.

Chapter Twenty
"A New Home"

Dr Paul Indrissi and his wife, Fatin, had been good parents to little Ahmed. They had tried for several years to have a child, but even fertility treatment had not worked. Eventually they had put their names down with an Arab adoption agency in Paris in the hopes that a suitable baby could be found. One evening, now some eight years ago, they had received a phone call, not directly from the agency, but from someone who had previously worked there. He explained that he knew of a baby that required adoption, but the true identity of the child could not be revealed, both then and forever. He also explained that there could be no financial support from the real parents for fear of tracing their identity. The baby was newborn. The adopting parents would never know who the parents were, nor would the child. In fact, the child must be raised believing forever that the adopting parents were the real parents and that the truth must never be revealed. This would be an illegal adoption, but all of the required paperwork would be supplied to make it appear legal. Once the baby had been delivered to the doctor and his wife, there would be no further contact with the caller nor the real parents who would remain anonymous. And finally, the baby could be delivered to their home "tonight".

The doctor and his wife panicked. They desperately wanted

a child, but these circumstances were, to say the least, highly unusual. If they took the baby, how would they overcome the fact that Fatin had not appeared to be pregnant? Some of their friends and neighbours were aware that they had signed on with an adoption agency, so maybe they would all just think that this arrangement had born fruit. They could, they supposed, just tell the agency that they had changed their minds and then just hope they never found out they had a child. The man on the phone was waiting for an answer. There was no time to think. "Is it yes or no?" the voice on the phone asked. "I can only give you two more minutes to decide." For a doctor to decide something of such gravity without possession of all of the facts was inconceivable.

For a doctor's wife, who desperately wanted a child, facts were not so important. What she did want to know was that the baby was healthy. "I have one question," she told the mystery caller, taking the phone from her husband. "Is the baby healthy? Does it have all of its fingers and toes?"

"The baby is three days old. It has everything a baby needs," came the reply. "Make up your minds!"

"Yes," said Fatin, without further consultation with her husband, "we will take it."

The doctor was stunned into silence. And so little Ahmed was delivered and, amazingly, everything worked out well. At first, Fatin and Paul were shocked that the baby boy was pale skinned with blue eyes. They had just assumed that the orphan would be a little Arab child, since that was what the agency the supplier had previously worked for specialised in. So, when a little white bundle was delivered to their doorstep, what were their options? They knew nothing about the baby; not where he came from or even who had brought him here. All they knew was that he was now in their home and once Fatin had lifted him from the basket, there was no going back. The much-loved son was soon accepted in the family and by friends and neighbours. Everyone assumed that the adoption agency had done its work. The agency assumed that the couple had changed their minds. Little Ahmed was a bright child. The baby became a toddler, then a robust little schoolboy, top of his class in most subjects, and the absolute pride and joy of his parents. Although the neighbourhood was predominantly Arab, there were quite a few white Eastern European immigrants, so Ahmed did not see himself as unique or special. Nobody knew the story of his conception or delivery to Versailles. The secret arrival had stayed a secret for so long it seemed it would do so forever. Until the day the detective agency called. There was no denying the facts. The detective agency seemed to have them all anyway. The question was, who else did?

Paul and Fatin were beside themselves with worry. The stability and happiness that had befallen their little family since the arrival of baby Ahmed was now at risk. They had to find out who had commissioned the detective agency. They had to protect their little boy. He would be shattered to find out they were not his biological parents. He would not understand why they had never told him the truth, although they realised that the day would soon come when they had to explain little Ahmed's white skin. They had decided to put off that day until he asked. Now their world was about to implode.

As soon as panic had given way to calm and logic, the doctor decided that it was necessary to meet the man from the detective agency. He and Fatin needed to know who had commissioned them and, more importantly, why. Maybe there was a simple explanation; maybe young Ahmed could still be saved from the truth, at least for a few more years.

As far as investigator Martin was concerned his brief from Constance stopped at locating the child. It did not include becoming involved in any action subsequent to the discovery of the facts. That was for the parties involved to decide.

So, when Dr Indrissi insisted on having a meeting with the agency, Martin had to be firm. "I'm not at liberty to disclose who my client is, nor his motives," he told the doctor, deliberately using a masculine rather than feminine title. "I'm afraid I cannot discuss the matter further. Should my client or his representative wish to take the matter further, I'm sure they will be in contact with you directly." With that he said goodbye.

The doctor and his wife were distraught. Somebody knew their secret and they had no idea who. It seemed there was nothing they could do, except carry on as normal. Little Ahmed must be protected at all costs.

Back in London, Constance had made contact with Julie, who, grasping the anxiety in Constance's voice on the phone, had agreed to take the day off and come up to London to meet with her. When Constance shamefacedly and painfully related the story of the baby's birth and subsequent events, Julie was truly shocked. She had previously thought of Constance as a bit of a whore. She had witnessed her behaviour at the gala night at the Vanilla Beach. She had heard the rumours of a conveyer belt of lovers and erotic films, but she could never have guessed that Constance could have sunk so low in self-preservation as to give up a child. Or to conceal the birth from the rightful father. "How could any mother do such a thing? How selfish can a woman be?" But despite her loathing of the woman in front of her she realised this was also painful for Constance, who was only now sharing the information in the interests of saving Roger's life. "Perhaps she's not all bad," thought Julie, "but whatever I think of her is irrelevant. If I can help her shock Roger out of his depression so he can defend himself, then that's the priority, not punishing Constance."

And so it was that Julie agreed to work with Constance to save Roger's life, without, they hoped, seriously damaging the life of the innocent little boy. Julie agreed to carry the secret of Constance's baby to Roger. Roger should know that the baby was his. Hopefully, this news would be stunning enough to rekindle his desire to live. It would be for Roger to decide whether the boy's life should be disrupted, just as, sooner or later, it would be the boy's decision whether he wanted to trace his real parents, once Paul and Fatin had explained the circumstances of his adoption. Maybe the knowledge that Roger had a son would be enough to give him the resolve to live. Julie agreed that she would take on the role of messenger. It was the least she could do to help save the life of the man she now knew she loved.

Constance, now satisfied she had chosen the right person to break the news to her ex-husband, thanked Julie profusely and notified the detective agency in Paris that their new and only contact going forward would be Julie, not herself. The necessary papers between the parties were signed and exchanged and the fate of the secret was now firmly in Julie's hands. The next day, Constance set off to the Comores, where Ahmed greeted her with the enthusiasm of a deprived husband. He had no knowledge that his secret "abduction" and placement of the baby was no longer a secret, and Constance was not about to tell him. If, as a result of her actions, Roger would survive and, ultimately, get to know their son, then God bless him. She would have to live with the pain of never knowing her son and that would be a lot of pain to carry for the rest of her life.

Chapter Twenty-One
"The Truth is Out"

Julie dreaded her next visit to Roger. She rehearsed how she was going to break the news to Roger a thousand times. Just how do you tell a man, who is already in a depressed state, that his ex-wife never told him she had conceived and given birth to his son. He probably would simply not believe her, or, if he did, would sink even deeper into depression on account of the fact he had been so easily duped and deceived.

The visiting arrangements in the prison were not ideal for the delivery of such momentous news, although Julie realised that some pretty shocking disclosures must have passed across the "no touch" tables of the prison visiting room before. Nevertheless, she considered the news she was going to impart was so serious, and because she had no way of knowing how Roger would react, that she requested a private meeting room. These, she had discovered, were made available from time to time when a relative or friend needed to impart such grave things to a prisoner as a death or accident. Julie's news was hardly a death, but she managed to convince the administrators of the jail, without telling them exactly what the news was, that it was sufficiently jaw dropping to merit a private room. The officer in charge liked Julie. He had long ago realised Julie was trying to shake the prisoner out of his malaise and he felt sorry for her lack of success. She was a lovely personality who brought the freshness of Devon to the prison each week. She had always been bright, cheerful and thankful to the guards, so why not do her this little favour?

From the second Roger was led into a private meeting room, rather than the communal hall, he realised something was up. He would need to be on guard. Julie was dressed in a pretty summer print. She looked fresh and lovely, thought Roger, but also quite tense. "What's up, Julie?" said Roger, "you look worried."

"I am," replied the housekeeper. "I have something important to tell you, but I don't know where to begin." She glanced nervously at the attending statue of a guard, as if looking for help.

He smiled encouragement and gave her a slight hint of a nod, as if to say, "go on; you're doing well."

"Just spit it out," said Roger, "nothing could shock me now."

"Well," started Julie, "I've found out that you have a son."

"Of course I don't," interrupted Roger.

"Please, Roger, don't interrupt me until I have told you the whole story. Let me tell you what I know."

Roger, suitably admonished, kept quiet. Julie, bit by bit, related the whole saga as she had understood it from Constance and from her double checking with the detective agency. She told Roger everything she had learned, including the location of the little boy and his adopted name. Roger sat in bewildered silence. It was a lot to absorb. After all those years of hoping to have a family, this news was incredulous.

"There must be some mistake," he started. "This is nonsense from Constance. She's just stirring it up. But God knows why?"

Julie reached out and touched Roger's arm. The guard stepped forward as if to stop her. But he had heard the story. He realised this was a lot for his prisoner to take in. He let Julie's hand stay where it was.

"I believe her," said Julie, as she squeezed Roger's arm. "I think it's wonderful news; the idea of a little Roger running around is marvellous. It's something worth living for."

Roger was silent for a long time, deep in thought. Then, just for clarity, he asked Julie to go over the facts all over again. As Julie spoke, Roger's mind was racing. "If this is true," he thought, "then I must see the little lad. I must see that he is alright, that he is happy, that he is taken care of..." And so on. "But, the little boy must now be eight or nine; he must be at school; he may not know any of this; he may think that his adopted parents are for real. What happens if I disturb his happiness? What the fuck do I do? And how could Constance have been so devious?"

By the time Julie had run through the facts, as she knew them, Roger believed her. "What do we do, Julie?" asked Roger.

Julie, delighted he had used the word "we", smiled. "We think about what to do very carefully. But, in the end, it will be your call, Roger. You must decide whether an interruption of this magnitude in the little boy's life is good for him. Whatever you do, you must think first of the little boy, your little boy."

"Well, of course, Julie. Of course, we must think of him. But I must know more about him. I must know what he looks like. I must know if he is happy or if he needs anything. I must know that he is being properly taken care of."

"You're right," said Julie. "But to do that, you must first get out of here. You must get out of this rotten prison. You must make the police and the courts see that you are innocent. Your little boy must not find out that his real dad is in jail. That would be an awful start."

Julie's little lecture sank in. Roger was again silent for a long time.

"Visiting time is up," said the guard, breaking the silence.

"Five minutes more, then I am afraid, madam, that you will have to leave."

Roger smiled at Julie. This was the first time he had actually smiled since he had been admitted. "Is the real Roger coming back?" thought Julie. She smiled back and her bright eyes sparkled. She wanted to hug him, but knew this was not allowed. "Roger," she started, "I'm so pleased for you. This is really something to live for. Think it over. I'll be back in one week, as usual. By then, I'm sure you'll have a plan." With that, she squeezed his arm, smiled her most lovely smile, thanked the guard and left.

Roger started to cry. His emotions were finally returning. They were tears of joy. The guard waited patiently, against regulations, for Roger to compose himself and then gently ushered him out of the room and back to his cell. Then, since he was already breaking the rules, the guard spoke directly to his captive, "If you want to talk to someone about this, let me know."

Meanwhile, in the suburbs of Paris, Dr and Mrs Indrissi had come to a decision. They had consulted a child psychiatrist about the situation they now found themselves in. They would sit little Ahmed down and tell him the truth. They would tell him the story of his adoption. They would tell him that they did not know who his parents were and that they had no way of finding out. They had known all along that this day would someday arrive. They knew from the day that the little bundle arrived on their doorstep that the child would, sooner or later, question the fact he did not look like his parents. Nevertheless, it was heartbreaking for them that the day had arrived, far sooner than they had hoped and far sooner, in their view, than was necessary. But now there could be no hiding the facts. They must prepare for the day that someone, somehow, would make contact with them about the boy. The person who was interested enough to pay for a detective agency to track down the child, must, clearly, be interested in meeting him. As far as Paul and Fatin were concerned, it was better that their son was forewarned.

It took Roger several days to get over the shock of learning that he was a father. His emotions see-sawed from joy to anger. He was thrilled that he was actually a dad, but angry he had missed the first eight years of his son's life. His anger was directed at Constance, but she was not here to admonish, shout at or punish. How could she have done such a thing? How cruel could she be? He did not "buy" the difficult circumstances she had found herself in. He did not care about her protecting her new husband's career. Her behaviour had been cruel; worse, it had been wicked and selfish. He could never forgive her. On the other hand, she had produced his son and, as far as he could tell from the information Julie had gleaned from the detective agency, the boy had been placed in a comfortable and loving home. But it was not his home. The boy was not where he should be – with him. But where was that? He was in prison!

During periods when the anger subsided, Roger tried to think rationally about what to actually do about it. Assuming the boy was happy with his adopted parents then Roger decided he must not do anything to destroy that. After all, it was not the "parents'" fault and certainly not the little boy's.

Before doing anything, Roger would have to find a way to ascertain the situation; he would have to find a way to see that his son was being properly raised without his intervention causing chaos. As these thoughts swirled around Roger's brain he came to realise two things. First, he should seek professional help about how to best handle situations like this. After all, it could not be unique that a long-lost father needed to reacquaint himself with a son. Second, he realised that, to do anything at all, he would need to get out of jail. He must stop feeling sorry for himself. He must stop wanting to die, because he now had something to live for. Constance's plan to come clean and shake Roger out of his depression seemed to have worked. Although Roger was yet to realise this, his saviour could in the long run be Constance. Yet it was Constance who had caused all of the trouble in the first place.

When Julie came back to visit, one week after her bombshell disclosure, she found Roger a different man. Roger wanted to meet his son, but he was now certain he would only do so after he had got out of jail, so it was clear to him that proving his innocence was the priority. He needed to destroy the case against him which, since he had not committed the crime, he knew was circumstantial. It should not be too hard to prove that one did not do something if it was true. What would help matters would be if he could identify the real killer, if there were one at all. So many people hated Mersky that the list of potential muderers could be quite long.

"Julie, my dear," announced Roger, over the nasty little desk in the visiting hall of the prison. "I want you to get hold of the lawyer, Green. You can tell him I'm ready to talk." His words echoed around the hard drab room.

"Of course, Roger. I'll do it immediately. I'm so glad you're going to fight." A small feeling of triumph flowed over her.

"There's nothing much to fight. Only myself. But one thing is indisputable. I didn't do it. I hated the man, but I didn't kill him. Nor do I believe any of the four men in my pact did either. I'm not sure he was even murdered, but, if he was, there are plenty of candidates for the job. He was the most hated man I've ever known."

When Roger's case went to trial several weeks later, it did not take barrister Green long to demolish the case against him. All the evidence was circumstantial. It would be impossible for the state to prove any of the actions that witnesses had seen Roger indulge in on the fateful morning of Mersky's death had actually resulted in the man dying. The jury was unanimous. It could not be proven that Roger was the culprit. After seven months in prison, Roger was a free man and the police were, once again, left scratching their heads. It seemed more than likely that, unless new evidence emerged, Mersky's death would remain clouded in mystery.

Roger and Julie celebrated the victory with a lovely dinner at the Savoy Grill. To anyone watching it would be clear that Julie was in love with Roger. But Roger, grateful as he was for her support and kindness, was not in love with Julie. His true love had died the day the aeroplane crashed in France. And, in any event, now was not the time for self-indulgence. Now was the time to meet his son.

When Roger landed at Charles de Gaulle, a flood of emotion washed over him. He was back in France, the land he had come to love, and the birthplace and deathplace of his lover. But now was not the time for reminiscence or recriminations. Now was the time to begin the process of meeting his one and only son. Roger's first meeting, however, was with the detective agency. Although they were bound to secrecy by the contract they had signed with Constance, they were quick to point out that, if they could get Constance to waive their non-disclosure agreement, then they would be free to provide Roger with the information he needed to locate the young boy. At first, Constance refused to take their calls. Her life with Ahmed senior had resumed and recaptured its earlier happiness. The last thing she wanted was for the world to discover her husband had spirited away a little white boy on the pretext the baby had died. She knew if Ahmed were to find out about her detective work behind his back in Paris, their marriage would, once again, be in jeopardy. Roger was quick to point out to the agency that Constance had signed away her rights in regard to their contract to Julie, but the agency people were still nervous of any disclosure. Constance refused to engage with them. Roger, who was angry at her for her disgraceful treatment of him in the first place was now even more so for her refusal to cooperate. "Constance always puts Constance first," he grumbled to Julie. "I'm going to tell her that her little secret will find its way to her husband unless she authorises the agency to cough up the details."

That tactic worked. A tearful Constance, on the phone to Roger, finally agreed to allow the agency to open their files. Roger promised she would never hear from him again, nor would her husband. She clearly had no interest in his son, but would he, Roger wondered, one day have some interest in her?

The first meeting between Dr Paul and Fatin with Roger went well. Roger and Julie had decided that Roger should, before attempting to make contact with little Ahmed, meet his foster parents. By all accounts they had done a wonderful job in raising the boy. It would not be fair to undermine their success or destroy their lives. Despite his determination to get to know his son, he did not want to upset his life, or that of the couple that had raised him. Their first meeting took place whilst Ahmed was at school. Paul and Fatin had been expecting the call. They knew their secret had been unearthed. When Roger showed up at their home they were relieved. He seemed a nice man and, since he expressed not only his desire to not rock the boat but also his deep appreciation to the couple, a huge burden was lifted from their shoulders.

Roger too was happy. He could see that his son was being brought up in a nice home by a loving couple. True, their culture was different from his, but, nevertheless, they seemed kind and caring. It was clear that Ahmed's life could have been vastly worse. As the worried couple showed Roger the boy's bedroom, Roger could see he seemed to be living a normal happy life. Was he right to be even thinking of interfering with it? "But, on the other hand," thought Roger, "he's already been told that Paul and Fatin are not his real parents. He must be wondering who they really are."

After a couple of hours' discussion and many cups of sweet tea, all three of the adults were in agreement. Ahmed should meet his father, but his father would do nothing to disturb the boy's lifestyle or adopted home. Roger would attempt to make it clear he was not there to disturb the boy's life, only to be available to him. They all agreed that Roger should start his relationship with the boy slowly and carefully. The boy's mental health and happiness was all that really mattered. The boy must come first.

Chapter Twenty-Two
"Revolution"

When Constance got back to Moroni after her lengthy stay in the UK, things had changed. Whilst she had been scheming to breathe fresh air into her ex- husband's desire to fight his corner and get out of jail, her husband, Ahmed, had grown restless and taken himself a new, and far younger, lover. It was only now Constance realised why Ahmed had not been pressing her to come home. Christina was the daughter of the French Ambassador to the Comores. She had been visiting her father, who had naturally introduced her to President Ahmed. Christina, at twenty-two, unlike Constance, looked more Spanish than French. Her skin was slightly darker than Constance's. She had jet black hair and brown sultry eyes. She was slim but shapely, and once seen by Ahmed, he simply had to possess her. Christina did little to discourage him and it did not take long for the sexy little French girl to be sleeping in Constance and Ahmed's bed. The staff at the Palace were not at all surprised nor dismayed. There was not a great deal of sympathy for Constance, who, somehow, had always been an outsider. There had been, however, much speculation amongst the help as to what would happen upon Constance's imminent return.

Ahmed's promiscuous lifestyle had never been a real problem to Constance, in fact, she even got some sexual stimulation from it. She, of course, was well aware of wives number one and two in the compound; this she accepted as a political necessity. She also knew of his sexual transgressions on his "political" trips around the country, some of which he even boasted about to make her jealous and, at the same time, arouse her. She drew the line, however, at an interloper and would-be rival sleeping in her marital bed and keeping her underwear in her drawers and her cosmetics in her bathroom. Although Christina was not actually in residence when Constance came home, the evidence of her presence was all over the place. Neither Christina nor AAM had made any effort to hide it. This, even above Ahmed's taking a lover in her absence, upset her more than the fact he had been unfaithful.

Ahmed did his best to placate Constance, but instead of falling into his arms and making love to him, as would be normal after a considerable time apart, she crossed her legs in anger. To Constance, Ahmed was still a handsome and desirable man, whom she actually loved. If she did not love him, she reasoned, she would not be so angry. She had not yet, of course, set eyes on her new competition, but, as she examined the girl's underwear, she imagined the bitch was probably quite attractive. Constance realised that her nearly forty-year-old body might not compare favourably with a pretty thing half her age, so if she was to retain Ahmed's love, she would have to be quite astute. She wondered just how she was going to compete, but she would not easily give up her handsome husband nor her cosseted and comfortable lifestyle.

Meanwhile, Ahmed's complicated love life was not his only problem. During his almost three terms as President, he had dragged the country, bit by bit, into the world. By carefully playing off the West against the East, Ahmed had reaped the rich rewards of financial assistance for his country from both sides of the globe. Vanilla and sugar plantations had proliferated and several factories had been started, mainly producing fashion accessories such as silk scarves, belts and handbags. It turned out that the women of the island were particularly skilled in this regard, and the major fashion houses of the world had seen the Comores as a source of cheap but skilled labour. Ahmed had also recognised that the world of IT knew no boundaries. He had encouraged major companies to set up telephone call centres in Moroni as well as support centres for major online gaming companies who were not allowed to operate in the more highly controlled countries of Europe and North America. This had brought wealth to a few Comorians and employment for many, but it had opened up a huge gap in incomes from the "techy haves" and the "have nots". Ahmed's political opponent, LOU, had continued to grow his support from the poor majority. Those that had benefited from Ahmed's commercially sensible programmes had, as is not uncommon, tended to display their wealth with a foolish ostentation. Many large new homes had been built, and imported luxury cars were sprinkled around the island, even though the roads were far too potholed to accommodate their use. In the jungle and the primitive villages, discontent among those who had not benefited from the country's economic improvements had been growing, as had the discontented, spurred on by the irreligious lifestyle of the island's rich. The Comores was predominantly an Islamic state and almost exclusively so amongst the poorer population. The growing dislike of the successful rich was not just based upon economic jealousy, it was born of a genuine religious teaching that greed and capitalism were ungodly and evil. The poor population of the Comores was a happy hunting ground for the revolutionaries under the spell of LOU, whose numbers had swollen hugely during the last term of Ahmed's rule. Whereas Ahmed had been saved at the last election by his charm to the women of the island, this advantage seemed to have dissipated.

LOU, however, was not prepared to take his chances at an election anymore. Twice before he had followed the rules and gone to the electorate. Twice he had lost, and he was now convinced that the counting of the votes had been rigged. As far as he was concerned, there would be no more elections. He would take the government by force. Quietly but steadily, LOU had been building up an armed force in the jungle. The support of ultra-religious States in the Middle East and the Stans had been easily obtained, together with military training. The result was that LOU, with his terrorist army, would soon be in a position to march on Moroni and throw out the "elected" leadership together with their whores and cronies.

Ahmed, of course, was aware of the build-up of opposition forces in the jungle. As far as he was concerned, he had two options: fight or flee. Having personally further enriched himself during two and a half terms in government, Ahmed saw no real need to fight. In fact, as a realist, he knew fighting could only lead to multiple innocent deaths and probably personal disaster for him and his family. In his view, he had done his duty well for the island and its people. He had created circumstances where those that wished to work hard could thrive. He could not fight a religion that frowned upon success, and one the majority of the population seemed to have fallen for. "If they think Allah will provide for them, then so be it," he would say. "I would rather trust in hard work." Ahmed had been a visionary leader in many regards, but ultimately his selfishness would prove greater than any altruism.

So, Ahmed, together with many of his locally enriched businessmen, had quietly but steadily been stashing money away in offshore bank accounts. Ahmed's hidden pile was sufficient for him to live in luxury for the rest of his life in France, together with his wives and children. He would insist on taking wives one and two because they were the bearers and guardians of his children, not necessarily because he feared for their safety once he had left. Whether Constance wanted to join him would be up to her. Despite her unhappiness over his recent dalliance with the sultry daughter of the French Ambassador, which he hoped he could carry on, he still loved Constance. Christina, his new lover, already lived in France.

By the time LOU's army was ready to march on Moroni and the Presidential Palace, Ahmed and his family were packed up and ready to leave. A jet was at constant readiness to whisk them all away. Ahmed had acquired a beautiful home in St Paul de Vence, nestled in the hills above Nice. The estate was big enough to house his complete entourage. Constance would now need to make a decision – a life of luxury, but from time to time shared with others, or a return to the family in South Africa. Despite her age, Constance was still a very attractive lady; attractive and clever enough, she reasoned, to be well placed to make a success of France.

When LOU marched into Moroni, with several hundred well-armed militia, he did not meet any resistance. The little roads were lined with apparently welcoming crowds. The low-paid workers from the factories which exported luxury goods to the world had come out in force. The men waved flags and signs. "Allah is great." The women all wore headscarves. The revolution was quick and bloodless. LOU did not move into the Presidential Palace, as expected. Within weeks its conversion to a state hospital had begun. Many of the squatters at the ruined Vanilla Beach quickly found their way into the abandoned villas of the rich who had fled. Grandiose villas were turned into grubby dormitories. The new regime had begun.

Chapter Twenty-Three
"Paradise Rediscovered"

Since that first dramatic meeting with his birth father under the watchful and nervous eyes of Doctor Paul and his wife, Fatin, Ahmed junior had known that he had actually been born in the Comores and, as such, could rightfully claim citizenship. At the age of eight this had not been a concept Ahmed was interested in. To him, his parents were the good doctor and his wife. Nothing would ever change that, not even the appearance of this nice man who apparently, unbeknown to both of them for a while, was his real father. To Ahmed, blood was not thicker than water. Paul and Fatin had taken him in. Paul and Fatin had showered him with love and affection. His birth mother had abandoned him and his birth father, apparently through no fault of his own, had known nothing about him. At first it had been hard for Ahmed to accept that Roger was completely ignorant about his birth. The whole concept of what had actually taken place was beyond the grasp of an eight-year-old. Roger had been disappointed at Ahmed's refusal to accept him as a father, but he was realistic about it. Over time, he argued with himself, the boy would come to terms with it. He realised the only constant in Ahmed's life had been Paul and Fatin. To burst that bubble could have been disastrous, but also cruel to the kindly couple. It was hard for Roger to have to stand back, but, as always, Julie's sensible and solid advice was invaluable. In this regard, Julie was the only other person who understood the situation; Julie was his only counsel, and his saviour.

By agreement with his guardians, Roger gradually increased his visitations with his son, sometimes with "Aunty Julie" and sometimes on his own. Money was not an issue for Roger. His gains from the sale of the house in Eze Bord de La Mer and the casino business had made him considerably wealthy. He acquired a small apartment in Paris so that he had a place to take his son on visitation days. He bought season tickets at Paris St Germain so he could share the experience of the games with Ahmed. He paid for his secondary schooling. But all these things he did cautiously and carefully, sometimes with the knowledge of Ahmed and sometimes not. At all costs, Roger was determined not to upset the deep bond between the young man and his illegal guardians, Paul and Fatin. Their appreciation and relief were palpable. They, over time, developed the deepest respect for Roger and would frequently consult with him on matters of Ahmed's education and wellbeing. Roger appreciated that, but yearned to have a closer relationship than he could with his only son.

Young Ahmed never asked about his mother. At the age of eight, when he had first been told that Paul and Fatin were not his birth parents, he had, of course been curious, but Roger, Paul and Fatin had agreed that they would not burden him with the truth at such a young age. They concocted a story that his mother had died in childbirth and, although saddened, the little boy seemed to accept this. Only later, when Ahmed was around fifteen or sixteen did Roger tell him the truth, but only after he had agreed this with Doctor Paul and Fatin. Before doing so the trio had sought professional advice, which strongly suggested the teenager was now ready to understand what had actually happened. Ahmed had been furious with all three "parents" for concealing the truth for so long. He had become moody and inward looking. For a few months he baulked at seeing Roger, who had, in his eyes, "lied" to him. But, as he matured, he came to accept that none of this was Roger's fault; he saw that Roger had been duped, even more so than himself. What his mother had denied him, she had also done to his real dad. They were now a team; they had both been deceived. So, with that clarity of mind, and urged on by Fatin, Ahmed had resumed his relationship with his birth father and their bond had gradually and eventually become strong.

In the years of Ahmed's development from child to young man, Roger had been active in real estate in the UK and France. He had been buying up vacant brownfield city centre areas on which buildings had once stood. He was not interested in constructing new buildings on the sites (too much hassle!) but did see them as a "land bank" from which he could make money in the short term, by turning them into parking lots, of which there was a distinct shortage in the major cities. It had turned out that the car parking business was extremely lucrative, far more so than the rents he would have achieved from any buildings, so the little company had grown and grown, until it owned more real estate in London, Manchester, Birmingham, Liverpool, Paris, Marseilles and so on, than almost any other. After attending university in Paris, Ahmed had a decision to make. Should he do what Paul wanted, to train to be a doctor, like himself, or should he join his birth father in business? He had chosen the later. Paul was disappointed but realistic. He understood that medical training was long and hard. Making money from renting out wasteland seemed to be a much easier way to make a living, if less altruistic.

In his mid-twenties, Ahmed Indrissi fell in love. The girl was English. When he introduced his new friend to Roger, his father was shocked. The young lady looked exactly like Constance. With her long blonde hair, sparkling blue eyes, and gorgeous figure, she could have been Constance's daughter or even, in a different age, her twin. "Christ," thought Roger, "the boy has found his mother." The partnership blossomed and Ahmed's young lady friend, Jilly, became entrenched. Roger could not get over Jilly's striking likeness to his ex-wife, but he kept this to himself. Jilly seemed such a nice girl that Roger did not want to do anything to rock the boat. And, in any event, Jilly's background, as a farmer's daughter from Essex, was so far removed from Constance's upbringing in Cape Town there was not the slightest possibility of the two women coming from the same stock. Or was there?

Jilly, of course, soon learned of Ahmed's complicated background, and it was not long before she was clamouring for Ahmed and her to visit the Comores. Up until then Ahmed had shown no inclination to visit the place of his birth, but Jilly was quite persistent, so a holiday was arranged. Just like his father, his first trip to the Comores changed his life.

All of Ahmed's personal documentation, of course, identified him as Ahmed Indrissi, born in Paris, so the likelihood of anyone identifying him as the son of the ex-President's third wife and the manager of the Vanilla Beach was negligible. Upon Roger's advice, Jilly and Ahmed junior decided to keep it that way.

It had been over twenty years since the volcano destroyed the Vanilla Beach. Roger had been fully compensated for his loss by the insurers but still owned the land as well as the beach cottage on the promontory. During all this time, Roger had not been able to summon up the will to revisit. Ahmed and Jilly, however, wanted to see the site of Roger's resort, the place that was the foundation of his fortune. They had heard the stories about the coup d'état, the French invasion, the cyclones, and the hijacked plane. They had heard about the hotel and the celebrity guests. They had heard about the difficulties of running such a place and, of course, its tragic end.

Now they could see for themselves where Roger and Constance had lived, loved and worked. The place where Ahmed had, almost certainly, been conceived. As they drove through the bush from Moroni to the hotel, they caught the first glimpse of the site from the top of the hill in the bush, just as Constance and Roger had done with Dusty from the South African foreign office and just as Roger and Brigitte had a few years later. The sudden appearance of the two wonderful beaches from the clearing on the hill was just as startling and beautiful to Jilly and Ahmed as it had been to Constance and Roger, and later to Brigitte. People come and go. Buildings are constructed and fall. But the natural wonders stay, if not forever, for a very, very, long time. From what they could see, the site was still as beautiful as it had been when Constance and Roger first laid eyes on it. From the top of the hill Ahmed and Jilly had a clear view of the two beaches. Intersecting them was the ruin of a building partially covered in black hardened lava. From their viewpoint it looked as if someone had spread a jar of dark treacle over it. Further away, along the beach, the structure seemed to be intact although pretty much smothered with jungle. The couple held each other tight as they absorbed the view. Ahmed was looking at the place where he had been conceived; it felt strange. After a few minutes of gazing, Jilly and Ahmed got back into the car and headed down the hill toward their destination. As they passed the area where the flow of lava had crossed the road, a new section had been built, but it was already riddled with pot holes. Soon, after a bumpy ride down the hill that really tested the shock absorbers on the rental car, they were at the Vanilla Beach. The place was deserted and completely silent.

What they found, upon arrival, was a wreck. The main buildings of the hotel had been completely destroyed by the lava flow, which had set fire to them and effectively burned them to the ground. Their still-charred remains were now overgrown with dense jungle plants. Even coconut palms had found a way through the ashes of the buildings and were bravely waving in the breeze. The scene was reminiscent of a Picasso painting: sad, but arresting. The natural shapes and curves created by the waves of hot lava were quite striking. Their strength and power must have been enormous to wrench down and consume the bricks and mortar they now imprisoned. The bedrooms near the main buildings had also been completely destroyed and, likewise, had spawned multiple green plants and colourful blooms. But, further along the beach, the charred and weather-damaged three-storey blocks still stood. Now apparently uninhabited, but littered with the detritus of human occupation. They were, without doubt, no longer habitable, but nevertheless still standing as an ugly monument to their mundane design. Just like his parents before him, Ahmed walked the length of the beach with Jilly, and, just like his parents, they were stunned by its beauty. The juxtaposition of the pure white sand with the glorious azure water was incredibly beautiful. Time and the volcano had done nothing to destroy that.

Their destination was the cottage on the point. This, they had been told by Roger, had been the marital home: a home, apparently, with many stories to tell about the relationship of Ahmed's father and mother. Arm in arm, Ahmed and Jilly meandered down the beach, carrying their shoes so that they could feel the soft sand between their toes. They were happy to be there. They had almost reached the end of the beach when Jilly stopped. "You know what," she suddenly said, "I'm going for a swim."

"But you don't have a costume," retorted Ahmed, "you can't swim now."

"Who cares?" said Jilly, "there's nobody here." With that she started to disrobe, handing, as she did, her clothes to Ahmed. When she reached her flimsy underwear, much to Ahmed's surprise, almost shock, she did not stop. With a cheeky grin, she flipped her bra and panties to him, raised her arms above her head to show him the full glory of her breasts, then turned and tip-toed off down the sand into the welcoming sea, her bottom wiggling provocatively at Ahmed as she went. Just like Constance, the warm Indian Ocean swept around her naked body, up her shapely legs, past her little patch of pubic hair, gradually reaching her beautiful breasts, the deeper she went. What she did not know was that there still remained several squatters in the building, who had relocated to the upper floors. Word of this new gift from Allah quickly spread and for the first time in over twenty years the other deserted bedrooms of the hotel started to fill with local men, some the sons of those who had been there to ogle Constance. Some only arrived as Jilly was emerging from the sea. What they saw was the glistening body of a Venus, but, unlike Venus, all her parts were there. As in all of Africa, people just appeared from nowhere, as if by magic. Allah was being kind again, after all those years. Maybe good things would be in store for the Vanilla Beach?

When Ahmed and Jilly reached the cottage, they were both ready to make love. There was almost no furniture left except the large double bed, which, presumably, had been too heavy or too awkward for the pilferers to take. However, much as the two lovers were ready to jump into bed, neither liked the idea of high jinks in the filth of the cottage. They resorted to the beach. They had never felt so close or so happy. Ahmed felt he had come home and, above all else, wanted to share his home with his lover. In the calm of after-orgasm the pair just lay in the hot sunshine, listening to the gentle lap of the sea at the point. They didn't care whether or not anyone had been watching them.

Suddenly, Jilly broke the blissful silence. "Don't you want to find your mother?" she asked out of the blue.

Ahmed was silent. He wondered why she, in the afterglow of lovemaking, had asked that question. She had never asked before. There was a long thoughtful pause.

"I mean," she continued, "she must have had a reason for doing what she did. No mother just dumps her child like that. She had to have had a reason."

"As far as I know, she was doing what her husband, who was the President, wanted her to do. It was a political move. What kind of woman dumps her baby for politics? Although, as I understand from my father, she wasn't even married to the guy. No, my darling, I really don't want to meet her. She has to be the most selfish woman alive; I don't want that to rub off on me."

Jilly knew it was not the time to continue down this route. She also knew that Ahmed would never be "complete" if he did not, one day, meet his mother. For the rest of the day, she and Ahmed busied themselves with tidying up the cottage, which meant tossing out the remaining bits and pieces of furniture. When they were done, Jilly had one more skinny dip whilst Ahmed watched her from the little beach at the point. Jilly did her best to coax Ahmed into the water but he steadfastly refused. Instead, he sat on the beach admiring his beautiful lover and thinking about his mother.

And so it was that Ahmed, son of Roger, became deeply involved with his birthplace. It did not take him long, upon his return to England with Jilly, to persuade his father to go back with him to the Comores. The thought of just leaving the family property there in ruins did not seem right. Ahmed saw it as work unfinished: a story half told. He just had to get his dad back there. Surely there was something they could do to utilise the site? Roger was shocked at what he found. Several years of ultra-religious rule under LOU had shattered the delicately poised economy. All the good work President Ahmed had achieved had been dissipated through the mismanagement and financial ineptitude of LOU and his religious cadre. The fashion-accessory factories had closed. Western capital had been withdrawn or discontinued. The vanilla crops had been wasted. The roads and other infrastructure had fallen into disrepair and, despite the pious teachings of the religion, the mismanagement of public enterprises had produced worse results than the previously corrupt managements. The Comores was no longer a country with sprouting possibilities; it was a plant that, untended, was withering away. Poverty and filth were everywhere.

Ahmed junior had seen this for himself on that first romantic trip with Jilly. But he was smart enough, and emotionally involved enough, to see that things could get better. "If you're at the bottom," he kept telling Jilly, "there's only one way to go." And the Comores was at the bottom – and many of the potential electorate could see that. What they desperately wanted was someone to lead them out of the misery created by LOU, or, as many would have it, by Allah himself.

Even Roger was shocked to see the devastation wrought by the volcano. The once-vibrant site was now a complete mess. He listened to his son Ahmed's exhortations that all was not lost, that the place could be rebuilt, that the old glories could be revived, but Roger was less than enthusiastic. "What's the point?" he kept asking his son. "The volcano could strike again."

"But that may not be for a hundred years," Ahmed argued, "and who's to say that, even if it did, it would head for here?"

Roger explained patiently to the impatient young man that he had been exceptionally lucky. "I got away with insuring against the volcano striking," said Roger. "They had to pay me out. There's no way that that'll happen again. No insurance company would touch it, and, without that, no bank will finance you."

"But you might," said Ahmed speculatively.

Roger just laughed. "Then again, I might not!"

Where Roger and his son did agree was on the state of the state. Roger had always seen potential in the islands. He had taken raw recruits and, with the proper training and leadership, had been able to establish a world-class product. Others, following him, especially in the garment industry, had also proven that the people of the Comores, particularly the women, could work as well and efficiently as anyone else in the world. Their journey down the path of a religious dictatorship had clearly been ruinous. They needed new leadership and a new vision. Maybe, thought Roger, just maybe, his son Ahmed could be that man. After all he was, technically and legally, a man of the Comores.

Chapter Twenty-Four
"Exiled"

Life for AAM in the South of France was comfortable. Ensconced in a mansion in the foothills of the Alpes Maritimes, his luxurious home spread across several acres of manicured land. The main house was huge, with sweeping views, over a massive pool and tiered well-kept gardens, of the famous coastline stretching from Monaco to Cap D'Antibes. From the extensive balcony of the house one looked directly down to the Baie des Anges, with its pyramid-like harbour buildings and a clear view of the runway at Nice airport. It was there that Ahmed conveniently kept his Challenger jet, among Europe's largest fleet of private planes. Dotted around the extensive gardens were various substructures, two of which had housed wives one and two. However, as luxurious as their surroundings were, both women, now no longer in their prime, were desperately homesick and troubled. Their once well-connected families in the Comores had been dispossessed of their property by LOU's army and were now living in appalling conditions in the villages. Their children by Ahmed were now almost all adult and, one by one, he had set the sons up in small businesses in France. The daughters rebelled against their imprisonment in their luxurious quarters and had spread themselves, sometimes literally, across French society. Wives one and two, for a while, were forbidden by Ahmed to leave the compound, but his visitations to their bedrooms had become less and less as they got older and his sexual interests became even more deviant.

Wife three, Constance, still regarded herself as wife one. In her middle age she had retained her figure and her panache. She still had the ability to turn Ahmed on, but she, notoriously, had not reserved that ability exclusively for him. She knew full well that he was, whenever the chance occurred, visiting with the Ambassador's daughter. Constance, too, could play at that game. For her, the South of France was a happy hunting ground, especially in the summer, when there were more multimillionaires per square mile than anywhere else in the world. Constance played the field. Ahmed liked to hear about her adventures. The whole thing was weird. Constance, for a while, thought this was fun, but, not far beneath the surface, her regrets were simmering. She knew she had made mistakes, and as the lines began to show on her face, she thought more and more about the utter shallowness of her life. It was depressing to realise there was no way back.

Since Constance had moved with Ahmed to the South of France, she had had no further contact with her ex-husband, nor had she attempted to meet her one and only son. She had, of course, been delighted to hear Roger had been released from jail, and was pleased and proud that she had played a part in that. There was little else for her to be proud of. She was often tempted to contact Julie for news but always had second thoughts and did not call. She yearned to meet her only son but knew he was off limits. "One day," she often mused, "he'll come looking for me." But he didn't.

Ahmed continued to make love to her, but his behaviour became more deviant. One day he announced he was going to produce an erotic movie. He was bored with the ones he had seen. He wanted to produce a movie with a real story. Constance, with her previous experience, should be in it.

Constance refused. Her body was still good enough to play the part but her mind had moved on. She didn't need to do this. Not even for her husband. AAM was not pleased. If she would no longer be his plaything, she would have to go. It would be worth a few million to trade her in for a newer model. And so it was that, less than five years after her flight with AAM to France, Constance found herself back in Cape Town, ready to start a new chapter in her life. Her topsy-turvy life with AAM was over.

Chapter Twenty-Five
"Reunification and Revelation"

Ahmed junior's persistence with his father, Roger, paid off. It had taken a while but Ahmed was determined, spurred on by Jilly, who just loved the idea of living in the sunshine. Jilly had now been with Ahmed for over five years. She loved him deeply but, even though they had been living together for the last four years, Ahmed had shown no inclination to get married. Jilly was patient and, in any case, marriage was not as fashionable as it had been in her parents' time. Who needed to get married? Jilly tried to convince herself, so she never raised the subject, nor that of having their own family. Deep down, Jilly knew that Ahmed's reluctance to commit was something to do with the blocking out of his birth mother. She was certain that he needed to meet her; he needed to get her out of his system.

Ahmed had become an expert on volcanoes. He had made several excursions to the Volcanic Studies Institute in the Massive Centrale district of France, where he had consorted and consulted with the world's experts in volcanic behaviour and history. His conclusion, and that of his learned friends, was that the possibility of Mount Karthala erupting again within the next one hundred years was infinitesimal. He knew that he would not be able to convince an insurance company of this, but he may be able to convince Roger.

Ahmed's plan was to build a different sort of resort from the old Vanilla Beach. The hotel industry had moved on since Roger's days. Whilst many large beach resorts existed and were still being built, there was also an emerging niche of much smaller and substantially more exclusive resort hotels that charged exorbitant room rates. Higher room rates meant offering considerably more in amenities and quality. They also needed to be constructed in very private places, where their well-heeled guests could have maximum privacy. The returns on investment in extremely exclusive get-away resorts, if successful, could be immense. Vanilla Beach offered everything a super-deluxe and exclusive resort could need. There were few places in the world that were so isolated, yet accessible, than the Comores and, within its territory, Vanilla Beach itself.

For Ahmed's dream hotel to become a reality, three things needed to happen. First the politics of the island would need to return to capitalism. The leftist and ultra-religious leadership of LOU would need to end and be replaced with a more business-friendly leadership. Second, the new leadership would need to embrace the idea that the Comores should not set itself up for mass tourism; it should only allow very high-end and exclusive developments. It should be the Saint Barts of the Indian Ocean. Less scarring of the landscape and higher returns. Third, Ahmed would need to convince his birth father to lend him the money to fulfil his dreams, because he was sure nobody else would.

After a tour of the few resorts in the world that lived up to Ahmed's dream, Roger convinced himself his son was right: to be able to charge ten times more for a hotel room that was only three times larger than the old Vanilla Beach rooms seemed to make economic sense. Sure, the cost per room and the cost of the common areas would be far higher than for a conventional resort, but, even so, the return on the investment looked very good. Also, unlike most other developers, the land cost would be zero, since Roger already owned it. Who could beat a boutique hotel set in the multiple acres of Roger's beachfront land?

What stood in the way of developing the Vanilla Beach site was the politics. LOU's revolutionary leadership had run out of steam, but he clung onto power until the coffers were empty. Discontent had been growing amongst the population as jobs disappeared and the economy contracted. Poor people were poorer now than they had been under AAM's economically successful regime and the rich ones had left with their money. Public services, bad or limited as they had been, had now all but disappeared. Crime was rampant. The young people, with no jobs, no future and no faith in the religion, had started to riot. The pressure on LOU to resign was growing daily. The call for a general election grew likewise. Then LOU had a heart attack. Two days later, he was dead. There was no strong man to succeed him, such was the nature of dictatorship. The acting President, LOU's deputy, did not like the heat. He called for a general election, which he did not really want to win; the problems were too great.

Ahmed junior decided to seize his chance and stand for election. He had no experience as a politician, but he had demonstrated his business acumen in running and growing his father's property empire. The older population of the Comores remembered his father, Roger, with immense respect, and had passed on their feelings to their offspring. The problem was, although Ahmed claimed he was Roger's son and had been born in the Comores, he could not furnish the proof, and without that, he could not stand as a candidate in the election. The only way to proceed would be to find his mother. She, and she alone, could testify that Ahmed had, in fact, been born in Moroni. This was a huge dilemma for Ahmed. Much as he had sworn to himself that he never wanted to know his mother, he now found himself in a situation where he needed her, for the first time in his life and, hopefully, he thought, for the last.

After much gut-wrenching debate with Jilly, Ahmed reluctantly concluded that, if his political career in the Comores were to begin, he would need the cooperation of Constance, at least for a fleeting moment. Constance would need to sign the necessary declaration to establish Ahmed's country of birth. There would be no point in approaching AAM, whom he knew lived in the South of France, because AAM, presumably, would want to keep the story buried. So it seemed there was no alternative than to approach his birth mother. Hopefully he would not even need to meet her. Someone else could get her to sign the necessary declaration. Jilly, secretly, hoped that there would be a meeting. This might lay the ghost to rest.

Jilly encouraged Ahmed to discuss it with Roger. Roger, too, had not had any contact with Constance for years, but Roger and Julie were still good friends. Roger had never really realised Julie actually loved him, or, at least, he had not wanted to acknowledge it. He regarded Julie as a friend: a very good friend, who had stuck by him for many years. She was still an attractive lady and Roger had often hoped she would find the right man to love her, but this never happened. Julie had not been clinging to Roger, but she had made sure he remained in contact and they had spent many lovely days together. Roger did not have an address for Constance, but he guessed Julie still might. After all, it was Julie that Constance had turned to when they prised him out of jail. Roger was right. Julie had never discussed this with Roger, but she had kept in touch with Constance for the sake of Ahmed. Now, she could help again.

When Roger reached out to Constance in Cape Town, Constance was delighted. It had been so long since she had heard Roger's voice. "What a fool I was to leave him," she thought as he explained the situation. "What a mess I have made of my life." Constance, had, upon returning to Cape Town, opened a fashion boutique. She had many friends there but now lived alone. The thought of Roger appearing again in her life excited her. Yes, of course, she would sign the affidavit. Yes, she would be thrilled to meet their son, after so many painful years.

"Well, it won't be necessary for you to meet," said Roger over the phone. "You just need to sign the papers in front of a lawyer."

Constance was stunned. "But I want to meet our son. Please tell him I really want to meet him. I promise I won't be a nuisance. I won't be a drag. I just have to see him."

"But he doesn't want to see you. He just wants you to sign a piece of paper."

Constance was hurt. Her hopes of seeing her only child were dashed. She was upset, but also angry. For a moment she thought she might refuse to sign unless Ahmed would see her, but then she realised this opportunity for a rapprochement would be dashed forever. "Probably," she thought, "it is smarter to cooperate in the hope that this small, but helpful, action will somehow open the door for a relationship in the future."

Roger patiently waited for a reply on the other end of the line.

Finally, Constance spoke again. "Alright, I'll sign the papers. But, Roger, please help me to see my son. I'm so unhappy. I need to see him before I die. Please!"

"I'll tell him what you said," said Roger, and that was that.

Armed with the document, Ahmed had the proof he needed. He had been born in the Comores. He could stand for election. On the other hand, AAM's reputation for duplicity had been uncovered. The story of Ahmed junior's birth and fake death astounded the people of the Comores. Although it had all happened a long time ago, it did nothing to enhance the reputation of AAM in the history books and it was dubious whether it really did any good for Ahmed junior's first political campaign. Luckily there turned out to be only two real candidates for the vacant leadership position and one of the two did not really want to win. Several weeks after LOU had died, Ahmed, son of Constance and Roger, was elected to the highest office in the land. Paul and Fatin Indrissi were thrilled that their name was now an indelible part of a nation, particularly one that worshipped Allah.

Ahmed and Jilly moved into the Presidential Palace. There was a lot of work to do. LOU had not cared for the Palace, which he had briefly turned into a hospital. This had not been practical, but the mess it had created was devastating. His attention to its maintenance had been negligible and the place was almost uninhabitable. Whilst Ahmed came to grips with the problems of state, Jilly busied herself with refurbishing their quarters. Ahmed was really impressed with what she achieved. So much so, that he asked her to put her mind to sourcing an architect and interior designer for the resort he intended to build at Vanilla Beach. For the moment he was far too busy to attend to private business. This was particularly frustrating since the initial reason for him entering politics was to pave the way for the redevelopment of the resort. Now that he had achieved the goal, he had no time to pursue the dream. The ruins of the Vanilla Beach remained untouched. After a year of frustration, Ahmed turned to his father for help and Roger, once again, found himself at the sharp end of a hotel construction project, this time working with his son's partner, who was the spitting image of Constance, who had laboured with him over the first Vanilla Beach. "How strange," thought Roger, as he and Jilly pored over the plans and designs for the new resort, "that I should be working with a Constance lookalike." It just seemed weird.

Roger, knowing he would need to spend most of the next two years in the Comores, decided to renovate the beach cottage. This time, he added an extra bedroom. He was still very much in touch with Julie; she had been so helpful to his son, Ahmed, and was always "there" for him as a friend. With Ahmed tied up with matters of state, Roger also needed to pay more attention to the real-estate business in Europe, so every month he needed to be there for a few days to administer his affairs; not that his car parks needed too much attention. Roger was lonely at Vanilla Beach. Working with Jilly was fine, but she was his son's girl. Working with architects, interior designers and consultants was also interesting, but, when they had all left to pursue their own private lives, Roger was lonely and alone. On the trips back to England, he always called Julie. Julie had the capacity to cheer up everyone she encountered. In the case of Roger, since she loved him, she leaped at the chance to be with him. Bit by bit Roger felt closer to Julie. She was a safe haven. Her bubbly personality never deserted her. She was good to be with and being with her was good for him. Julie was still working as a housekeeper, but now for a London hotel. She was available every time Roger beckoned. They played Scrabble together, and cards. They went to the theatre and to their favourite restaurants. They enjoyed each other's company, but, other than a hug of greeting or farewell, they never physically touched, even though Roger touched Julie's heart. Oh, how it touched her.

When, on one of his trips back to Europe, Roger suddenly said to Julie, "Would you like to come back to Vanilla Beach with me? I've restored the little villa on the beach. I've added a bedroom. It would be lovely to have you there", Julie could not understand what he was actually asking her to do. Did he mean for a holiday? Did he mean permanently? Was he asking her to give up her job? What was he really saying? She needed to know.

"Roger, my love, what are you asking? Are you asking me to live with you? Are you asking me to be a companion? Are you—"

He interrupted, "No, Julie, I'm asking you to marry me. I've been a fool. I love you. I've been blind, or stupid. I should have asked you long ago."

Julie's heart was pounding. Of course, she wanted to marry him. Of course, she wanted to live with him. But she knew that she was not a blonde nymphomaniac like Constance, nor a film star, like Brigitte. She was just little old Julie. He had to understand that Julie was Julie. You got what you saw. She needed to know that he wanted to live with her because he loved her, not because he was lonely; that wouldn't work. She needed to be sure. She did not want her heart broken. On the other hand, this is what she had always wanted. The question was, was it what he really wanted?

"I do love you, Roger. You know I do. I've loved you for many years. But I need to be sure you really want to marry me; that you're not just lonely. I need to think about it."

Roger was disappointed, but not surprised. Of course, this sudden declaration of his love had come as a surprise. After all, he had never even really kissed her. He understood that to woo her might take a little time. He could have whisked her off to bed and made passionate love to her, but, strangely, he thought she might prefer to do things the old-fashioned way, to wait until they were married. "I understand," he said. "I understand you need to think about this. I'm disappointed, but I do understand."

She leant forward and kissed him. She had not kissed anyone like this since her late husband many years prior. It was a long, tender, loving kiss. She wrapped her arms around him and pulled him tight. She could feel his firm body against her breasts. It was a wonderful feeling. One she had not had for many years. He responded by squeezing her tight. They stayed that way for several minutes. "Roger, I must go now. I do love you. I always have; but give me some time."

Three weeks later, Roger and Julie were married in the Chelsea Town Hall. There were no other guests. There was no fuss. They did not even tell Ahmed and Jilly until they arrived shortly thereafter at Vanilla Beach. The second bedroom was not required.

Between Jilly, Julie and Roger, and a handful of the world's best consultants, they designed and built the most fabulous hotel resort in the world. Thirty bungalows were spread along the beach which had previously housed three hundred rooms. Each little residence was luxuriously furnished with the utmost "island" good taste. Each had a private swimming pool, an inside and outside bathroom, a media room, a comfortable lounge with deck overlooking the blue water and personal bar. The wood they used was sourced in the Comores, the power came from solar panels hidden in the spectacularly landscaped gardens. A helicopter landing circle was positioned at the far end of the site so passengers could be whisked in from the airport, but an afternoon tea deck was installed at the very site on top of the hill from which Constance and Roger had first sighted Vanilla Beach with Dusty Evans, so many years ago. The central buildings of the hotel were stunning; the blue water from the ocean lapped all around the dining and drinking areas. Every guest had so much space, but, knowing that people like people and people like to see other people, the hub of the hotel was an active place, with good viewing from everywhere – good viewing of everything and everyone. There was not a spot in the whole "village centre" of the hotel you could not watch or be seen from. The whole effect was spectacular.

Ahmed was extremely happy with the end result. It was even nicer than he had envisaged. He was so grateful to his dad and Julie for their hard work and organisational skills.

But he was also so very proud of Jilly. He knew she had played a huge role in creating his dream hotel. He, like Roger and Julie, recognised her talent and was grateful. "I am so proud of you, my love," he whispered in her ear one evening in bed. "I want to give you a gift to thank you for all you have done. Of all the things you could possibly have, what can I get for you?"

"It's not what you can give to me," replied Jilly, "it's what you can do for me."

"What can I do for you?" said Ahmed, now intrigued.

"You can invite your mother to the opening of the hotel. That's what you can do. Forgiveness is a wonderful thing."

And so it came to pass that Constance and her long-lost son were reunited. Good looking as she still was, Constance did not try to be the star of the opening festivities. And Jilly did not dress provocatively as Constance had done all those years before. She looked wonderful in the simplest and most chic Armani dress. So wonderful, in fact, that Ahmed, finally, that night, asked for her hand in marriage. She did not hesitate to say yes. She was so happy.

What Constance did not tell her new daughter-in-law to be, nor anyone else, was that her new husband's father was not Roger. In fact, nobody, not even the man himself, knew who Ahmed's father actually was, only Constance. It would be a secret she would take to her grave. It suited her to let Ahmed senior believe the man who had impregnated her was Roger, and, it suited her to let Roger believe the same. At least it had got him out of jail; in fact, it had saved his life. The lie had also, eventually, been a blessing to young Ahmed; who could have asked for a better father than Roger? And what the real father never knew he could never regret.

Meanwhile, as Roger and Julie danced to the new Mauritian band at Ahmed and Jilly's wedding, back in Europe, a tall thin mean-lipped old man was dying. He had asked for a priest. There was something he needed to confess, something he needed to get off his chest before it was too late. That man was Hans Ofal, the prickly assistant manager at the Sloane Towers. When the priest arrived, the old man confessed, "I once murdered a man. I got away with it. Throughout my life I have never regretted it, but neither have I admitted it. I want to set the record straight. The man I murdered was Antoine Mersky."

Author's note

The characters in this novel are entirely fictional. Any resemblance to persons alive or dead is purely coincidental.

However, almost all of the events at the Vanilla Beach hotel are based upon actual and real occurrences at one or other of two hotels in the Indian Ocean islands of the Comores or Mauritius.

The Galawa Beach Hotel in the Comores was built at the time of the "Apartheid" government in South Africa's search for friendly islands where they could land South African aircraft for refuelling. Initially the hotel failed due to poor management and lack of airlift to support tourism. The South African government then asked the legendary hotelier, Sol Kerzner, to see if he could make a success of the property, which he subsequently did, through his company, World Leisure. During World Leisure's management, under the watchful eye of the long-suffering hotel manager, Christian Antoine, many of the instances and events described in the book actually took place, including several Grande Mariages, the crashing of a hijacked Ethiopian Airways jet liner, the planning of a Coup D'État and mercenary takeover. The hotel beach was subsequently the landing point of the French army troops who re-established the rule of law.

The commercial success of the Galawa Beach was very

much due to the cooperation of Emirates, the airline chaired by Sheikh Ahmed Maktoum and operated by Sir Tim Clark.

Many of the other stories, fictionalised for the book, are based upon real events at the Saint Geran Hotel in Mauritius. These include the barracuda attack on a hapless hotel guest, the collapsing beds, various damaging cyclones, the hotel manager's foray into adult movies, the high jinks of the band, the chef's erratic behaviour, and so on.

The book was inspired by a previous novel, *Don't Stop the Carnival*, written by the great novelist, Herman Wouk, to whom this author is grateful.

As far as the author is aware, Mount Karthala has not erupted for over a hundred years.

Also by Peter Venison

Managing Hotels
Heinemann Professional Publishing (London)
1983,1984,1986,1988

100 Tips for Hoteliers
I Universe, 2005

In the Shadow of the Sun
I Universe, 2005

100 Ways to Annoy your Guests
Clink Street Publishing, 2020

Out of the Shadow of the Sun
Clink Street Publishing, 2020

The Lottery
Clink Street Publishing 2020

The Extraordinary Life of Niv Bloom
Clink Street Publishing 2021

When the Rainbow Turns Black
Clink Street Publishing 2022